Julian Symons is primarily remembered as a master of the art of crime writing. However, in his eighty-two years he produced an enormously varied body of work. Social and military history, biography and criticism were all subjects he touched upon with remarkable success, and he held a distinguished reputation in each field.

His novels were consistently highly individual and expertly crafted, raising him above other crime writers of his day. It is for this that he was awarded various prizes, and, in 1982, named as Grand Master of the Mystery Writers of America – an honour accorded to only three other English writers before him: Graham Greene, Eric Ambler and Daphne du Maurier. He succeeded Agatha Christie as the president of Britain's Detection Club, a position he held from 1976 to 1985, and in 1990 he was awarded the Cartier Diamond Dagger from the British Crime Writers for his lifetime's achievement in crime fiction.

Symons died in 1994.

BY THE SAME AUTHOR
ALL PUBLISHED BY HOUSE OF STRATUS

CRIME/SUSPENSE:
THE 31ST OF FEBRUARY
THE BELTING INHERITANCE
BLAND BEGINNINGS
THE BROKEN PENNY
THE COLOUR OF MURDER
THE GIGANTIC SHADOW
THE IMMATERIAL MURDER CASE
THE KILLING OF FRANCIE LAKE
A MAN CALLED JONES
THE MAN WHO KILLED HIMSELF
THE MAN WHO LOST HIS WIFE
THE MAN WHOSE DREAMS CAME TRUE
THE NARROWING CIRCLE
THE PAPER CHASE
THE PLAYERS AND THE GAME
THE PLOT AGAINST ROGER RIDER
THE PROGRESS OF A CRIME
A THREE-PIPE PROBLEM

HISTORY/CRITICISM:
BULLER'S CAMPAIGN
THE TELL-TALE HEART: THE LIFE AND
    WORKS OF EDGAR ALLEN POE
ENGLAND'S PRIDE
THE GENERAL STRIKE
HORATIO BOTTOMLEY
THE THIRTIES
THOMAS CARLYLE

The **End** of **Solomon Grundy**

Julian Symons

HOUSE OF
STRATUS

This edition published in 2001 by House of Stratus, an imprint of
Stratus Holdings plc, 24c Old Burlington Street, London, W1X 1RL, UK.

www.houseofstratus.com

Typeset, printed and bound by House of Stratus.

A catalogue record for this book is available from the British Library.

ISBN 1-84232-923-5

INTRODUCTION

The French call a typewriter *une machine á ècrire*. It is a description that could well be applied to Julian Symons, except the writing he produced had nothing about it smelling of the mechanical. The greater part of his life was devoted to putting pen to paper. Appearing in 1938, his first book was a volume of poetry, *Confusions About X*. In 1996, after his death, there came his final crime novel, *A Sort of Virtue* (written even though he knew he was under sentence from an inoperable cancer) beautifully embodying the painful come-by lesson that it is possible to achieve at least a degree of good in life.

His crime fiction put him most noticeably into the public eye, but he wrote in many forms: biographies, a memorable piece of autobiography (*Notes from Another Country*), poetry, social history, literary criticism coupled with year-on-year reviewing and two volumes of military history, and one string thread runs through it all. Everywhere there is a hatred of hypocrisy, hatred even when it aroused the delighted fascination with which he chronicled the siren schemes of that notorious jingoist swindler, Horatio Bottomley, both in his biography of the man and fictionally in *The Paper Chase* and *The Killing of Francie Lake*.

That hatred, however, was not a spew but a well-spring. It lay behind what he wrote and gave it force, yet it was always tempered by a need to speak the truth. Whether he was writing about people as fiction or as fact, if he had a low opinion of them he simply told the truth as he saw it, no more and no less.

This adherence to truth fills his novels with images of the mask. Often it is the mask of hypocrisy. When, as in *Death's Darkest Face* or *Something Like a Love Affair*, he chose to use a plot of dazzling legerdemain, the masks of cunning are startlingly ripped away.

The masks he ripped off most effectively were perhaps those which people put on their true faces when sex was in the air or under the exterior. 'Lift the stone, and sex crawls out from under,' says a character in that relentless hunt for truth, *The Progress of a Crime*, a book that achieved the rare feat for a British author, winning Symons the US Edgar Allen Poe Award.

Julian was indeed something of a pioneer in the fifties and sixties bringing into the almost sexless world of the detective story the truths of sexual situations. 'To exclude realism of description and language from the crime novel' he writes in *Critical Occasions*, 'is almost to prevent its practitioners from attempting any serious work.' And then the need to unmask deep-hidden secrecies of every sort was almost as necessary at the end of his crime-writing life as it had been at the beginning. Not for nothing was his last book subtitled *A Political Thriller.*

H R F Keating
London, 2001

CONTENTS

Solomon Grundy
Born on Monday
Christened on Tuesday
Took ill on Wednesday
Worse on Friday
Died on Saturday
Buried on Sunday
This is the end
Of Solomon Grundy

The Nursery Rhyme of Solomon Grundy

PART ONE

Chapter One *The Weldons' Party*

Grundy's hands, large, strong and hairy, rested on the steering wheel. The hairs, reddish and curling, sprouted abundantly from the confinement of his cuffs, covered much of the backs of his hands, and extended above the knuckles to his fingers. The lights changed to green and he turned out of the High Street traffic into the quietness of Brambly Way, with its squat Victorian blocks on one side and symmetrical Georgian façades on the other.

Three hundred yards down Brambly Way the blocks were broken by a sign that said in sans serif capitals THE DELL. Beneath it, in upper and lower case, the sign said: "5 Miles an Hour, Please. Children Playing." Twenty yards from this sign the houses began, built on both sides of the gravel road in small terraces of four or six, with identical picture windows but each with its differently-coloured front door. Each house had its own small garden and front gate, and outside the gate strips of green, narrow as carpet runners, separated the houses from the gravel road down which the car jolted, small stones crunching under the tyres. The hundred houses that made up The Dell stretched as far as the eye could see, some of them parallel and some at angles to the road and to each other. They were intersected at several points by other gravel roads and by stretches of green public lawn on which a few children were still playing at the end of this mild September day. Grundy drove round three-quarters of The Dell, then parked his old Alvis beside other cars on a patch of waste ground, and walked across the waste ground to his house. He opened the magenta front door. The time was eight o'clock.

Marion was in the bedroom in slip and knickers, making up her face. He bent over her. "Don't kiss me," she said. "You'll spoil it."

He stared at the two faces in the glass, hers a little haggard but darkly pretty, intense and eager, his own freckled, ginger-coloured, rough.

"What are you getting ready for?"

"The Weldons' party. I told you this morning."

"I forgot."

"You never remember anything. You're late."

He waved one hand. "I got caught up."

"They said eight o'clock."

"It doesn't matter about time with them, you know that. Besides, you're not ready."

"What was the point of my getting ready when you hadn't come home?"

This almost meaningless bickering had become part of their lives.

Grundy washed his hands and face and then went down into the living-room, drew the curtains over the picture window, put the first record he picked up on the record player, and sat down in an arm-chair with thin metal legs and a circular back. The record was from *My Fair Lady*. He turned it down until he could hear the words only as a murmur, returned to the chair, sat back and closed his eyes.

Ten minutes later Marion stood before him, ready for the party. She wore a dark green silk dress with a pearl necklace and earrings that he had given her ten years ago.

Her eyes sparkled with the expectation of enjoyment, as they always did before a party.

"Are you going in that suit? Aren't you even going to change your shirt?"

"For Dick and Caroline, no." Grundy got up, turned off the record player. "You look nice. A little snifter before we go?"

"We mustn't get there stinking of drink." But she took the large whisky he poured for her, pirouetted on a shapely leg, sat down opposite him. Reproductions of Rouault, Dufy, Segonzac, Utrillo, looked at the pair of them. "Dick's asked Kabanga."

"Who?"

"That Jamaican or West African or whatever he is, you know he's just come to live on the corner, No. 99. Edgar says there are too many of them coming to live here, they'll put down property values."

Grundy swirled the whisky in his glass. A little slopped on to his thumb, and he sucked it. "Edgar's a bastard."

"It doesn't matter, does it?" Marion leaned forward, her eyes bright. "I mean, colour shouldn't be anything to do with it. Nor should money. That's what I think's so wrong."

"I don't know what you mean."

"I mean, Dick's just asked him out of curiosity, because he's coloured."

Grundy put down his drink. "Let's go."

They went out, walked a hundred yards to the right, crossed the road. From the Weldons' house, which was similar to but a little larger than their own, came a confused roar of talk, music and laughter. The door was open, but they rang the bell.

"Sol. Marion. My darlings. So glad you could make it."

"We had a long way to come," said Marion, responding to this old Dell joke.

Dick Weldon looked from one to the other of them, his large nose slightly raised as though scenting – what? – a scandal, an indiscretion, some infelicitous note indicative of marital disharmony? By profession an architect, Dick was a man who felt a natural, proprietorial interest in other people's affairs. This interest was not malicious. It was simply that to be unaware of what was going on in the neighbourhood – not to know who had moved into the house left empty three months ago, or who was running the raffle for the Church or nuclear disarmament funds, or who had been knocked off his bicycle in Brambly Way – pained him like a nagging tooth. Over the years Dick's great blunt nose had developed a beautifully delicate susceptibility to news that might interest him and now he stood, pointing as it were, for a moment, before he stood aside for them to pass him, bellowing: "Caroline, Caroline."

The roar was louder, a turbulent dynamo of sound. Dick made a placatory gesture towards it, like a man apologising for the boisterousness of his loveable dog. "Get you a drink," he said, and disappeared. Marion added her coat to the pile in the hall, and they pushed their way into the living-room. A couple of feet inside they were checked by a fat-faced boy who thrust at them a tray of bits of sardine, olives, smoked salmon, meat and cheese on strips of toast. They each took a strip.

"Hallo, Cyprian," Marion said. "It's a bit hard on you having to carry this tray around."

"Mummy told me to. I'm staying up." "That's nice for you. Do you like the party?"

"I think it's bloody awful. I want to watch TV."

"What's that?"

"It's a programme about an African tribe. They still have human sacrifices and initiation ceremonies. In one initiation they cut open a man's stomach –"

Cyprian was waylaid by a girl in a mauve dress. Marion chewed her bit of smoked salmon and shuddered slightly. "Horrid little boy."

"I'll get us a drink." Grundy turned on his heel. Within the vortex of the room he was sucked into a pool of sound and physical contact. He knew most of the fifty people there, since almost all of them lived in The Dell. They were men and women like himself, accountants or advertising men or architects or actors. He knew that their wives, in appearance plain or pretty, tarty or timid, were generally faithful to their husbands even when they were flirtatious with other people. Yet such is the transforming power of a party that these people now seemed strange to him, as though they were all in process of becoming what they believed to be their real selves, selves more witty, profound, elegant and desirable than was ever apparent in the knockabout of everyday life. As he pushed through the scrum, his thighs brushing against a woman's buttocks, the skin of his hand feeling the texture of suits smooth or hairy, sentences and phrases came through to him through the deep general wave of sound, rather as though the crackle on a wireless set were intermittently shut off in favour of intelligible speech.

" – in any theory of graduated response –"

" – a wonderful hock, fruity and fragrant –"

" – a disgrace, of course, the whole garage question, and the committee –"

" – *Beyond the Fringe,* yes, I loved the one who –"

" – Late again, I said to the porter, and he said –"

" – if overkill, I mean, why not underkill –"

" – kill in any case –"

" – either you deliver on Thursday, I said, or I cancel the order –"

" – you can't go wrong with the '59 –"

" – the Macmillan sketch was extremely funny –"

" – that's right, you can't go wrong with the '59 –"

" – an outmoded concept, have you read Schlesinger –"

" – part of the price we pay for living here –"

" – don't shoot the committee, they're doing their best –"

A voice said in his ear, "Don't shoot the committee, eh?" Edgar Paget grinned up at Grundy, a little marine growth of a man, thick dark hair smooth as seaweed, features pudgy and malleable as though seen under water.

"I'm looking for a drink."

"Here." Paget wriggled aside, and behind him there was revealed a table with a cloth on it that served as a bar. Bottles of several kinds, full, half-full and empty, stood upon it. Grundy took a glass and one of the bottles, and tilted it. Suddenly

Caroline Weldon, her face flushed, popped up from the other side of the bar.

"Darling Sol." She leaned over and kissed him gently on the cheek. The bottle jerked a little, liquid flowed over the cloth.

"Very sorry."

"Doesn't matter. Are you having fun?"

"I've only just got here."

"I'm having fun, I'm a barmaid." And indeed Caroline, brawny-armed, deep-bosomed, hair some quite honestly artificial shade of blue, did look at home behind the bar. "Where's Marion? Has the poor darling got a drink?"

"I'm not sure. I'll take her this one."

There was a tug at his sleeve, light but positive and persistent, like that of some small animal determined to attract attention. Edgar's face wavered a shoulder's height below his.

"Wanted to have a word, old boy, just a couple of minutes, in here."

Grundy allowed himself to be led out of the door into the adjoining small dining room. People at parties congregate in one room and for no apparent reason ignore another. So at this party there were no more than half a dozen people in the dining room, talking quietly and earnestly to each other. Edgar took Grundy to a corner of the room where they talked beneath one of the near-Calder mobiles which Caroline made to express her uncertain artistic aspirations.

"I expect you can guess what it's about." Edgar smiled lopsidedly. Whisky could be smelt upon his breath. Grundy absent-mindedly gulped the wine he had got for Marion.

"The garages? There's a committee meeting tomorrow, isn't that right?"

"Not the garages. This African chap."

"Kabanga?"

"Yes. Dick's asked him along here, that's all right, shake hands with the fellow, quite all right. But there's a bit too much of it."

8

"What do you mean?"

"He's moved in, you know that, I expect. Four of them living here now."

"Well?"

"I'm an estate agent, old boy, believe me I know what I'm talking about. There was just one living here twelve months ago, four now, maybe twenty in another twelve months. You've got no colour prejudice, all right, neither have I, but I'm telling you – speaking as an estate agent, mind you – if that happens the value of your house is going down *and* down. Right or wrong, that's the way it is." He wagged a finger. "Tell you another thing. Keep my ear to the ground, you know that. This Kabanga's no good."

"What do you mean?"

"A word to the wise. He's no good, that's all."

Grundy tapped the mobile above his head. Little gold and silver blobs on the ends of the wires moved round. He drained his glass. His voice, hoarse but powerful, came like rusty water out of a tap.

"Marion and I were talking about this before we came here. Do you know what I said? I said to her, 'Edgar's a bastard.' "

Edgar's face wobbled, the eyes staring fixedly in their jelly of flesh. He began to say something, then put down his glass on a table and turned away. Grundy began to laugh. The Weldons' daughter, Gloria, a girl of thirteen, came up carrying a tray of sausage rolls.

"Have one of these. Mummy made them, and I've made them hot. Isn't this party just marv."

"Marv." He took a sausage roll.

By ten o'clock Marion had drunk three large whiskies, two glasses of white and one of red wine, and had eaten a number of biscuits and bits of things on toast. She had seen her husband's ginger head only once or twice across the room, but this was not unusual. They were after all, as she often said, independent

9

beings, and you didn't go to a party just to talk to your husband. So she had talked to Peter Clements, the TV producer, whose general air of extrovert normality made it all the more surprising that he kept house with Rex Lecky, a young actor who seemed to be nowhere about. She had talked to Jack Jellifer, who was a professional expert on wine and food, and to his rather tarty wife Arlene. She had had a long conversation with Dick Weldon, in which Dick had told her that he often worried about the kids, particularly about the language Cyprian used.

Marion shook her head. "Doesn't matter."

Dick was serious, even solemn. "Honestly, sometimes I wonder whether a psychiatrist is the answer."

"Trauma. Just a trauma."

"You think so?"

"If you've got a good relationship, you and Caroline, that's what's important to – to Gloria and Cyprian. Home example, that's the thing."

"I expect you're right." Dick nodded, with what in another man might have been called complacence.

"I mean to say, when you've got a relationship like that you can feel happy about – anything."

She became aware that her voice was a little high. Dick's large nose pointed upwards, his brown eyes looked at her speculatively. To avoid his gaze she lifted her glass. It was empty.

"I'm being a bad host." He filled her glass with white wine and moved away. From the dining-room there came the sound of music. Marion moved towards it and stood in the doorway. Somebody had turned out all of the lights except one, and had placed a thick bit of material over that. In the semi-obscurity half a dozen couples moved around. Marion saw Jack Jellifer dancing with Caroline Weldon, and Arlene moving round with her head resting on the shoulder of a stranger to the Dell, whom she vaguely recognised as a guest of the Weldons. She did not see her husband.

"Would you care to dance?"

This was another stranger, a slight smiling man. His teeth gleamed whitely, his dark suit fitted him snugly, a white handkerchief peeped out of his breast pocket.

"Thank you." She was dismayed to hear the hint of a giggle in her voice. She looked round for somewhere to put her glass, and in a moment he had taken it from her. Then she was in his arms. There came from him some faint semi-sweet semi-astringent smell, perhaps a blend of hair oil and eau-de-Cologne. He murmured something which she didn't hear.

"I'm sorry."

"I love the name of The Dell. It is well chosen for a little oasis of peace."

"It's a real little community, yes. A paradise for children, five miles an hour for cars, they can play in safety."

"You have a family?"

"No."

"I suppose most of the people here are part of the community?"

He had a pleasant voice, low and melodious. "Why, yes. Someone or other in The Dell gives a party pretty well every month, and of course they ask their neighbours. I suppose you might call it a bit dull in a way, but we don't think so."

"How could it possibly be dull?" He smiled, and pressed himself very slightly against her. The music stopped. They separated. He recovered her glass and handed it to her with the hint of a bow. They leaned against the wall. "I am sure I shall not find it so."

For a moment what he had said did not sink in. "You live here?"

"I am what you might call a new boy. Tony Kabanga."

"Of course. How silly of me. I'm Marion Grundy. We – I don't know where my husband is – we live at No. 70."

His teeth were gleaming. "I know almost nobody here, that was why I so much appreciated Mr Weldon –"

A woman screamed, a noise that pierced the noise.

Marion was startled, and more startled to find her wrist suddenly and painfully gripped by Mr Kabanga. She looked down, and in the dim light it seemed to her that the hand placed on her wrist was dark. "Where did that come from?"

"Upstairs, I think. Probably somebody's spilt –"

But he had left her, moving smoothly and sinuously into the large living-room and through the crowd that had now perceptibly thinned. She followed him, out into the entrance hall from which a self-consciously elegant staircase went up to the three bedrooms and bathroom on the floor above. She looked up the stairs and it seemed to her that what she saw would be printed on her mind for ever.

Coming down the stairs was a young woman she had never seen before in her life. She was perhaps twenty five years old, she had a high colour, her eyebrows were thick, her nostrils flared boldly, her glossy dark hair was piled up in a beehive. She wore a dress that glittered as though it was made of fish scales, with slits up the side of each leg. This dress had been torn on the left shoulder, and the tear extended down the front. She was doing her best to hold the tears together, without much success. On the fine pure marble of her left shoulder there could be seen red marks.

At the top of the stairs, glowering down, stood her husband, hands hanging ape like. He looked enormous, seen from below. His collar and tie were pulled a little to one side, his suit was rumpled, and upon his cheek there were four thin red vertical lines.

This was the scene that stayed with Marion Grundy unblurred by the nightmare events of the following days and weeks. In fact, no doubt, there never was a moment of time frozen like this, in fact the girl must have been moving down the stairs, Grundy must have been in the act of taking out a handkerchief to dab at his cheek, but the picture stayed in her mind as though fixed permanently by a camera. Then it splintered as though the camera print had been dissolved by acid, everybody began to move and speak.

The young woman came down the stairs, even in these difficult circumstances, with natural grace. Tony Kabanga moved forwards from the people in the hall just as gracefully and Marion saw now that his skin was a very light coffee colour, so that he could never really have passed for white although he was a long way also from the dusky African of her imagination.

"Sylvia," he said.

"Tony." She descended the rest of the stairs, put her white arms round his coffee-coloured neck.

He said nothing but, by some masterly strategy produced from an inner pocket a small gold safety pin. With this he repaired the worst ravages to the silver fish scales. Dick and Caroline were now on the scene – when had they got there? – Dick's nose high and eager. Kabanga, with what seemed miraculous speed, had discovered their coats.

"You're not going?" Dick's nose swung from side to side in quest of information.

Kabanga said with courteous gravity, "Yes, we must go."

Caroline moved forward, looking at the tear in the girl's dress. Grundy came down the stairs. He did not look at his wife, but held a handkerchief to his cheek. Dick glanced from one to the other of them, then said heartily: "And now, Caroline my dear, how about a bowl of soup? Did I smell something quite intoxicatingly delicious brewing in the kitchen?"

"Not unless Gloria's doing it."

Cyprian's fat face appeared from somewhere. "Did she scratch his face?"

"Just see how Gloria's making out, will you, my dear?" Dick said with transparently false bonhomie.

"You tore her dress, didn't you?" Cyprian asked Grundy.

"You just shut up, young man," his father said.

"High time you were in bed."

13

He hustled Cyprian upstairs, Marion and Grundy got their coats. Just before they left she heard Cyprian's voice from upstairs: "But it's interesting. Was he trying to rape her?"

When they got indoors Grundy poured himself a large whisky and drank it neat. Marion indicated her own refusal of a drink by a sharp shake of the head. It would have been against her principles to criticise her husband for drinking, although she thought he had had enough.

"What worries me is why you had to do it," she said.

"I mean, I've always thought we had a good relationship. Of course I quite accept that you can be attracted to somebody else, although I didn't think she was – well, your type."

"Let it alone."

"I can't. It worries me."

"You're so beautifully bloody rational."

"What's worrying is that it must show we're badly integrated." He burst out laughing.

"If you want to know, it wasn't what you're thinking at all."

She sat down. Her voice was consciously patient.

"Please, Sol. I know what I saw on the stairs. I won't say I don't mind, but we're civilised people. Please don't be childish about it."

"You're too good to be true."

"I'm going upstairs." She got up, swaying slightly, just a little drunk. At the door she turned and spoke, almost defiantly. "I don't see that it's all my fault if we don't have a good relationship. If you'd like –"

"No, thanks."

Grundy poured himself some more whisky, and went upstairs half an hour after her. The light in their room was out. They slept in separate beds.

The departure of Tony Kabanga and his friend, followed by that of the Grundys, destroyed the rhythm of the party. People were not exactly embarrassed by what had happened, and indeed, as is always the way on these occasions, most of them were not sure just precisely what had occurred. Was it that somebody, drunk, had hit somebody else upstairs? A woman had slipped and fallen down that treacherously elegant staircase, tearing her dress? Grundy had had a fight with the coloured chap? Whatever it was, people wanted to talk about it, and they felt that this would not really be proper in the Weldons' house. The party therefore began to break up immediately after the Grundys' departure, and had completely disintegrated before midnight. Edgar Paget and his wife Rhoda were among the first to go, and they took with them their daughter Jennifer. The Pagets lived just outside The Dell, in Brambly Way, but Edgar had been responsible for selling several of the houses in The Dell, and exercised such a near-proprietorial interest in them that he was generally invited to parties.

Jennifer, who was seventeen, spotty, and much larger than her parents, was silent on the way home, and remained silent while her father opened the cocktail cabinet and poured for himself and his wife their ritual night-cap. She longingly watched her father recork the whisky bottle. It was understood, but not by her, that she was too young to drink more than an occasional glass of sherry or white wine.

Edgar settled himself into a chair, crossed one little leg over the knee of the other, and swung it jauntily. "Shows what happens when you make the mistake of letting in our coloured friends."

"And their fancy ladies." Rhoda Paget was no taller than her husband, and was indeed an almost square little lady, but where Edgar's features were malleable, capable of constant change, Rhoda's solid trunks of legs, square figure, firmly defined features, might have been made out of metal. "It wasn't Kabanga, though, there was some sort of row upstairs."

"Shouldn't let 'em in. Great mistake to let them in to The Dell."

"Don't see how you can stop them."

"Not stop them?"

"One man's money's as good as another's, I suppose." Rhoda was fond of making such apparently bold statements.

Her husband did not reply directly to this remark.

"You can always stop them. There are ways and means. I was saying to that lout Grundy, when you let them in, what do they do? Cause trouble."

"It was Grundy who caused the trouble." At this speech of Jennifer's her parents, for the first time, gave her their attention. "He attacked her, tore her dress."

"You weren't upstairs," her mother said sharply.

"I was. I was in the lav, and I heard her scream. Then when I came out she was standing in the doorway of Caroline's room and her dress was torn. She came out and there he was behind her. She'd scratched his face, it was bleeding."

"The dirty dogs," Edgar said. "The dirty dogs." It was not clear to whom he was referring.

Rhoda fixed her daughter with a heavy, steely glance.

You didn't actually see him do it?"

"Do what?"

"Attack her."

There was a fractional hesitation before Jennifer replied. "He had his hand on her shoulder. You know, pressing it, trying to hold her. But she broke away from him."

"I expect she led him on." Edgar got up, walked over to the modern tiled fireplace which was empty of heat, and put his hands behind his back. "I can't understand the women who go about with these coloured chaps…"

They listened to him, Jennifer looking modestly down at the carpet, Rhoda staring sometimes at her daughter.

The Jellifers were among the last to leave, and before they went they had heard from the Weldons as much as their hosts could tell them of the scene on the staircase. They lived in the next block of houses, and it took them only a couple of minutes to walk home across the path that separated them. Jack Jellifer felt, as always, a slight stirring of self-satisfaction as he stepped into their own hall and appreciated the good taste with which it was furnished, the appropriateness of the prints about eating and drinking on the walls, the rightness of the one good original picture in their living-room, a sort of abstract with a central shape strongly suggestive of a fish. Little bits of rather good furniture, ingenious standard lamps, unobtrusive carpets, blended into one harmonious whole.

"People say these houses haven't got any individuality, that they're like each other," Jack was fond of saying. "What they don't understand is that a house is simply a machine for living. You want it to be comfortable, warm, easy to run, like these houses. Then you stamp your own individuality on it." Now in his early forties, and just a little jowly and paunchy from conscientious adherence to his duty of eating and drinking, Jack had been extremely good looking in youth, and he retained still a fine fleshy operatic handsomeness, a ponderous elegance of manner that was impressive in its way. Arlene, when she had gone upstairs to make sure that their son Charles was sound asleep, came down and stood smiling at him. Arlene had a style too, the style of a beautiful parrot. Her clothes blared at you, her dark eyes signalled what seemed an invitation to pleasure, her cheeks were brightly-coloured as a doll's. She waited expectantly while Jack poured the brandy. Should it be aerated in gargantuan goblets or put into vessels more modest? Jack, who firmly believed – and had often said so on radio and television – that one shape of glass was suitable for almost any drink, poured the brandy, stuck his nose into the glass, gravely approved, offered it, sipped, rolled the drink on tongue and palate, swallowed, spoke.

"Rather a curious business. What can old Sol have been up to?"

"He's frustrated."

"Would you say so?"

"He's got every right to be. Who'd be warmer in bed, Marion or an icicle?" Arlene's laugh was rather surprisingly coarse and jolly.

"You really think that?" Jack frowned at his brandy.

"Still, feeling frustrated is one thing, tearing a girl's clothes off is another."

"Our Solomon has blotted his copybook, has he? You'd never do such a thing yourself, of course."

"Certainly not," Jack said with stiff pomposity.

"I hope I can take my pleasures in a civilised manner."

"I'm sure you can." Arlene's gaze was brightly mocking. "All the same, I do agree it was a bit queer. I mean, you only do that sort of thing when you're pretty tight, and it didn't seem to me old Sol was all that tight. Do you suppose he knew her already?"

"I've no idea." Jack conveyed the distastefulness of this sort of speculation.

"I shouldn't be surprised."

"I don't see you've any reason to say he did or didn't."

"Oh, don't be such an old stuffed shirt. Come to bed." Half-reluctantly, half-willingly, he allowed her to take his hand and pull him out of the living room.

"My God, what a shambles." Cigarette butts stubbed out in plants, dregs of drink left in glasses, bits of half-eaten sausage rolls, all the characteristic debris of a party, confronted Dick and Caroline Weldon. Gloria and Cyprian had been sent to bed, and they were smoking a last cigarette.

"We ought to do some washing up." Caroline leaned back on the sofa, stretched like a cat.

"Saturday tomorrow. Leave it till the morning."

Tentatively, a cat probing at some possibly forbidden feast of delicious fish, Caroline said, "Rather a flop tonight, I'm afraid."

"Oh I don't know. Do you know, I think I'm going to have my pipe." Caroline watched with pleasure as he put out his half-smoked cigarette, stuffed tobacco into the pipe bowl, tamped it down, lit up and puffed. That pipe smoke rising at the end of the day had been the herald of some of their most cherished confidences. With the pipe properly going, Dick conceded: "It wasn't too good. Not really our fault, though. After all, if you have chaps like old Sol going berserk, it's enough to break up any party. I must say I thought it was rather much."

"I really don't know what got into him."

"Pretty girl, wasn't she?"

"If you say so."

"You're the one for me, you know that." Dick leaned over and patted her sizeable thigh. "I just say she was a pretty girl, that's all."

"He's a knock-out, Tony. I wouldn't mind him knocking *me* out." She coiled her legs under her.

"Naughty." Dick wagged his pipe. "Still, he is a bit of a knock-out, I agree. Wonder where he found Sylvia." With an archness not unusual to him he added, "Who is Sylvia, what is she? And what exactly happened to her for that matter? I'm still not clear."

"I don't know either, dear. There seems to have been a scream, and then there she was with her dress torn and Sol with his face scratched."

"Still, I suppose there's no doubt about the essential facts. Sol was looking for a bit of slap and tickle and got turned down. Might have happened to any of us. Great mistake to make it so public, though. Hard on Marion, I must say."

"Oh, *Marion.*"

"I'd like to know what you'd be saying if I'd been playing games with Arlene."

"She wouldn't have screamed."

Dick advanced in a mock-threatening manner upon his wife. "And what about you, would you have screamed?"

She looked up at him, smiling. "Try me."

Later, when they were in bed, he said, "All the same, there's something queer about old Sol."

Sleepily, she asked, "How's that?"

"I don't know. Sometimes he talks to himself, walking along the street I mean." Caroline made no reply. She was evidently asleep. Dick said to the ceiling, "He's a queer fish, old Sol, he really is a queer fish."

Chapter Two *Family Lunch and the Garage Committee*

On Saturday morning Marion got up at the same time as usual. It was not yet nine o'clock when she called out sharply: "Breakfast." Grundy came down in his dressing-gown, ginger hair rumpled. They sat in the eating annexe with its picture window, which looked out across grass to the house opposite, where Peter Clements sat eating his breakfast. The television producer showed his big teeth, and waved. A couple of minutes later he was joined by the slender figure of Rex Lecky. Rex also waved. Marion and Grundy waved back. This was almost as much part of the routine of breakfast as brown toast popping up, Cooper's Oxford, the electric percolator, crunch of solid, slurp of liquid, crackle of morning paper. On this morning, however, Grundy lowered his paper earlier than usual.

"I ought to explain. About last night."

Marion said nothing. He buttered a piece of toast, spoke carefully and slowly.

"I went upstairs to the lavatory, but someone was in it. That girl – what's her name, Sylvia – called to me from Dick's bedroom. She said the zip on her dress had caught in those frilly curtains round the dressing-table, could I get it free. That's why I went in there. Are you listening?"

"Yes."

"The zip is at the back of her dress. I couldn't get it free, I tugged it and as I tugged I tore the dress. Under those fish scales

21

it was very thin stuff. When I did that she swore at me, screamed, then scratched my face."

"There was the mark of your hand on her shoulder."

"I got angry when she scratched my face, and I must have gripped her shoulder. I said something too, I can't remember what it was. Then she ran out and down the stairs."

Marion's voice was painfully patient and reasonable.

"Please, Sol. I was at the bottom of the stairs. I saw the way you both looked. As I said last night, we're both civilised people. We ought to be able to discuss these things sensibly. If you sometimes feel you want to make a – I suppose you'd call it a pass – at another woman, I can understand. We both know that monogamy isn't –"

"Oh, for God's sake." Grundy flung down his newspaper. It knocked his cup on to the floor. The cup broke. Liquid flowed from it on to the wood block floor. "For an intelligent woman you certainly are a bloody fool."

He got up and went upstairs. Marion called after him, "Don't forget Mum and Dad are coming to lunch." Then she picked up the broken cup and wiped the floor. From across the way Peter and Rex watched with interest.

Marion's father, Mr Hayward, was a big jovial red-faced man who looked as though he should have been a publican or a butcher, although he had in fact been the accountant to a firm of timber merchants. At the age of sixty he had retired, and he and his wife had sold their house in Croydon, and bought one just outside Hayward's Heath. The coincidence of names never ceased to please him. "Doesn't belong to me, this Heath, you know," he would say to friends, adding with a mock-rueful shake of the head, "Wish it did," or in a variant of this ploy he would say solemnly, "Used to be mine, this whole area, they even named it after me, did you know that? Had to sell it, though, when money got tight." His wife was a little wispy woman, who was generally silent, but upon certain subjects became extraordinarily voluble. To outsiders it seemed remarkable that Marion, cool, logical, progressive Marion, should have had such parents, should be extremely fond of them and should call them Mum and Dad. To Grundy, however, who remembered the quiet, docile young librarian he had courted thirteen years earlier, a young woman who had been perfectly at home in what her family called the good residential part of Croydon where they lived and had been intent to console them for the loss of her elder brother Robert who had been killed on the Normandy beaches, what seemed strange was the metamorphosis of the Marion he had married into the woman who now sat opposite to him at meals. In the presence of her parents Marion was transformed again into the docile young lady of Croydon, the treasure her parents had been so unwilling to lose.

"You like this, then, do you? You like it here," Mr Hayward said as he had said several times before, with a note of surprise. "Wouldn't do for me, I can tell you that."

Grundy nibbled nuts, drank sherry, made no reply. It was Marion who said, "Of course we like it, Dad, or we shouldn't have come here."

Mr Hayward walked over to the window, jingled the coins in his pocket. "No, wouldn't do for me. Sharing everything with your neighbours, haven't even got a bit of garden to call your own except for that pocket handkerchief out there. Living in a goldfish bowl."

"It wouldn't do for us all to like the same things though, would it?" Mrs Hayward said boldly.

"No, it wouldn't. You're just about right there, it wouldn't," her husband assented.

"I'd better make sure nothing's boiling over." Such a remark from Marion invariably preceded a lengthy period of absence.

"Well, Solomon, how are things?" Mr Hayward always spoke Grundy's ridiculous Christian name in full, and did so with a sense of its absurdity, which was not less obvious because it was always repressed.

"All right."

"Our little girl looking after you properly? That's one thing she was brought up to do at home, isn't that so, Mother? Got to feed the brute." His tone changed.

"What have you done to your face?

"A cat scratched me."

"Puss puss," Mr Hayward called. "You haven't got a cat."

" A neighbour's cat. Have some more sherry."

They had some more sherry. Mr Hayward kept up a monologue about a holiday in Spain from which they had just returned, until Marion came back, becomingly flustered, to say that lunch was ready. They ate their steak, chips and salad sitting in the picture window. Peter and Rex were in their places opposite.

"That chap, he's a TV producer, I think you told me," Mr Hayward said. "Does he do *Emergency Ward 10*?"

"No. Plays of different sorts."

"Ah. You get a lot of arty types here, don't you? Shouldn't care for it myself."

"One man's meat is another man's poison." This was Mrs Hayward.

"We get all sorts. Professional men mostly, I should think you'd call them." Marion offered the remark, as it were, to her husband, but Grundy was not disposed to call them anything. Mr Hayward's eye, which did not lack keenness, followed this exchange or lack of exchange.

After lunch, back to the living-room for coffee. "You don't have to hurry away, do you?" Marion said, but her parents had promised to have tea with friends near Reigate. There was a lot of traffic on the road, Mr Hayward said, and they must start soon. The word *traffic* might have been a spring that released his wife's tongue. She began to speak at once.

24

"The traffic I call a disgrace, really I do. What are they doing, putting more cars on the roads when they're not fit to take the ones we've got already, that's what I ask. And the learners, they should be kept off the road for a year if they fail their tests, they're a real danger. This morning, we'd just come through Redhill and were turning on to the Banstead road –"

"Didn't come through Redhill this morning," her husband said.

"You know what I mean. It was just after we'd passed that black and white farmhouse –"

"Glyte's old house, you mean?" Marion was leaning forward attentively.

"You turn down All Souls' Lane, and then take the second right by Barrington Church –"

"Glyte?" her father said to Marion. "You mean old Ronnie Glyte? He never lived there."

"No, no, not Ronnie. His cousin, the one you used to call Chappy. You took Robert and I there for the day once, don't you remember? He was a friend of someone you knew, Dad, was his name Fairclough?"

"Yes, I remember. But his name wasn't Fairclough. Let me see, now –"

"Just after the church there's a sharp bend and this man, this learner, I don't believe he had anyone with him in the car, was on the wrong side of the road."

"There's no left turn after the church, Mother," Mr Hayward said severely.

"Of course there is. Not a turn, a bend. You go right round the churchyard."

"Round Easonby Churchyard?" Her husband's face was purple. "How can you go round it?"

"Not Easonby, Barrington."

"Barrington. But that wasn't where we met the chap."

"Fairweather," Marion said triumphantly. "His name was Fairweather."

"Going out for a walk," Grundy said. "Got a headache. If you'll excuse me."

There was silence, then Mrs Hayward said, "I think we ought to be going, Dad." Her husband agreed.

He took Grundy by the arm, led him outside. "I must do a Jimmy Riddle before I go. Everything all right?"

"Why not?"

"Thirteen years you've been married now, is that right? They say the first twenty-one years are the worst." They were standing outside the door of the lavatory. Mr Hayward laughed, then became grave. "I want my little girl to be happy. Is she happy?"

"You'd better ask her."

"I shouldn't like it if I thought she was worried by – cats." Mr Hayward's face lost its usual beefy jovial look, and became almost menacing. Then he stepped into the lavatory and locked the door. Five minutes later he and his wife had crunched away in their Rover down the gravel drive of The Dell.

Marion waved them away, smiling. When she came back into the house, she said, "Why do you have to spoil everything?"

"I don't know what you mean."

"How often do they come to see us? Once a month, for a few hours. Can't you be polite to them even for that little time?" Her voice was as cool as usual, but a note of strain moved through it like a red thread in a neutral pattern.

"I had a headache."

"You can't bear to see me enjoying myself, why not say so?"

"I can't help it if your father and mother are bores, and you know very well that they are."

Now her voice did rise, as though the thin red line had widened, was spreading over into the neutral part of the pattern. "Bores, are they? And what did you say that was so brilliant?"

"How can you be brilliant with bores? They wouldn't understand."

Her upper lip was raised from her teeth, she was snarling at him like an animal. "What makes you think you're anything but a bore yourself? What are you but a cheap commercial artist doing a comic strip for morons, a sort of prostitute –"

His large hand, swung back from a distance, struck the left side of her face. It was the first time he had struck her.

"Oh," she said. "Oh." She put one hand to her cheek as though he had wounded her, then ran out of the room and upstairs. Grundy began to collect the coffee things, his big hands placing them gently upon the tray.

That evening Grundy attended a meeting of the garage committee. The question of the garages had become a matter of increasingly bitter discussion during the past months. When The Dell had been built seven years earlier, neat modern garages had been provided for the houses numbered 1 to 50. The houses numbered from 51 to 100 had not been ready for occupation until eighteen months later, and by that time the price of land had increased. The SGH Trust, the company which financed the building, had suggested that part of the ground which had been designed as a lawn should be used for garages, so that they might save the cost of the extra ground, belonging to a man named Twissle, which would have to be bought. This proposal had, naturally enough, been resisted by the residents of the houses with numbers above 50, since through it they would be losing the amenities of a large lawn. The matter had drifted on from month to month, and even year to year, with nothing done. What should have been a green lawn was a patch of waste ground, on which what were understood to be temporary car ports had been erected. These car ports, roofed with corrugated iron, were undoubtedly an eyesore, but they did provide garage space, and the price of the ground on which the garages might in the first place have been built increased every year. The SGH Trust now demanded an extra sum from each resident if they had to buy this ground and use

27

it for garages. They offered to put up permanent garages to replace the temporary ones on the waste ground, but this met with strong objections, especially from those who lived in the houses that faced the car ports. It was possible theoretically for any householder to attend committee meetings by giving notice in advance, but in practice this right was never exercised. Twice a year a public meeting was held, at which severe criticism of the SGH Trust and of the committee was voiced. One or two committee members resigned each year, and new blood, which soon grew as thin as the old, was injected.

The garage committee met that evening in the Jellifers' house. The members, besides Jellifer, were Dick Weldon, Peter Clements, Felicity Facey, Grundy, and Edgar Paget. Felicity Facey was the wife of a local chemist with artistic inclinations. She was herself an enthusiastic painter of abstract pictures. The Faceys lived in one of the houses directly opposite to the waste ground. The Jellifers, the Weldons and the Grundys all lived in the upper numbers, and so were directly concerned with the garage question, Peter Clements, who was not, had been included to show that those lucky enough to possess proper garages were sympathetic to the fate of their unfortunate neighbours. Paget was present as a representative of the SGH Trust. Finally, the committee chairman was Sir Edmund Stone, a retired civil servant who lived in Brambly Way and thought The Dell architecturally detestable, but had taken the position of chairman because he felt it his duty to preserve local amenities.

The Committee meetings were informal. They sat around in chairs and on sofas, grouped to face the abstract painting with its suggestion of a fish, its vaguer hint of a bottle. Arlene came in with a tray of varied bits of liver sausage and salami and cheese, placed on slices of rye bread, and decorated by fragments of pickled cucumber. When she had departed Jack solemnly made coffee in a machine with a special filtering device, which he said produced the only coffee worth drinking. While he superintended this, poured the coffee into minute cups, and handed it round, Edgar Paget was talking. Almost every meeting ended with Edgar reporting back to the SGH people, and the next meeting began with their reactions.

"I've been asked to repeat that the SGH Trust has no intention whatever of backing out of its contractual obligations. At the same time, it's got to be understood that the time has gone by when it was possible to get Mr Twissle's land for any figure which would make the erection of garages an economic proposition. We must be realistic, that's what I have to impress upon you, ladies and gentlemen, the need for realism. Any proposals submitted by me on behalf of SGH –"

"Are there any proposals?" Felicity Facey boomed. She was a big horse-faced formidable woman, with a mane of coarse black hair.

"I am coming to that." Edgar swayed a little but recovered, like one of those shot-based toys that resume their position however hard they are hit. Once he was on his feet it was impossible to get him down in much less than ten minutes. It was necessary for the committee to sit through his recital of SGH's good faith, and his analysis of past negotiations, before coming to their present offer, which was to purchase Twissle's ground and erect garages on part of it absolutely free of all charge. A little sigh of pleasure was exhaled at this point by two or three committee members. Edgar rocked a little, swayed but not bowled over by this sigh, and added that there was one condition. The residents paid a sum of £25 a year each for upkeep of the lawns and paths. In view of the heavy additional costs involved, it would be necessary to double this sum for all of the householders, not only those directly concerned because they lived in Nos 51 to 100.

The sigh became a gasp. Edgar rocked a little in response to it. "If you want my advice, I tell you frankly that this seems to me a very good offer. I strongly advise acceptance."

Peter Clements showed his big teeth, more in anger than in amusement. "Speaking for myself, I must say I find it hard to see why on earth our upkeep figure – and I'm really speaking I'm sure for the rest of us who already have garages – should be doubled. If you could tell me why that has to be so, Paget, it would help me to, what shall I say, sell this idea."

Sir Edmund tapped with a pencil on his saucer. Jack Jellifer viewed the tapping with alarm for the saucer.

"Just address your remarks to the chair, Mr Clements."

"There are some things I should like to know," Felicity boomed. "First, Mr Chairman, can Mr Paget assure us that Mr Twissle is prepared to sell?"

Edgar replied, "At a figure, yes."

"Next, are the garages to be built according to the design submitted by us?"

"Absolutely, just that design."

"All right, then. Bill and I are sick of looking out at a dump with some cars on it. It's blackmail, but I'm in favour." She bit decisively into salami and cheese.

"I don't think one can be in favour of blackmail." That was Jack Jellifer.

"Please." Sir Edmund looked down his long thin nose. His general appearance was that of a perfectly preserved waxwork, and he brought a breath of old-world superciliousness into everything in which he engaged. "It is really not necessary to use such language."

"Call a spade a spade," said Felicity.

Sir Edmund looked at her with barely concealed distaste, as if wondering how such an obvious representative of trade had got into their midst. Then, fixing a monocle into his left eye he addressed Edgar with little more warmth.

"There is one point about which I am not altogether clear, Mr – ah – Paget. Supposing this proposal is – ah – rejected, what would be the attitude of the Trust about the upkeep question?"

"Glad you asked me." Edgar was on his feet again at once. "Quite frankly, the costs of upkeep are becoming impossible. They'll have to go up."

Dick Weldon's long nose was in the air. "I'd like to know what authority there is for an increase."

"In the leases," Edgar said promptly. "All in the leases. I know, I helped to draw 'em up."

"Read the small print," Felicity barked.

"Not at all. I resent that remark. It's not a question of small print, just of reading the leases."

There was a sense of strain. Sir Edmund looked at Felicity, then dropped his monocle as though in acknowledgement of the folly of expecting anything else but brash remarks from a tradesman's wife. Grundy cleared his throat. They all looked at him as though he were a wild animal about to be unleashed.

"Some things I'd like to know. First, we've all heard rumours that Twissle's already sold his land to the Trust. Is that true?"

"Certainly not. Quite inaccurate."

Grundy lowered his big head. "He hasn't sold it to you, has he?"

It was unusual for Edgar to flush, but he did so now.

"Mr Chairman, I resent, I very much resent, that remark."

Sir Edmund put in his monocle again. "Most improper. Mr Grundy, I really must ask you to withdraw it."

There was a general murmur, whose exact import could not easily be interpreted. "Let him answer," Grundy said. "If he doesn't, we shall know what to think."

"Perhaps, after all, Mr Chairman, our friend Edgar might – " Jack Jellifer began richly, but Edgar was on his feet again.

"I shall not stay here to be insulted, particularly when the insults come from a man who thinks nothing of assaulting the woman friend of a ni–coloured man." He reached the door and fired a parting shot. "I can tell you that SGH Trust takes a serious view of all these coloured people coming to live in The Dell. It's letting down the neighbourhood, I can tell you that."

"Please, Mr Paget," Sir Edmund said with what, for him, almost approached agitation.

"No disrespect to you, Sir Edmund, but I'm not coming back till I've received an apology." He was gone.

Sir Edmund looked about him like a man who can smell something unpleasant, without being able to tell quite where the smell is coming from. "I don't quite know – I am not sure whether there is any purpose in continuing this discussion –"

"I must say I hope it won't be broken off," Jack Jellifer said. "I think that I for one might be prepared to reconsider."

"Reconsider?"

Jellifer was looking at the fish picture. His gaze dropped for a moment and met the militant stare of Grundy. From this he hastily averted his eyes, looking instead with some intentness at the thick horse hair of Felicity Facey. "I think it's necessary for the good of the community that we should come to a settlement, and personally I think we've had enough of those disgusting temporary garages. I am in favour of accepting the offer."

"You called it blackmail five minutes ago," Grundy said.

"I suppose we are allowed to have second thoughts," Jellifer said in a voice both irritated and ponderous.

"I'm with you. And I don't think driving Mr Paget away has helped." That was Felicity. She added with a slightly spurious forthrightness, "I think he's got a point about the coloured people too. Of course I haven't any personal objection, we have a very pleasant coloured family, the Belandos, living only two doors away from us. But the fact remains that if we get another half-dozen coloured families living here it's going to affect the value of our property seriously."

Grundy's long legs were stretched out so that his shoes scuffed the mushroom-coloured carpet. "One of my best friends is a nigger, but I don't want more than one."

"That was quite uncalled for," Felicity barked.

Dick Weldon spoke, his tone pacific as always. "There really is no need for this, Sol."

"Isn't there? Why aren't they represented, then?"

"Represented?" Dick was momentarily foxed.

"There are four coloured householders here now, the Belandos, the Mgolos, the Challises, and now Kabanga. Three of them have the same rotten temporary garages that we've got. Don't they have a right to be represented?"

"Oh, Sol, Sol," Dick sighed. In the distance there could be heard faintly the Jellifers' tuneful door chimes.

"You really are being difficult, old chap."

"Do you want to restrict coloured immigration to The Dell? Shall we fix a percentage limit?"

"I hate to have to say this, but I wasn't the cause of Tony Kabanga and his friend leaving the party last night, was I?"

Sir Edmund, who had been following these exchanges with increasing bewilderment, now tapped again on his saucer. "This has gone far enough. I really don't know what you're talking about, but if this bickering goes on I shall have to close the meeting. We are here to consider garages, not coloured people. Mrs Facey and Mr Jellifer have said that they are in favour of Mr Paget's suggestion. Will you let us have your views, Mr Weldon?"

It was at this moment that the door opened and Arlene appeared, looking, for one of her general assurance, almost nervous. Behind her, in a lightweight light-coloured suit, stood the smiling figure of Tony Kabanga.

The members of the committee stared at him, open-mouthed. Sir Edmund, who had never met Kabanga, looked the least surprised. He stuck in his monocle.

"Good evening. Can we help you?"

"I heard that there was a meeting. Is it permitted to come to it?"

Grundy laughed, a raw sound. Jack Jellifer said ponderously, "I don't think you know our chairman, Sir Edmund Stone. This is Mr Kabanga, who has just come to live in our community."

Kabanga smiled, showed his very white teeth. "I am delighted to make your acquaintance. I heard that there was a meeting, and decided to attend. You must inform me if I am out of place."

A chorus of sounds avowed pleasure at his presence. With thin superciliousness Sir Edmund said, "It is unusual for residents to be present at our deliberations, but I am sure there will be no objections. Please sit down."

Kabanga sat, placed one leg over another, and offered Russian cigarettes, which nobody except Jellifer accepted.

"We were discussing an offer made by the SGH Trust in relation to the – ah – vexed garage question."

"Not correct." Grundy shook his ginger head. "We were talking about coloured people living here."

"You are out of order."

"I said there were four coloured residents, and they ought to be represented. Most of them seemed to think four families were three too many."

"You will please stop." Sir Edmund's voice had risen. and issued now in an unfortunate squeak.

"This is absolutely too much," Felicity cried.

Grundy grinned at her. "Didn't you say another half-dozen coloured people coming here would seriously affect the value of our properties?"

Felicity's face was red. "Oh, you're insufferable."

Kabanga stood up, put out his cigarette, then walked over to Grundy, who looked up at him.

"I have tried to ignore what happened last night, but you will not allow me to do so. Please will you understand that all we wish is to be left alone."

"You don't understand. I'm on your side, boy."

In his soft, classless voice, Kabanga said, "If you make trouble for me, Mr Grundy, I shall make trouble for you." He turned to Sir Edmund. "I think it is better that I should go. I am sorry."

When he had gone Sir Edmund tapped on his saucer once more. "I am closing the meeting. And I must say, Mr Grundy, that the way in which you have comported yourself has made this an extremely painful occasion. Extremely painful. In a lifetime's experience of committee meetings I cannot say that I have ever known one so – " He seemed to search for some really explosive word, but the one that came was tame, "– unsatisfactory."

"Sorry about that. Don't see what I've done, beyond sticking up for our coloured neighbours, but there's only one thing to do about it. Dick, you're secretary, will you accept my resignation from the committee here and now."

Nobody expressed distress. The meeting broke up. Dick Weldon and Grundy walked home together. When they reached Dick's house he said, "Come in for a drink, Sol."

"No, thanks."

Dick had lighted his pipe as soon as they left the Jellifers'. Puffing away, he said, "What's up?"

"Don't know what you mean."

"That was a queer show you put on in there. Do you want to put everybody's back up?"

The night was fine, filled with stars. "I don't mind either way."

"I see." The remark was quite untrue. The idea that one might not care about the social attitudes adopted by fellow human beings towards oneself was totally incomprehensible to Dick Weldon.

Grundy looked up at the stars. To his left there shone one of the specially designed Dell street lamps, which cast a spectral light upon them both. "I don't belong here."

"You've been here five years," Dick said, too logically.

"Even so. Sometimes the whole place is too much for me."

"How do you mean?"

"The whole place, community living, what anyone does is everybody's business, little committee meetings to blather away about garages. Too much bloody *order*."

"Why don't you move, then?"

"Not possible."

"Not *possible*. Why not?"

Under the lamp Grundy loomed above him, a giant.

"What you do is something that happens to you, do you understand? It changes you. You come to live here, very well then, that's the sort of person you are and you can't get away from it. It's not what you think that matters, it's what you do."

"I see," Dick said again, untruthfully. "But you can do something else."

"You can try." Grundy's voice was deep, hoarse, despairing. "But what's happened is part of you, you're part of it. You can never cancel what's happened to you, you have to accept it."

"Suppose you can't?"

There was silence for a moment. "You have to. You have to try. If you can't – " Grundy scuffed with his foot and did not finish the sentence.

Dick took out his pipe, looked at it, put it back again, and brought the conversation down to good firm practical ground. "But you want proper new garages, don't you?"

"Oh, sure. By all means."

"Well, then. Sure you won't come in for a drink?"

"Sure."

"We've known each other five years, Caroline and I, you and Marion. We'd be sorry if – what I mean to say is, if there's any trouble, I hope you'll let us help."

"Thanks. There's no trouble."

Dick ventured a joke. "Guffy McTuffie been playing you up?"

Grundy laughed, a bellow that was an unseemly disturbance of the peace of The Dell. "That's right. Guffy McTuffie's been playing me up."

Chapter Three *Sunday in the Dell, Monday at the Office*

If the inhabitants of The Dell had been asked what characterised them as a group, most of them would have been inclined to reply a little indignantly that they were not a group but individuals. Why, otherwise, would they have answered the advertisement in *The Observer* which appealed to "Individuals, who want to live in a community, but one that does not confine but actually enhances their own individuality; those who believe that a residential housing project – abominable phrase – can be a means to gracious, civilised living?" They would have claimed for themselves that they were liberal, unorthodox, tolerant – or rather, they would not have made the claim but would just have accepted it as a fact that they were forward-looking modern people who had no religious, sexual or other prejudices. Yet The Dell had its own orthodoxy, and a sociologist making an examination of the people who lived there, and in the dozens of other Dells built in England during the past few years, would have come to some firm conclusions about its inhabitants, although those conclusions would have been modified by the particular district in which each Dell was set. A Dell in semi-suburban Surrey, like this one, no doubt attracted different people from a Dell on the outskirts of a provincial town, but the similarities were more notable than the differences.

Dell-dwellers, the sociologist might have said in his report, were mostly those who regarded themselves as professional men, rather than tradesmen or manual workers. Their average age was the early thirties – the garage committee, which was composed of particularly responsible members of The Dell community, was distinctly over average age. Such occupations as advertising, architecture, medicine, the law, and technological engineering were well represented among them. There were a few artists and more near-artists, and a cluster of lively fresh-looking young business men who held managerial jobs in enormous corporations. A Dell-dweller would not be among the higher reaches of his profession, for as his income grew and his hairline receded he naturally moved on to a detached home of his own at Hampstead, Sunningdale or Gerrard's Cross. He would have no more than two children, because the houses in The Dell were not built to accommodate larger families. He would own a number of books, but not too many because, as he might wistfully say, there was no room for them. He would have pictures on his walls, but they would probably be reproductions rather than originals. He almost certainly possessed a record player, and was fond of music. In politics some Dell-dwellers liked to call themselves Socialists, many were Liberals, few admitted to Conservative votes or feelings. About religion the Dell-dweller was generally agnostic, although he tended to go to church at Harvest Festival or Christmas time. He was a moderate drinker, he owned a medium-sized popular car, and he was tolerant in theory of much that he disapproved in practice, like anarchism or drug-taking. This was the male Dell-dweller. His wife, who very often had artistic feelings or inclinations, was totally in accord with her husband's view that Dell-living was pleasant, labour-saving and comfortable. It left her time to prepare little meals which might almost – but not quite – have been prepared in France or Italy or Spain, to read reviews of books in the weekly magazines, to collect or work for at least one good social cause, and generally to play a part in the social and intellectual life of the community.

Dell-living, the sociologist might have summed it up, represented a progressive, leisured and easy way of life for a rising national group with cultural inclinations above their intellectual stations.

The Dell orthodoxy, of clothes and conduct, was apparent at week-ends. On Saturdays husbands and wives went out to shop together in the High Street, the husbands looking slightly raffish in corduroy trousers, cravats and rather jaunty caps, the wives uniformed in jeans and sweaters. On Sundays the heavies – that is, the serious weekly papers – were read to a late hour in the morning. Later the husbands, wearing tremendously informal but really rather smart old clothes, washed cars and played with children, while their wives cooked lunch. After lunch came washing up, after that visits to friends for tea.

On the Sunday after the garage committee meeting Dick Weldon, pipe in mouth, was washing and polishing his car in the gravel driveway outside his house. He was using a new flexihose combined washer-polisher which was not working very well. His neighbour Felix Mayfield, an advertising executive, came and watched.

"I hear we may be getting some real garages at last."

"You do?" Dick grinned. "The grapevine's been working overtime."

"Arlene told Steffie there'd been a bit of bother." Stephanie was Mrs Mayfield. Dick said nothing.

"What's Grundy been up to now?"

Dick put down the flexihose, looked at his pipe, which had gone out, rubbed his nose with the pipe stem. "I don't know that he's been up to anything."

"He really is a bloody barbarian."

"Sol sometimes has an unfortunate way of putting things, that's all."

"If he's trying to stop us getting garages –"

"Look, he wants garages, we all want garages. There was a stupid argument about coloured people, nothing else. Sol puts people's backs up."

"I'll say he does. And he wants to look out for himself with that coloured chap, Kabanga. I hear he was with that woman of Kabanga's last night."

"Who was?"

"Grundy."

"That's nonsense. You can take it from me. I said good night to him at about half past nine. He was going home then."

"This was later, about eleven."

"Where did you hear that tale from?"

Felix looked a little uncomfortable. "Never mind. They were together, over by the shrubbery near Kabanga's house. He was kissing her. That's the story."

"I don't believe a word of it." Dick Weldon was naturally polite, but now he very nearly turned his back on Felix Mayfield, and picked up his flexihose again.

This bit of gossip had been given to Felix and Steffie Mayfield by their fourteen-year-old daughter Jill. Just off the High Street there was a coffee bar called the Aficionado. The interior of this bar was filled with posters of bull fights, around the walls were photographs of matadors, and the bar was a meeting-place for the local teenagers. Jill Mayfield had gone there that morning with Adrienne Facey, who was fifteen, and Jennifer Paget. It was Jennifer who had broken into her juniors' discussion of pop music with the news.

"What were they doing?" asked Adrienne, a girl startlingly like her mother.

Jennifer looked down at her coffee. "Well, you know." Adrienne whispered. "Oh, no. You know, they were – he was holding her tight."

"Kissing?" asked Jill.

"Yes, they were kissing. And he was holding her."

"I don't see how you could see them," Adrienne said. "It's jolly dark."

"Well, I could. I'd taken Puggy out for a walk."

"You must have been close."

"I was close enough. You can't mistake him, with that ginger hair."

"In the dark?"

"The street light isn't that far away, and Puggy went near them."

"I think he's very attractive for an old man," Jill said dreamily. "I mean, I like old men myself."

"How could you see it was that girl? If she was kissing him, I mean," Adrienne asked.

Jennifer's spotty face was flushed. "I could see and it was her. I saw them both."

The subject was dropped, but both Jill and Adrienne repeated the story when they got home, Jill delightedly and Adrienne sceptically. It was already a subject of discussion in the Paget household.

"I do quite honestly think that chap's a bit much," Peter Clements said.

"What chap?" Rex Lecky was reading the script of a new television play in which he had a part. He sat sideways in a great vessel of a chair, with one leg cocked over the side. His shoes were hand-made, his trousers tight and narrow. He looked even younger than he was. His dark hair was brushed forward in a manner currently fashionable.

"Grundy. He really wrecked that meeting last night. I said we ought not to agree to pay more money for those garages. Those of us who'd got them already. Of course it's not really a charge for the garages, it's for upkeep. I wonder if I was right." There was silence. "You might say something."

Rex looked up. "Sorry. I thought it was Clements soliloquising."

"After all, we're part of a community, and I suppose it's not unreasonable really. I wonder if I ought to have a word with other people to see what they think."

"Dear Peter. So public spirited." Peter glared at him. Rex put down his script. "He's a terrific roughneck, Grundy, but in that roughneck way he's got a lot of charm, wouldn't you agree?"

"You're just trying to needle me."

"No, I honestly think it. A tremendous lot of charm."

"I'm going out." Rex nodded, and returned to his script. At the door his friend paused. "I think Grundy's a boor and a bore."

Peter picked up his rather elegant walking-stick, which stood in the hall, and went out into the September sunshine. He spent the next hour and a half in calling on several Dell-dwellers who lived in the numbers between 1 and 50, telling them about the committee meeting and Grundy's atrocious behaviour, and asking whether they would be prepared to pay the extra money involved. To his surprise most of them felt that the waste patch was such an eyesore that they would do almost anything, including paying the extra upkeep cost, to get rid of it.

Grundy spent that afternoon with his friend Theo Werner, in the first-floor room that in most Dell houses served as a bedroom, but which Grundy had turned into a working study. They discussed the problems of Guffy McTuffie.

Guffy was a child of the small agency which Grundy had started when he came out of the Army after the war and discovered his complete lack of any obvious commercial talent. His father had been a moderately successful Irish actor, a big magniloquent expansive extroverted ginger man who never tired of telling about the part he had played in the glorious days of the Troubles, a part which varied from a major role in the storming of the Post Office to exploits as what he called the good right hand of Michael Collins. Holding out his own hairy freckled hand in front of him, Pat Grundy would repeat the words that Michael Collins had used so often: "I'd sooner lose this right hand than I'd lose Pat Grundy." His hearers in bar rooms and boarding houses were only occasionally enthralled, and the small ginger-haired boy who knew the stories by heart passed through the usual stages of fascination, adoration and repulsion. He had been given the name of Solomon partly because of the nursery rhyme, which appealed to his father's simple sense of humour, but also because Pat hoped that his son would combine, as he said with wearisome frequency, "the wisdom of a Solomon with the courage of a Grundy."

Solomon Grundy spent his childhood in theatre dressing-rooms, among bits of stage scenery, in boarding houses, and in railway station waiting-rooms. His mother, an Irish woman who was frail, pathetic and often ill, could not bear that he should be parted from her. Sometimes he went to school, once he went to a boarding school for a couple of terms, but for the most part she educated him herself, teaching him to read and write. She took refuge in her son from the drunkenness and unfaithfulness of her husband. Pat Grundy made only a few appearances in the West End, but he could always obtain a place in touring repertory companies. Mrs Grundy died of cancer when her son was sixteen years old, and Pat was killed during the blitz on London, when a bomb scored a near miss on the shelter in which, a trouper to the end, he was entertaining the shelterers with dramatic impersonations of characters from Dickens. Solomon was called up, fought in Africa, Italy and France, took a commission and reached the rank of captain. In the mess his colleagues found him reticent and self-contained. He rarely joined in the good-natured horseplay that is common among soldiers, and when he did there was nothing good-natured about his violence. After he broke the arm of a fellow officer who had played a practical joke on him, everybody became a little afraid of Solomon Grundy.

He had read a good deal in the Army, and when he came out wrote a number of short stories, none of which was printed. He drifted into advertising, and after a couple of years as a copywriter started an art agency with an artist who worked in the same firm, Theo Werner. The agency led a struggling existence for some time, before the birth of Guffy McTuffie.

Guffy was a comic strip character. The essence of him was that, although a coward by nature, he was led to perform courageous actions. When, for instance, a gang of teenage bandits took over Slumside, where Guffy was paying a visit, he went down to their headquarters and talked to them, chattering with fear. When the gang attacked him, Guffy overthrew them with judo. When they practised judo on him it turned out that he had become proficient in oduj, a higher form of wrestling. This particular adventure ended with Guffy raising funds for a community centre, which, as created by Archie Accurit the architect with the new build-it-in-a-day material Prefab-constricuct, proved such an attraction that leaders of industry put up new factories, concert halls and theatres were erected, Slumside was transformed, and Charlie Corncrackle the teenage gangster found himself isolated, saw the error of his ways, became a missionary in the Noncongelical Church, and was last heard of in Congojumbaland where he was helping the natives to rule their own country.

Who had thought of Guffy McTuffie? This was something that Grundy himself could no longer remember. He had been elaborated in casual talk, drawn by Theo as a little man with a big head, an inquiring look and a single lock of hair that would never stay down, and had been sold at once to a national newspaper. As time passed Guffy had come to occupy more and more time, and to provide a larger share of Grundy's and Theo Werner's income. Guffy's activities were protean. He had solved the problems of young lovers, obtained a new drainage system for Middletown, rescued a would-be suicide from the top of a tall building although terrified of heights himself, and exposed an atom spy group. Guffy had become much more concerned lately with politics, the fate of the world, and nuclear disarmament, and in the new series that was now being designed and drawn, "Guffy's Sooperdooper Bomb", he was going to bring the world leaders to a disarmament conference and then compel them to make peace by the threat of using his Sooperdoopernootral Bomb, designed by his friend Snowy Syentist, which had the effect of neutralising all other bombs and rendering them useless.

Comic strips are prepared long in advance, and Theo had been drawing some of the final scenes of this particular series. Theo Werner was a few years older than Grundy, a puckish little Austrian whose family had fled from his country when Hitler took over. He pranced round the study now, showing the big drawings he had put on card.

"Here you are, Sol my dear, here's Krosscross talking to Johnno, they're going to shut Guffy up, Krosscross wants to seal him in the Crumlin, Johnno's going to bury him in Castle Knocks. And there's Hum-hum." Theo giggled with pure enjoyment. Krosscross and Johnno were deep in discussion, and stiff-necked Hum-hum trailed behind them, holding up a tiny model of the Tower of London, saying: "Let's stuff Guff in here."

Grundy laughed half-heartedly. Werner broke off.

"What's wrong, Sol? You're not up to the mark, as they say." Theo liked occasionally to drop in an "as they say" or "as you put it" to show that he was a foreigner.

"Nothing."

"Yes. You haven't got your usual zing, my dear. I shall tell Marion."

"Perhaps she knows already."

"What have you done to your face?"

"A cat scratched it."

"We are in rapport, you and I, eh? When anything bothers you I know it."

"Perhaps. These are fine. Clacton's got the outline."

Clacton was the editor of the paper that ran the strip, and he had the whole new story in rough outline. These were the finished drawings that would appear in the paper.

Werner cocked his head to one side. "And you do not know why he has asked to see us tomorrow, eh?"

"To talk about the next series, very likely. But he didn't say." Grundy rose from the desk, shook his shoulders as though he were dispersing rain. "Let's have a drink."

"A sooperdooperexcellent idea."

Marion liked Theo, who always paid her extravagant compliments which she enjoyed, although she publicly disapproved of them. Theo stayed for half an hour talking to them both, had two drinks, then said, "I must get back to my Lily of Laguna, as they say." Lily was the latest of the series of mistresses in occupation of his Earl's Court flat.

Marion had become quite animated. "They don't say anything of the sort."

"Don't they? I am an Austrian idiot." He kissed her hand, then her cheek. "Goodbye, my charming hostess. Farewell, old Sol. See you in the morning."

Grundy showed him out, then returned to the living room. He looked at Marion, seemed about to speak, then poured another drink. Then spent Sunday evening in finishing the papers, drinking, and watching television.

On Monday morning The Dell was transformed from its weekend leisure. From eight o'clock onwards affectionate fathers said goodbye to wives and children, and hallo to those other much-loved children, their cars. Slick, spry, jaunty, some wearing suits of uncommon elegance and carrying umbrellas, others a little more bohemianly dressed, they put on their business faces, got out their cars, revved them up, turned into Brambly Way, and were sucked into the metropolis. Dick Weldon went to his architect's office, Felix Mayfield, smartest of the smart, to the elegant Georgian house recently acquired by his advertising firm, a local doctor to his surgery, and a dentist to face the array of bad teeth in his waiting-room. Jack Jellifer went to an appointment with an editor to whom he hoped to sell a series of articles on "Great Dishes of the East." Mr Belando, one of those disturbing horses of a different colour, went to a job in his country's consulate, and Mr Kabanga went – well, nobody yet knew exactly where he *did* go. Sir Edmund, watching the cars turning out of The Dell from the bow window of his house in Brambly Way, deplored the vehicular – as he deplored the architectural, the moral, and almost all the other – habits of the age. The Dell children went to school, the Dell wives did the necessary jobs around their wonderfully labour-saving houses, in which many of them were helped by dailies who obliged for a couple of hours. Then they went shopping in the High Street or arranged flowers or read the papers or went in for a chat over a cup of coffee. Their lunches were light, for the children stayed at school, and all except a few local husbands were up in London. Dinner was the meal of the day, dinner preceded by a cosy little drink, and it was towards dinner that the Dell wives bent their culinary thoughts.

AdArt Associates, the firm owned by Grundy and Werner, occupied three rooms on the second floor of a street in the dubious area between Long Acre and the Strand. Two girls, or women, or secretaries sat at typewriters in the outer office, and the partners had a small room apiece. Since AdArts' business consisted essentially of selling the work produced by other people, nothing more was necessary. On this Monday morning Theo Werner, bow-tied, and wearing a dashing cardigan and what almost looked like winkle-picker shoes, was ebulliently cheerful, Grundy more uncommunicative than usual. They went together to see Clacton.

Clacton was a big rumpled man, an able editor who, like so many editors in these days, exercised little real power. When challenged about this in a television interview, Clacton had said that he made his own decisions, and no doubt in a sense this was true, but it was truer and more important that his individual decisions had to accord with the policy of managers who had a collective, not an individual, face. As soon as they entered his office, Grundy, whose sensibility in such matters was acute, realised that Clacton had something disagreeable to tell them. Theo, who was oblivious to such fine shades of feeling, was still smiling when the blow fell. Clacton delivered it with the briskness which is really kind. The paper didn't like "Guffy's Sooperdooper Bomb," and wasn't going to use it.

Theo's look changed almost comically. "Not to use it? But it was agreed, you agreed yourself. It has been drawn, it is finished."

Clacton nodded. "I know. It's tough."

"But what is the matter with the series?"

"It doesn't *feel* right." Clacton hesitated. "I'll tell you what's been said upstairs. It's subversive."

"Subversive." Grundy laughed. "A comic strip. How timid can you get?"

Theo, however, looked thoughtful, even grave. *Subversive* was a word he understood, one that carried a heavy weight of emotional meaning from the past.

"That's all very well, Sol, but you've got to see it their way." Clacton was earnest. "Krosscross is Kruschev, right, and Johnno is Johnson. You're putting them on the same level, aren't you, the same moral level I mean. They both do everything they can to stop the chap who wants disarmament. We're a radical paper, you know that, but they don't like it upstairs and I can see what they mean."

Grundy roared with laughter. "Come off it, Clack."

"I'm serious."

Theo also was serious. "So we change this a little and make it okey dokey, as they say."

"I'm afraid not. They've turned down the whole of this one, just like that."

49

Grundy was about to speak, but stopped as a boy came in with coffee. When the door had closed he said, with brow corrugated and lower lip thrust rebelliously out,

"This is all balls, Clack. We've got a contract."

"Yes. For a year."

"Supposing we push it, suppose we say that we like this and we don't agree to scrapping it."

Theo made a deprecatory gesture. Clacton looked lugubrious.

"There's something else I ought to tell you boys. There's a general feeling that the whole tone of Guffy over the last year or so hasn't been right. That one about the elections, you remember, and the series about the crooked building contractors, they weren't right."

"You've changed your mind. You liked them at the time," Grundy said sarcastically.

Clacton spread out his hands. "I'm on your side, boys, you know that. But we all have to face the facts of life."

"You mean you haven't got a mind to change, they make it for you upstairs?"

Clacton was not a man to lose his temper, but his voice hardened perceptibly. "All right. You don't want it easy, you can have it hard. The view upstairs is that the last four Guffy stories stink. They're preaching some sort of phoney radicalism, and what's worse they're not funny any more. This isn't just somebody blowing off, it's based on several samples of reader reaction. You can try to get back to your old style if you like, though they doubt if you can do it. So do I, to be frank. Otherwise we finish with the story that's running now, and you'll get a cheque for the rest of the year."

"Why, you crumby lot of bastards," Grundy said.

"Sol. Please, Sol." Theo had his hands clasped in entreaty.

"That goes for you too, Clacton." Grundy in anger, ginger-haired and red-faced, arms hanging apelike out of a jacket that seemed too small for him, was a terrifying figure. "I thought you were one of the editors with guts around Fleet Street. I see I was wrong."

"Please. He doesn't know what he is saying," Theo said.

Clacton stood up. "I think you'd better get out."

Grundy glared at him, his mouth and eyebrows twitching. Then one of his big hands swooped down, as though it was a creature with a life of its own, picked up a glass ashtray on the desk and flung it. Clacton ducked but in any case Grundy's aim was bad. The ashtray crashed through one of the glass panels behind the editor, and landed with a clatter in the press room outside. Grundy marched out like a Great Dane, trampling broken glass. Theo, a protesting poodle, followed him.

Mrs Langham, who liked to think of herself as a sort of confidential secretary, was really rather shocked by the events of that day, after the partners had returned from their interview with Mr Clacton. There was first of all the sound of angry argument in Mr Werner's office, argument of a kind she had never heard there before. Then, just after midday, Mr Grundy burst out of Mr Werner's office, grabbed his coat, barked something unintelligible at her, and went out, slamming the door. Two or three minutes later Mr Werner came out, and he – he who was always so pleasant, so happy, so much one for a joke – brushed past Mrs Langham and her associate Miss Pringle, without so much as a word. He was wearing his camel-hair coat and his smart little Tyrolean hat, and when he turned at the door they could see that his bow tie was sadly out of place. "I shall not be back today," he said.

Mrs Langham did not reply, feeling that least said soonest mended. But Miss Pringle could not resist remarking, "Your tie, Mr Werner, it's not quite straight."

"My tie," he responded with an agonised look, "is *ruined*, Miss Pringle, ruined." Then he was gone.

The stresses of the day were not yet over. Half a dozen people rang up during the course of the afternoon, artists and people from advertising agencies, and Mrs Langham had to employ her stalling technique of saying that both partners had been called out urgently in connection with something – as she hinted, naming no names – really big. It was five o'clock when Mr Grundy came back and he was obviously, as Mrs Langham discreetly put it to herself, the worse for wear. When she told him about the messages he looked at her with bloodshot eyes and said nothing. When she said that Mr Werner would not be back, and suggested that he should make some telephone calls he spoke one word only: "Later."

At half past five she and Miss Pringle put the covers over their typewriters, and she opened the door of his office. He glared at her, and said again: "Later."

Mrs Langham was offended. "Miss Pringle and I are going, Mr Grundy. Shall I put the line through direct to your office?"

He smiled, and she melted at once. She thought he had a very nice smile. "Sorry to be snappy. Had a hard day." His speech was just a little blurred. "Put the line through. And let me have the Guffy file, the drawings."

She took in to him the Guffy McTuffie file, which contained the last four series of Guffy strips, covering a year. When she closed the door he had propped them on the desk and was staring at them.

Grundy often had a drink with an artist on the firm's books after office hours, but he was usually home by seven. It was a quarter past seven on that Monday evening when he rang Marion and said that he would not be in to dinner.

She had spent part of the day in brooding on the defects in their relationship and had decided, as she often did in his absence, that they were largely her own fault. His call left her determinedly unruffled.

"It doesn't matter a bit," she said. "It just does not matter one bit."

"I hope you haven't made anything special."

It would have been the part of wisdom, no doubt, to say that there was only cold meat and salad, but honesty demanded that she should mention the rice dish, with lobster claws, mussels and chicken, that was in the oven.

"Oh," he said. "Sorry."

To ask exactly what he was doing would have been against Marion's principles. She said obliquely, "You'll be having dinner?"

"I'm in the office working on Guffy. There's been a bit of trouble with the paper."

"Oh, well. You'd like something when you get back."

"Don't bother. I'll have some sandwiches."

"You'll be home about ten." Again she refrained from putting it in the form of a question.

"I expect so."

He rang off. Marion ate the rice dish alone. It occurred to her while she did so that he had sounded a little odd.

Jack Jellifer had had an agreeable day. The series about "Great Dishes of the East" had been approved in principle, he had spent the afternoon in looking up some of the dishes and subtly modifying the details in them so that they became his own. He had then met Peter Clements in company with some other television administrators to discuss the idea of a programme called *Two Minute Meals,* and this too had been favourably received. Since Arlene had gone to see her mother and Rex Lecky was rehearsing in some distant part of London, Jack took Peter Clements to dinner at a new and rather special little restaurant. They discussed – it was almost impossible for Dell-dwellers not to discuss – the errors of Grundy, and they had only just stopped talking about him when they emerged into the street. Jack felt on good terms with the world as they walked down Curzon Street towards Shepherd's Market. He strode along jauntily, looking about him, not paying much attention to Peter Clements who was saying something rather boringly technical about television.

"Good lord," he said suddenly, and halted. Such out-of-date exclamations were not uncommonly used by him. "Speak of the devil. There he goes."

"Who?"

"That old open Alvis. You can't mistake it." He pointed to the tail end of a car that, a moment after, turned a corner.

"Grundy, you mean?"

"I certainly do. I wonder what he's doing round here at this time of night."

Peter resumed his monologue. What Jack Jellifer saw on that September evening was to be the subject of argument later on.

Marion watched television, which she regarded as her secret vice, and then went to bed and to sleep. She was woken by something – what? – the sound of heavy breathing perhaps. She switched on the light. Grundy was getting into his bed. It was midnight.

"You're late," she said sleepily.

"Working." He came over and kissed her on the cheek. She could smell whisky, rather disagreeable. "Night."

"Night." She turned away, and in five minutes was asleep again.

PART TWO

Chapter One *Body Discovered*

Cridge Street is a narrow street of rather elegant terrace houses that runs off Curzon Street. Cridge Mews is, naturally, narrower still, a cul-de-sac of a kind not unusual in this part of London, containing some twenty garages with mews flats above most of them. The flats are small and, for the accommodation they offer, expensive. Most of them are rented rather than leased, and a continual flow moves through them of actors, actresses, dress designers, models, and others who are professionally involved within or on the fringe of the world of art. At nine-fifteen on Tuesday morning a cleaning woman named Mrs Roberts trudged on her bad feet into Cridge Mews, put her key into the door of No. 12, said good morning to the young chauffeur who was washing the Daimler outside, took in the milk, and puffed slowly up the narrow stairs.

"Miss Simpson," she called in her hoarse voice.

"I'm here, Miss Simpson."

She turned right into the sitting-room which, as so often, was in a mess, glasses on tables, cigarette stubs in ashtrays, cushions dragged off sofa on to floor, dirty knife and plate lying on floor, electric fire left on. Mrs Roberts grumbled subterraneanly about this as she opened the window, switched off the fire, took out dirty things to the kitchenette. Clatteringly, mutteringly, she washed up, and then went to look at the French clock in the sitting-room. It said twenty to ten, and that meant it was time for Miss Simpson to get up. "I sleep like the dead, Robby," she often said. "But you've got to wake me up, I *want* to wake up, whatever I say, d'you see? So you just do it, and don't mind me."

Mrs Roberts went to the little passage at the top of the stairs and called her. Miss Simpson, she called, and not Estelle, although she had been told to use the Christian name. There was no reply, and no reply either when she knocked, even thumped, on the door. When she opened the door and saw what was inside, she began to scream.

She went down the stairs screaming, and almost fell into the arms of the young chauffeur, whose name was Harrison. He ran up the stairs two at a time after hearing what she had to say. Estelle Simpson lay on the floor in the bedroom, her face discoloured and her tongue hanging out. She wore nothing but a pair of frilly black knickers. The room was in disorder. Harrison stood looking at it for a moment, then went into the sitting-room and telephoned the police.

They arrived before half past ten, in the persons of a detective-inspector and a sergeant. During the course of the morning, as the case developed and its shape became apparent, reinforcements were called for and appeared, little men carrying black suitcases from which they produced odd pieces of apparatus, some of which looked as though they might have been useful to an astronaut in his space capsule, big men who carried photographic equipment, others who seemed merely to stand about gossiping at the door but were suddenly galvanised into action as their special skills were required. The men sniffed about over the flat like dogs, taking pictures, making chalk marks on the floor, covering surfaces with fine dust and then taking pictures of what appeared in the dust. The little flat had ceased to be the habitation of a human being who lived, was happy, suffered, had the right to say yes or no. She had become an object, something to be looked at and prodded by a surgeon, taken here and put there, speculated and joked about. And the place that had sheltered her, that too was now an object, one of interest simply because it might contain the answer to a problem.

The boss, the chief, the big noise, the man with the answers, in a word the super, arrived after these preliminaries had been carried out, as the star of a musical comedy appears only after a suitable introduction by the chorus and a song or two from minor members of the cast. His name was Manners and he belonged to the newer school of detective – superintendents, those who never eat peas with a knife. Jeffrey Manners had been to a good grammar school and a redbrick university, and he had chosen a career in the police quite deliberately because he thought it offered more opportunities to his particular talents than a job in a large corporation. Now, in his early forties, he was a slight, dark, handsome man with a certain aloofness that did not endear him to subordinates. He stood in the sitting-room and listened with a frown of concentration to grizzled, toughly amiable Inspector Ryan.

"Dr Worthy's in there now, but there seems no doubt she was strangled. Marks on her throat. He didn't wear gloves, but too confused to be any good for prints. Lots of prints around in the bedroom and here, but most of 'em are her own or belong to the cleaning woman, Mrs" – Ryan looked at his notes, – "Roberts."

He took a breath and continued. "So, who was she? She'd been here four months. Mrs Roberts says she had some sort of a job modelling clothes, sometimes firms would ring up while she was here and make appointments for her to come along. No reason to doubt her, but not much doubt either that the girl was a bit of a tom on the side, like a lot of them."

"What makes you say that?"

"Did you see her knickers, sir?"

"Her knickers?"

Ryan had them brought in, and handed them to Manners. They were ordinary black knickers, but wording was printed on them in a pattern that ran upwards in a pyramid. The wording said: "Oh please do not touch me. Oh please do not touch. Oh please do not. Oh please do. Oh please. Oh."

"Then there are these, sir. Found them in a drawer of her dressing-table."

Manners looked at the photographs with distaste.

"These are not the girl herself?"

"No, sir. But a girl who keeps things like this in her dressing-table –"

"Yes."

"At the same time Mrs Roberts says there was never a man here in the mornings and the chap who runs the garage down below, his name's Seegal, says he doesn't think she had men in during the day. So does the chauffeur, uses the garage, name's Harrison. Of course we shall be asking other people in the Mews. It could be that she only receives in the evening. Or could be that she's not a tom at all, just broad-minded."

A tall man with a fine head of grey hair came into the room. This was Doctor Worthy, the Home Office pathologist.

"All pretty straightforward from the look of it. Manual strangulation from behind. Girl didn't have much chance to put up a struggle. Wasn't wearing shoes, so she didn't even have a chance to kick out. No sign of sexual interference."

"She still had her knickers on," said Ryan, who liked a joke.

Manners said sharply, "Her clothes may have been removed afterwards. What about it, Ryan? Any sign of tears, anything like that?"

Ryan sobered at once. Manners, although polite, could be unpleasant. "Nothing like that, sir."

"The way it reads, then, is that this was someone she was preparing to make love with," Manners said in his unemphatic voice. "She'd undressed. Perhaps he had, we don't know. Then he got hold of her from behind, strangled her."

Worthy nodded. "It's easier to strangle anybody manually from in front, of course. It's possible that they fell to the ground and his grip shifted, but the main pressure was exerted from behind. Indicates a good deal of strength."

"Time of death?"

"Difficult to be more than approximate. Say about twelve hours ago. Between nine o'clock last night and one o'clock this morning would cover it, with a preference for some time between ten and eleven. But that's only a guess, mark you, picking out that hour." He paused.

"Something else I ought to mention. I knew the girl."

"You did?" Manners was not often surprised, but he frankly stared.

Doctor Worthy said rather awkwardly, "Only to say good morning, nothing more than that. I live just round the corner, in Charles Street, and I garage my car here. The young man who telephoned you, Harrison, is my chauffeur. Occasionally when I go out to dinner I bring the car back here myself, and sometimes I get it out myself in the morning. I've seen her – oh, not more than half a dozen times."

"You haven't seen any men here, or leaving the flat?"

"I haven't seen a man around at all, although no doubt there was one. She was an attractive girl, full of vitality."

"We think there was more than one." Ryan showed the doctor the photographs.

"Yes, I see. You think she was a prostitute. I can only say I saw no sign of it. She spoke" – *He* had been about to say *pleasantly but without refinement,* but recollected that Ryan was not conspicuous for refinement, – "like anybody else."

"I suppose it's possible that Harrison saw more of her than you did."

"Perhaps. Ask him by all means. But of course Harrison drives my wife as well, so he doesn't have all that much spare time."

He waved a hand and was gone. Ryan mimicked him, " 'Of course Harrison drives my wife as well.' It's that *of course* that gets me."

"You've talked to Harrison?"

"And to Seegal, the chap who runs the garage. Got nowhere. But here are two interesting things, a letter and a postcard. We've got prints off them, the girl's of course, and one or two others, rather smeary but they may be some use."

Manners read the letter first. It was written in green ink on grey paper which was headed "Petersham Club," with an address in Chelsea. The letter said: "Darling, Yesterday was wonderful. Missed you in the evening, though, what happened? Hope to be able to fix up something for you in the next few days. Ring me. T." The letter was undated, and gave no indication of the day on which it had been written.

The postcard was on ordinary stiff white card, and the few words on it were in an upright, angular hand. They were: "Monday evening. Same time, same place, same object." The card was not signed, but at the bottom there was a rough drawing of a little figure. Manners turned it over, saw that it was addressed to Estelle Simpson at the address in Cridge Mews, and that it had been posted in London, WC, on the preceding Thursday afternoon.

"Well," he said non-committally.

Leaves me to do the work, then takes the credit, Ryan thought without particular malice. "Both from boy friends, wouldn't you say? One finding her a new job, the other arranging to see her on the night she was killed. Be nice to talk to that joker who signs himself with a little drawing." Ryan paused, laughed. " 'Same object,' I like that. Suppose Mr Petersham Club found out that Miss Simpson had been having a spot of same object with Mr Drawing, he might not have been pleased."

"Too much theory, too little fact," Manners said, but he spoke mildly. "When we've finished here, try to find out who T is. But it's the other one that puzzles me."

62

"You mean, why sign with a drawing instead of a letter or a name? Kind of a code? Some special reason why he didn't want to use his own name. That what you mean?"

"I don't know. There's just something – I don't know." Manners dismissed it, went into the bedroom, stood looking down at the girl now decently covered with a cloth, the girl who yesterday had been attractive and full of vitality and today was an ugly piece in a sordid puzzle. The bed was untouched, uncrumpled. Two detectives were systematically examining the contents of a wardrobe.

"Where were those photographs?"

Sergeant Jones, who was conducting the examination, answered. "In the dressing-table drawer, sir. Not even hidden."

"And the letters?"

"Desk in the sitting-room, along with a lot of other stuff, mostly bills. Nothing else personal at all."

"She was certainly attractive," Manners said, looking at a head and shoulders portrait on the dressing-table. He went on thoughtfully, "If the chap who sent the postcard killed her, you'd think he'd have looked round for it. It pins the day on him. No sign of a search?" Jones shook his head. "All right. I'll talk to Mrs Roberts and the others."

He talked to them, but got little information. Mrs Roberts obviously had no love for the police, and would say nothing more than that Miss Simpson had been a lovely lady to work for, never complained, was always grateful for what you did. No men came to the flat, nobody rang up except firms who wanted Miss Simpson to model for them, and she could not remember any of the names.

Seegal and Harrison were more helpful. Seegal, small and swarthy, told them that he had a lease on a row of four garages in the Mews, three of which he rented out while he ran the fourth as a repairs business. He wiped dirty hands on a piece of waste, and talked about the dead girl.

"I saw her most days, except weekends that is, and she was a nice girl. Friendly, you know, you liked to talk to her. ' Call me Estelle,' she said. Nothing stand-offish about her."

"Was she a prostitute?"

Seegal scratched his dark chin. "Well, I don't know."

Ryan said aggressively, "You told me she didn't have men in during the day. You too, Harrison."

The chauffeur, a big freckled young man, touched his hand uneasily to the peaked cap on his head, and looked appealingly at Seegal, who spoke again.

"You know how it is. She was a nice girl, you don't want to make trouble, but – well, there were men called on her sometimes. Not many, often none at all. I don't think she was on the game, but I couldn't be sure."

"Some of them were arty types, they could have been to do with her acting," Harrison said.

"Acting?"

"Yes, she'd done some acting. In the provinces and on TV. That's what she said, anyway."

"She didn't tell you where? Any parts, any people she knew?"

Harrison said apologetically, "Afraid not."

"And how long did they stay, these people who came to see her?"

The two men looked at each other. Seegal was their spokesman. "No special time, ten minutes, half an hour, perhaps two hours. We didn't notice specially, you understand."

"You confirm that?" Ryan said to Harrison.

"I just don't know. Most days I'm not here more than an hour or two. I just know men did come to see her sometimes, that's all."

That was as far as they got. Seegal was doubtful whether he would recognise any of the men. They were mostly arty types, wore suede shoes and tight trousers. Their faces seemed to have impressed him not at all. He had shut up the garage at seven o'clock on Monday night and gone home. Altogether, Manners and Ryan left Cridge Mews knowing little about Estelle Simpson beyond her name.

Chapter Two *Background of a Victim*

The Petersham Club was in the basement of a street off the King's Road. Ryan walked down half a dozen steps and found himself in a room very much like that of any other small drinking club at half past three in the afternoon. There was a bar, music played quietly from a radio, a man and a woman sat in unspeaking communion on stools at the bar. The barman was a young negro. Police records showed that the owner of the club was a Mr A Kabanga, and Ryan showed his warrant card and asked to speak to him. The negro took him through a door which was concealed by a curtain, along a passage, then tapped on another door and opened it. "From the police," he said.

The police were obviously not unfamiliar here. Ryan thought, "Hallo, someone's been taking dropsy," but that was no part of his present concern. The man who rose from behind a desk was small, handsome, rather too elegantly dressed. He greeted Ryan politely, raised his brows when he looked at the warrant card, offered a drink. Ryan refused it. He believed in a direct approach and now he showed the man, whom he had classified instantly as a coffee-coloured spade, a photostat of the letter found in the flat. He watched the other's reaction carefully.

Kabanga showed no emotion other than annoyance.

"This is a copy of a letter of mine. Where did you get it?"

"You wrote it?"

"What have my relations with Sylvia to do with you?"

"Sylvia?"

Kabanga waved a neat, manicured hand. "Sylvia Gresham. Estelle Simpson is her stage name."

"Yes." Ryan felt himself on uncertain ground. Then this reference to fixing up something –"

"What has it to do with you? Sylvia and I have done nothing wrong."

"She was murdered last night. In her flat. That's why I'm here."

Kabanga put his hands palm down upon the desk in front of him, and his dark eyes increased in size and became swimmy. He's going to cry, Ryan thought incredulously, damned if the spade isn't going to cry. But Kabanga did not cry. He said in a flat, almost conversational tone, "My God." He got up, went over to a cupboard, poured himself a drink. Then he said, still in the same calm tone, "What do you want to know, Inspector?"

"How long had you known her?"

"Seven weeks."

"She was your mistress?"

"Yes. We were hoping – we intended to get married."

"How did you meet her?"

"She came here with a man, I don't know his name, a film man perhaps, somebody she hoped would give her a job. They had drinks, we talked. The next day she came back alone. She liked me, you see. She could tell that I liked her."

"You went to her flat in Cridge Mews?"

"Yes, I have done. And she stayed with me in my new house, it is in a good residential area." Ryan had a job to repress a smile at the phrase, as Kabanga told him where The Dell was.

"You own this club?"

"I have half a dozen clubs, Inspector. You have only seen the bar, but there is another room for dinner and dancing. They are profitable, my clubs. I do nothing wrong, you understand, but they are profitable."

"What did you mean by being able to fix something up for her?" Ryan drew a bow at a venture. "She told you she was pregnant and she'd asked you to arrange an abortion, that's right, isn't it?"

"Certainly not. What kind of man do you think I am?"

"I'd rather not say," Ryan replied, deliberately insulting. The remark had its effect. Kabanga for the first time seemed concerned about his own position.

"You do not think I had anything to do with her death? I loved her. I have friends in the theatre, and I was trying to find a job for her, that is all. Sylvia was a singer. Unfortunately I do not have a floor show myself, but –"

"Was she any good?"

"I think so, yes. She had been unlucky, that is all. She was out of a job for quite a time. It worried her."

"So that's what she was doing for a living."

"What do you mean?"

"She was a tom and you were poncing for her, isn't that a fact?"

Kabanga got up and came round the desk, hands clawing at Ryan, dark eyes moist not with tears now but with anger. Ryan pushed him away. When Kabanga came forward again he caught and shook him, not gently.

"You didn't know about it, all right, but it could be true. How often did you see her?"

"Three or four nights a week."

"What was she doing the rest of the time?"

Kabanga shrugged. "I was not her keeper. We would have lived together, she would have given up her flat and come to live with me, but I was not her keeper. She had her own life, her own friends."

"You saw some of them?"

"I do not think I could tell you their names. Some of them were in the dress trade, there was a man named Tom, a woman named Mina, who came in here once or twice. Some were I think in films or television. I remember an actress – what was her name – Susan Strong. She is in one of those plays that have been running for years. *The Worm Will Turn*, I think it is called."

"Where were you last night?"

"I was here, at this club, in the afternoon until six o'clock. Then I went to another of my clubs, the Windswept, and had dinner and spent the rest of the evening there."

"Where's this other place?"

"In Clarges Street, Mayfair."

"Ten minutes' walk from where the girl was murdered."

Kabanga looked very straight at Ryan. "Do you really believe, Inspector, that I had anything to do with Sylvia's death?"

Ryan had known several criminals who specialised in looking a detective straight in the eye and telling outrageous lies, but he was inclined to believe Kabanga. "You understand we have to make these inquiries," he said, much more politely. "Do you know of any enemies Miss Simpson, Miss Gresham, had?"

"She had no enemies," Kabanga said positively.

"Somebody killed her."

The head and shoulders photograph of the dead girl was released to the Press, and appeared in the afternoon editions. At four o'clock Sergeant Jones, who had been interrogating the other inhabitants of the Mews, returned to New Scotland Yard to report lack of progress.

"One or two of them aren't at home, sir, including the one who lives opposite to her, man named Leighton, but nobody that I've talked to noticed anything in particular about her visitors." He said a little resentfully: "Trouble is some of them are what you might call bohemians so they really wouldn't notice unless there was a knife fight in the Mews or something like that. There was one little chap who'd often visited her in the past few weeks, but nobody seemed able to describe him except to say he was a sharp dresser. Somebody said she'd seemed friendly with Seegal and that chauffeur, Harrison. But it doesn't seem to mean much, she was friendly with everybody, would always stop to talk if she met anybody in the street. There's one old bitch who said she was sure the girl was no better than she should be, everyone else seems to have liked her." Jones hesitated. "Those pictures could have been planted by whoever killed her."

"And the knickers too?" Manners asked mildly.

"I suppose not." Jones hesitated again. "Do you read the *Blade,* sir?"

"No, I don't. Should I?"

"Just struck me that little figure on the card looks like a figure in a cartoon strip they run. Character called Guffy McTuffie."

"Guffy McTuffie?" Manners was incredulous.

Jones brought in the paper, and they compared it with the card. Certainly the little figure, with its single curl of hair, looked very similar.

"I think you may have something," Manners said. "Good work, Jones."

"Thank you, sir."

"You've got something, but what does it mean?"

The telephone rang. "Was it her pet name for a lover, he signed the card like that because she called him Guffy? In that case, what would his real name be?"

"Gussie?"

Manners picked up the receiver. The, switchboard operator said, "A Mrs Gresham on the line, sir. To do with the Cridge Mews murder this morning. Says she's the girl's mother."

"Put her on."

The voice on the telephone was warm, agitated, girlish. "I am poor Sylvia's mother."

"I beg your pardon."

70

"Her photograph was in the paper, my husband showed it to me. They called her Estelle Simpson, that was the name she passed under."

"I see. You are Mrs Gresham."

"Melicent Gresham." Girlishly the voice said.

"Melicent, not Millicent, Sergeant. Melicent with an 'e'."

"This is Superintendent Manners, Mrs Gresham. It's good of you to telephone. I'd like very much to talk to you as soon as possible."

"But of course. I had no idea that I was talking to a *superintendent*."

"Could I have your address, Mrs Gresham." Manners wrote it down, then said, "I'll come out myself. Yes. Goodbye." He sat staring at the address. "The Home of Supra Peace, Tooting. Have you heard of the Home of Supra Peace, Jones?"

"No, sir."

"That's where the mother lives. I'm going to talk to her. You come along too. Perhaps at last we're going to find out what this girl was like."

"I'll tell you what she was like. She was one of nature's victims," Susan Strong said. The matinee of *The Worm Will Turn* was over, and she sat in her dressing-room talking to Ryan in the looking glass while she cleaned her face, a babyish-looking blonde in her twenties. Ryan watched the operation with interest.

"I'm not sure that I understand."

"Well, I'll tell you. We met, oh, about eighteen months ago, we were both in the chorus of some mouldy little musical, both wanted to be a success. But the way Estelle – that's what I always called her, too late to change now – the way Estelle went about it, she never had a hope. She'd turn up late for rehearsals, go out for a night of heavy drinking and look really shagged the next day, fall for any man who spun her a story. Producers don't like that sort of thing, and you can't blame them."

"You're saying she was a tramp?"

"No, not exactly." She turned round, lit a cigarette, offered him a drink. Ryan accepted. "She just believed what people said, that's all. She couldn't tell when they were lying to her, and she hadn't got any self control. During the run of this musical she started sleeping first with one man in the cast, then with another. She was surprised when the first one was upset, and the second one didn't care about her anyhow. She was the original girl who couldn't say no."

She was a tramp in my book, Ryan thought, but didn't say so. Instead he asked: "Had she any talent?"

"Not much, but when did lack of talent stop any girl who wanted to get on?" She drank, went on. "Estelle wasn't a fool. But she was silly, if you see what I mean. Now, I'm not like that. I may look silly, but that's purely for stage purposes. I know what I want, and I mean to get it."

I'll bet you do, Ryan thought. "Who was she carrying on an affair with – just now?"

"Some African creep who runs half a dozen clubs. His name's Kabanga. I didn't like him, told her he was a creep, but she took no notice."

"Was there any second string?"

"Not that I know of, but she mightn't tell me. We weren't that close. Last week she said she was going to marry Kabanga, but I didn't pay much attention, she'd said that sort of thing before."

"We have some reason to think she was a prostitute." She stared at him. He told her about the knickers. She laughed.

"If I may say so, Inspector, you're a little bit old-fashioned. There are a dozen shops in the West End selling knickers like that, and they're sold to perfectly respectable girls. It's like that old music hall joke, you know, 'Which of your relations do you like best?' 'Why, I like sex relations best.' You'll be hearing that any day now on BBC television. You're just slightly out of date."

Ryan was nettled. He told her about the photographs.

"Am I out of date about those too?"

"No." She sat staring. "She wasn't in them herself?"

"No."

"Because that, in a way, I can imagine. I can imagine her doing something stupid like that if she liked the man, or getting trapped into it somehow. But otherwise – no, I can't explain it. She wasn't a prostitute, though, and don't let any one kid you that she was. She liked sex too much for that."

"Tooting," Manners said reflectively in the car, as they passed through South London's suburbs. "How can a place be called Tooting? It's ridiculous. You'd think nobody would ever live there. 'I live at Tooting, I live at the Home of Supra Peace, Tooting.' It's unbelievable."

Jones, who lived at Cockfosters, was not impressed by this observation. He was also inclined to think that the Super had slighted his Guffy McTuffie discovery. He made no reply.

The Home of Supra Peace turned out to be a large ugly red brick Victorian house, set in its own considerable grounds, just off Tooting Bec Common. Manners and Jones were shown into a room lined with bookcases, where a few rugs were thrown about on a parquet floor. A tall man with a deeply lined face got up from behind a desk littered with papers. His eyes were dark and intense, his handgrip painfully firm, his smile singularly sweet.

"My name is Kronfelder, and I am the director of this Home."

"I was expecting to see Mrs Gresham," Manners said flatly.

"Melly will be here in a moment. She spoke to me after telephoning you, and I thought it best that I should speak to you first to avoid any misunderstanding."

"What sort of misunderstanding could there be?"

Kronfelder put his hands one over another. They were very white, plump hands, at variance with his appearance. Behind him a garden could be seen, with people moving about in it. "I don't know how much Melly told you on the telephone." Manners stayed unhelpfully silent.

"Did she say that Sylvia lived here?"

"No, she didn't tell me that."

"A grave decision had to be taken about Sylvia, Superintendent, to decide what would be truly in her own best interests. I don't suppose you know very much of our work here or of the teachings that inspire the Supra Peace movement. Ouspensky, Subuh, Gurdieff, do these names mean anything to you?" Manners shook his head, Jones moved his feet. Kronfelder's voice had grown warm, rich and expressive as he talked. "Our doctrines – yet they are not doctrines so much as beliefs not beliefs so much as instinctive certainties, mystical if you like to call them that – are a synthesis of these teachers and of others we respect, Christ, Buddha, Mahomet. They offered peace, but we try to reach something that is beyond individual peace of mind, utter harmony with the whole created world, what I call supra peace. We do this by means of group meditation, days of silence, manual labour, long periods of solitude. You may say that others too have done this, but we –"

"What has this got to do with Mrs Gresham's daughter, Mr Kronfelder?"

"Doctor," the big man said with his sweet smile. "I was a specialist in Stockholm – a doctor of the body before I understood that it is more important to cure the mind."

There was a knock on the door. A large, shapeless middle-aged woman came in. "The Group of Second Servers are ready for you to address them, Doctor."

"I shall be with them in five minutes. You know the rules, Irene, they will meditate together without speech. And when I go I wish you to take these gentlemen to Melicent. She is in her cell. You will see her quite alone," he assured Manners, who nodded his head.

"You must forgive me for trying to interest you in our work, but I have made more unlikely converts than police officers." Again that smile. "You asked what our work had to do with Sylvia. Simply this. She came here with her mother and father

74

when she was eight years old, and stayed until she was sixteen. At that time it was decided that she should leave."

"Who decided it and why?"

"The decision was taken by Melly and her husband Charles."

"On your advice?"

"They consulted me, certainly."

"And why was she – would expelled be the word?"

"Indeed it would not." Doctor Kronfelder put his arms on the desk, leaned forward and stared direct at Manners while managing somehow to include Sergeant Jones also in his gaze. "We accept everything that happens in the universe, but we are striving always towards the ideal of supra peace. We recognise high spirits, youthful unruliness, fornication, but we cannot permit them to disrupt the life of our community. Sylvia was a liar, a fornicator, one who had no conception of any Way beyond the Way of pleasure. We decided that for some years her life should be passed in the world outside this Home."

"We means you, isn't that so, Doctor Kronfelder?"

The doctor shook his head. "In myself I am nothing. I am the expression of the General Will."

Manners stood up. His voice was harsh. "I should like to see Mrs Gresham now."

Kronfelder rose behind his desk. Jones, rather belatedly, got up too. "I want you to understand the position. Sylvia's life here was over long ago. It can have nothing to do with her sad death. I hope there may be no need for public reference to her life here."

He came out of the room with them and strode away along a passage. The shapeless Irene took them up two flights of stairs, answering almost monosyllabically their questions about the length of time she had been there and the sort of work she did. Her tongue seemed unlocked as they passed through a baize-covered door like that of a doctor's waiting-room, into another part of the house. There were numbered doors on either side. An elderly man using a mop with a notable lack of enthusiasm smiled at them.

"These are the meditation cells," Irene said. "We use them when someone wants to come to an important decision, or after they have had a shock. Like Melly now."

Jones was walking beside her. "Did you know Estelle – Sylvia?"

"I knew her." She said fiercely, "She was corrupt."

"Corrupt?"

"She wished to defile everything." She opened the door of room number eleven, said, "Here are the policemen," and was gone.

The room was comfortable, shabbily but decently furnished, more like a bed-sitting-room than a cell for meditation. There were folkweave curtains and a bed with a cover in the same pattern. Melicent Gresham half-rose to greet them out of an arm-chair, then sank back into it. She was a fattish woman of fifty, with one of those good-looking, unlined, yet characterless faces frequently owned by those who have managed to absent themselves from the stresses of the world. She gestured with a plump ringless hand towards the other chair that the room contained. Manners took it. Jones sat down gingerly upon the bed.

Melicent Gresham's voice was high, fluting, without depth, the voice of somebody present corporeally but in spirit half-absent.

"You'll hardly believe me, Superintendent – Manners, isn't it? – but I have had a presentiment that something was about to happen to Sylvia. I said so to Charles and to Percy, but they did not believe me. It shows what I have often said, that true immersion in the Way brings instinctive perception of the outer world." Manners began to speak, but she interrupted him. "I should like to offer you some tea, but –" She let the sentence trail away. Jones, who was thirsty, wondered what the ultimate clause would have been.

"Who is Percy?"

"Doctor Kronfelder. Those who have known him a long time call him Percy." She waved a hand limply. "We have been here fourteen years. We had been drifting through life, Charles and I, without purpose. Do you have a purpose in life?"

"Catching criminals. Tell me how you came here," Manners said hastily, as Mrs Gresham seemed about to reflect on his occupation.

"Our time came when a surgeon, three surgeons, three of the leading surgeons in London, said that I must have an operation. I will not embarrass you with details, but it was a very delicate internal operation." She looked at Manners and then at Jones, who found himself staring at the worn carpet. "At that time Charles had this job with, I don't know, an export firm – oh, quite a good job, Superintendent. We lived in Highgate, a very pleasant house, everything quite comfortable, we were like any other people you meet in the street, you would have seen no difference. But there was a difference. *I knew that I was not meant to be cut by surgeons*, do you understand me? I was not aware of it at the time, but I was seeking for the Way."

The stuff I listen to in the cause of justice, Manners thought. Aloud he said, "Sylvia was with you?"

"We took her to a meeting. Percy did not often hold public meetings even then, and now he has given them up, but something drew us to that one. He talked of the Way of Peace, and while I listened –" A little shiver ran through Mrs Gresham's large frame. "– I cannot express my feelings. But I knew. I understood – oh, not intellectually, don't think that, Charles is the clever one – but through all my senses I knew what Percy calls the Isness of Becoming. I asked Percy's advice – he is also a doctor, you know that – and he told me that the operation was quite unnecessary. He treated me, not through medicine but through talk, prayer, meditation, and within two weeks the very distressing symptoms of my illness had vanished. We had found more than the Way of Peace, we had found Supra Peace."

"Your husband too?"

"He Understands but he has not Become," Mrs Gresham replied cryptically. "It is a saying of Percy's."

The interview, Manners saw, was likely to be a long one. He persevered, trying to extract from Melicent Gresham's tangled web of mysticism the thread that would lead to her daughter. The conversion, he gathered, had been complete. Charles Gresham had given up his job and they had come to live at the Home of Supra Peace. The principles of the Home were that all labour was voluntary and that those who volunteered received payment according to their needs. For those who lived in the Home, however, the needs were few. One of the great blessings of the Way of Supra Peace, as Melicent Gresham observed, was its absolute freedom from all monetary encumbrances, and Manners gathered that all such encumbrances in the form of house and savings had passed to the Home. Sylvia had gone to a local school, and had lived at the Home. Some twenty families lived there, the number fluctuating as new disciples were gathered and old ones strayed away.

But there had always been something alien about Sylvia, her mother said. The Isness of Becoming was something that she never apprehended, and the simple life and food of the Home seemed insufficient for her. She began to show an interest in boys. There was one other boy of her age at the Home, and when she was fourteen she had been found at night in his bedroom – or so Manners gathered, for Mrs Gresham spoke of' the incident so circuitously, and with such a number of tangential observations on Sylvia's incapacity to understand the Way, that he could not be sure. After that there had been an incident with a married man, a man who had left the Home abruptly. And after that Percy himself had been tempted, and – here Melicent Gresham used language of such mystical obscurity that Jones looked totally bewildered. But it had been decided that Sylvia should go.

"Go where?"

"Away." She made one of her limp hand movements. "She belonged in the world of cinemas and theatres and – sex. The Way of Peace was not for her."

Jones felt that he should say something. "You sent her to a relative?"

"We have no relatives." She amplified this. "We do not acknowledge them."

"But then –"

"She belonged in the world. We had taken her from it, but she wished to return. We did not prevent her. Percy found her a job."

"What sort of job?"

"Something, I don't know, it was in some kind of shop, a department store I believe. He also arranged for her to stay with a very suitable family, one that attended our meetings sometimes although they were not residents. But she did not stay more than a week or two with them, she did not stay in the job Percy had found." She made another of those indecisive gestures. "She belonged to the world, she returned to it, it destroyed her."

Manners could hardly trust himself to speak. Indignation rose in his chest, strong as heartburn. "She was your daughter."

She bent her direct yet absent gaze upon him. "Here we regard earthly relationships differently."

"You owed her something." She merely looked at him. "You did nothing – nothing at all to see whether she was happy, looked after?"

"She had rejected us. She had rejected the Way of Peace. She had rejected this Home."

Home, Manners wanted to say, do you call this mausoleum for decaying cranks a home? But there was no point in saying it. "Did she ever come back?"

"At first she came here sometimes to see us, three or four times a year perhaps. She said she was a model, then an actress, that she had good parts. Whether it was true or not –" She got up, wandered to the window, touching bits of furniture, "– I don't know. It all seemed to us very trivial."

"Your husband shared your opinions?"

"Of course."

"Had you seen her or heard from her in the last few months?"

"Oh, certainly we had letters. And a card at Christmas. But I have not kept them. They would tell you nothing, they were – trivial."

Jones coughed, leaned forward on the bed. "Can you suggest anybody who might have had a reason for killing her?"

She bent her gaze upon him, stared at him rather as though he were an insect. "It was one of her lovers," she said placidly.

"How was she when you found her, had she been – attacked?"

"She was strangled," Manners said shortly. "There was no sign of sexual interference." They got up to go.

The elderly man's idle mopping had carried him to the head of the staircase where he stood, hand on mop head, staring at one of John Martin's monumental religious scenes. "She told you what you wanted?"

"I wouldn't say that. Did you know Sylvia Gresham?"

He cackled. "I'm her father."

From the dismissive way in which Melicent Gresham had spoken, Manners had thought her husband was dead. Now he said, "You agreed when Sylvia left this place?"

"Not much use doing anything else. When Melly makes up her mind to something, that's what happens."

"But you were her father. You were responsible."

"I came here for peace. That's what I've got." He lifted the mop, touched the end of it, grinned.

"Did you hear from her?"

"Heard from her all right. Letters are trouble. Never answered."

"What did she say?"

"Can't remember. Some stuff. Always asking me about things." He turned bleary eyes to Manners. "You're as bad as she was, don't seem to understand. I just want to be left alone, that's all. Let them run everything, Percy, Melicent. Just leave me alone." He looked at the painting, in which hundreds of tiny figures cowered under an enormous rock which was being split by lightning. Some vast heavenly presence filled the sky.

"That's a fine picture. I like looking at it."

Manners's heels positively clattered as he went down the stairs, he went so fast across the hall and out to the car that Jones could hardly keep up with him. In the car, as they drove back, he spoke with a bitterness the sergeant had never heard in his voice. "The poor little devil, slung out to look after herself before she was sixteen. With a mother and father like that, what chance had she got? It would have been a blessing for her if she'd been brought up in a slum."

Chapter Three *Some of the Witnesses*

When Manners returned to the Yard he found Ryan waiting for him. The inspector had the glint of achievement in his eye as he told of his conversations with Kabanga and Susan Strong. Manners was unimpressed, and said so.

"That's not the end of it. Kabanga lives in Surrey, in a place called The Dell, sort of a high-class housing estate, only they don't call 'em that out there. She stayed there with him once or twice. Right? Now, a chap called – " Ryan looked at a memo pad, "– Paget has been on the blower to say that he remembers seeing this girl at a party there last Friday. She was with Kabanga, called herself Sylvia, he doesn't know her other name –"

"Sylvia Gresham. Estelle Simpson was her stage name or whatever you like to call it."

"Gresham, all right. At this party the girl had some sort of row with a man named Grundy. Paget says she smacked his face."

"Yes. I still don't see any cause for excitement."

"Wait. We're not at the end yet. You know Jones left someone checking up on that idea of his about the strip cartoon. Here's the result."

Manners took the memorandum Ryan handed to him, read:

> *Subject.* Guffy McTuffie strip cartoon. This appears six days a week in *Daily Blade,* has done so for three years. Have talked to editor, Mr Clacton, who says it was recently decided to rest the series. Decision was

82

communicated yesterday to T Werner and S Grundy, who are jointly responsible for it.

T Werner and S Grundy are partners in AdArts, firm of advertising art agents, also produce Guffy cartoons. Understand Grundy has ideas, Werner is artist, but need to check. Suggest investigation both men, see if associates of Estelle Simpson.

Manners read and re-read it. "Grundy was at the party."

"Right. And the girl smacked his face. And he lives in The Dell. A visit is called for, don't you think? Here are two things that could have happened. One, Kabanga killed her because he found out she was having an affair with Grundy. His club is only ten minutes' walk away from her flat, it's perfectly possible. Two, and I like this better, she was a tom. Grundy is an old client and when she meets him she tries to put the black on him, that's what causes the trouble at the party. She increases the pressure, threatens to tell his wife, he kills her." Manners smiled faintly, said nothing. "I know, theorising without facts. Still, it's worth seeing Grundy and this Paget, who sounds a nasty bit of work by the way."

"Yes, you're right." He was still thinking of Sylvia Gresham's parents, and the Home of Supra Peace.

"Whose manor is it?"

"Bobby Clavering's."

Five minutes later Manners was talking to Superintendent Robert Clavering, chief of the CID in the district where The Dell was to be found. The call was made partly as a matter of courtesy, partly in the hope of obtaining information. Clavering, a big bluff man who kept his nose to the ground, had little to give. The Dell, Manners gathered, was an estate similar to several that were being built on the outskirts of London and other big cities.

"They knock down perfectly good old places, put up these damned glasshouses, people go and live in 'em because it's fashionable, pay the earth for three poky rooms, all mod cons of

83

course, landscaped gardens, all that. The Dell's one of those. Don't know how some of the people afford to live there, I know I couldn't. Wouldn't want to for that matter, I like a garden of my own."

Manners was not interested in where Clavering lived or wanted to live. He asked about Paget and Grundy. "Edgar H Paget, F.A.L.P.A., yes, I know him." Clavering's jolly laugh boomed down the telephone. "Estate agent, does very nicely I should think. Biggest busybody in the district, always writing to the local paper about civic rights, ringing up the Council about refuse collection, that sort of man. What's our Edgar been doing?"

"Nothing he shouldn't, as far as I know. He rang us with a bit of information about that job in Cridge Mews. Just wondered what his standing was."

"Solid citizen, very much so. What was the other chap's name, Grundy? Don't know him at all. You coming down here?"

"I think so, yes."

"Come in and have a noggin."

Manners promised to do so, rang off, looked at his watch, and sighed. He ate a hurried meal, collected the sergeant who had been gathering the material in the memo, a man with the improbable name of Fastness, made sure that Paget was in, and set out on the half-hour car journey to see him and perhaps to pay a call also on Grundy.

"Mind you, Superintendent, I'm saying nothing, I'm making no accusation. Just giving you the evidence of my own eyes." Edgar Paget flung himself back in his chair, a man exhausted by the performance of his duty.

"And what you saw with your own eyes was Miss Gresham coming down the stairs –"

"He'd torn her dress."

84

"Her dress was torn," Manners said patiently. "You didn't see him tearing it. And Mr Grundy was at the top of the stairs, dabbing at his cheek."

Paget bristled a little, evidently feeling that these refinements were unnecessary. Manners turned to Jennifer Paget, large, spotty, awkward, and considered her for a moment. Then he spoke gently. "Now, Miss Paget, I'll just recapitulate what you've said. You were in the lavatory upstairs, and you heard a scream. You opened the door and you saw Miss Gresham standing in the doorway. Mr Grundy was behind her. His hand was on her shoulder, and he was trying to detain her." Manners noticed a glance, a mere flicker of a glance from upraised and then downcast eyes, directed by the rock-faced Mrs Paget at her daughter.

"You're sure of that?"

Jennifer had increased in assurance with the length of his stay. She spoke boldly.

"Quite sure."

"Was her dress already torn?"

"Yes. She was holding it up with her other hand, her right hand."

"Then she broke away from him and came down the stairs? Mr Grundy followed her?"

"Yes."

"And what did you do?" Manners asked suddenly.

Two spots of colour showed in her pudgy cheeks. "I was frightened. I went back into the toilet."

"Would Mr Grundy have seen you?"

"I – I don't know. I just stepped back. He might not have done."

"And now just tell me again what you saw on the following night, Saturday night."

She told them with composure, in a slightly sing-song voice. "It was about – between half past ten and eleven, and I was taking Puggy, that's our dog, out for a walk. We went up

85

Brambly Way and to The Dell and at the entrance to The Dell
Puggy tugged me that way and I let him pull me along. Just a few
yards inside the entrance I saw Mr Grundy and the lady I'd seen
at the party. They were standing off the path and he was holding
her and saying something, but I couldn't hear what. Then Puggy
pulled me back into Brambly Way again, but I looked back and
they were going together into No. 99, that's where Mr Kabanga
lives. That's all I saw."

Was the girl telling the truth? Manners was not sure. But
Fastness wrote out the statements and they signed them, Paget
with a flourish, his daughter in a round girlish hand.

"A drop more whisky?" Manners shook his head.

"You understand, I'm just doing my duty as a citizen. And
my daughter too."

"I understand."

Marion's attempts to preserve an integrated relationship with
her husband took three forms, cooking a meal with particular
care, talking about something that she thought would interest
him, and making it clear that she was sexually available. When
one or all of these stratagems failed she was inclined to relapse
into her more frequent feeling that such things were
unimportant. Tuesday evening was a relapsed period. They had
frozen fishcakes and frozen peas for dinner, with sauce made
from a packet, and afterwards cheese and fruit.

Grundy had said little, but now he paused in the act of coring
an apple, tapped the evening paper. "That girl's been killed."

"What girl?"

"The one whose dress tore at the party."

"Well." Marion took the paper from him, read the story. "It
says here her name's Estelle Simpson, but it does look like the
same girl. You can see what sort of girl she was." She got up,
cleared away the plates, spoke from the kitchen. "That
incident's closed, agreed?"

"There wasn't any incident."

She came to the door of the kitchen, dishcloth in hand, and spoke with elaborate patience. "I don't want to know anything more about your relationship with her, do you understand?"

"There's nothing to know."

Her patience now barely masked an irritation that she felt as acutely as if it were flannel chafing her skin. "Don't try to treat me like a child, as though I didn't understand. I fully realise that at certain times –"

He broke in. "You don't realise any bloody thing at all, so shut up."

Was it worth making a retort on this low level? She was still trying to decide when the door bell rang and provided a reason for ending the conversation.

"Mrs Grundy?" said one of the two men at the door.

"Good evening. Is your husband in?"

She had begun to say a hesitant yes, when she was aware of her husband's voice behind her. "I'm Grundy. What do you want?"

Almost but not quite smiling, and moving forward without in the least seeming to push his way in, the man in front said, "Detective-Superintendent Manners, sir, and this is Sergeant Fastness. Is it a convenient time to have a word with you?"

Somehow, after a moment or two, they were both inside, and she found herself closing the door after them. They all sat down in the living-room. The superintendent, she saw, was a refined, almost ascetic-looking man, one who might well have been a member of the district's Art or Archeological or Musical Societies. The sergeant was, well, he was very much like what you would expect a sergeant to be. Now the superintendent was saying, after glancing quickly at the evening paper on the table, "I wonder if you noticed the story in the paper this evening?"

"About that woman, Estelle Simpson, you mean?"

Grundy said. "We were just talking about it as a matter of fact, speculating whether she was someone we'd met –"

"Last Friday night, here at a party?" Manners nodded. "Yes, she was."

"She didn't use the same name there."

"No. Sylvia Gresham was her real name." He looked from Grundy to Marion, nodding again, pleased as Punch. His pleasure did not diminish when he was offered a drink. The four of them sat sipping whisky. Then Manners continued, still with an air of finding his own questions slightly absurd.

"Did either of you know Miss Gresham – I mean, before the party." Their negatives came together. "But I believe, sir, that you had something of an argument with her there."

"No." Grundy added, in a tone of vicious sarcasm.

"Is it your idea that because of this supposed argument I killed her? Is that what you've come to ask?"

Manners looked, and indeed was, shocked. People didn't, shouldn't, say such things with such crudity. Why had this big bruiser-like ginger man said it? He felt a certain artificiality in the words, as though Grundy were trying to force an issue that had not been reached. He said placatively, "Certainly not, sir. We're making inquiries into Miss Gresham's death and this incident has been reported to us, that's all."

"And I can guess who's reported it."

"Would you care to tell us just what happened, sir?"

"Nothing to tell. I was upstairs, tried to go to the lavatory but someone was in there, and she called to me from the bedroom. The zip on her dress had got caught in the dressing-table curtain. She asked me to do it up, I tugged it, tore her dress. She swore at me, screamed, scratched my face. Then she ran downstairs."

"I see."

"That's all. Never seen her before, never seen her since."

"Did you see anyone come out of the lavatory after you left it?"

"No."

"Or standing in or beside the lavatory door when you came downstairs after Miss Gresham?"

"No."

Manners said carefully, "There is a witness who said that you put your hand on Miss Gresham's shoulder, tried to detain her."

"I didn't see this witness, but that's right. I did put my hand on her shoulder. I was pretty annoyed when she scratched my face. Forgot to mention it."

Manners had now to make up his mind whether he should mention the identification made by Jennifer on Saturday night, and the postcard found in Cridge Mews. Such decisions are taken almost intuitively, and he could not afterwards have said why he mentioned the second of these but not the first. He took a photostat of the card from an envelope and asked Grundy whether he had written it.

The photostat lay on a small occasional table. The big man bent over to look at it. His wife got up from her chair and came over to look at it too. Then, lips pursed, she went back to her chair.

Grundy shook his head. "Nothing to do with me."

"That little figure on the bottom. It's been suggested that it looks very much like your cartoon character." Manners paused, then pronounced the words with an effort. "Guffy McTuffie."

"So I see. But that doesn't mean I drew it, or wrote the card."

"Of course not."

"I'm telling you I didn't. I take it the card has something to do with the murder."

"It was found in her flat. The appointment made in it is for Monday evening, last night, the night she was murdered. We'd like to know who wrote it."

"I can tell you I didn't, although as a matter of fact it looks rather like my writing." He went to a desk, took out two sheets of paper which had some notes on them, and handed them to Manners. The writing certainly looked very similar to that on the postcard. My word, he thought, this is a cool customer. Let's see how cool he is. He said. "I wonder if you'd mind writing something for me."

"All right."

He dictated the words on the postcard. The big man wrote them, unmoved.

"By the way, sir, where were you yesterday evening after – oh, after eight o'clock say?"

Grundy's smile was grim. "At my office working on this strip cartoon series. Alone. I got home about a quarter to twelve."

"The thing I really feel is that one's got a duty." Jack Jellifer sipped the new bedtime drink he had invented, a drink compounded of hot rum and lemon plus dashes of not one but two liqueurs to add pungency and puzzlement. "This has something. Shall I call it a Jellifer Goodnight?"

"I hope not." Arlene, perched on the arm of a chair, studied him thoughtfully. "I think you're being a bit of a nosy bastard about this, my old love. Now don't get on your high horse, it doesn't suit you. I like Sol."

"So do I," Jack said untruthfully. "But that's hardly the point."

"I should say it's very much the point. Let the police do their own dirty work."

"That's an outrageous attitude."

"After all, what did you see? Somebody in an old Alvis, you don't know who it was."

"How could I see? The hood was up."

"Did you spot the number, do you even know Sol's number?"

"Of course I didn't look at the number. Why should I have done?"

"Well then." She drained her glass. "If you ask me this drink is rather disgusting. Sickly."

Jack Jellifer was not capable of being really angry with his wife, whom he prized as his most precious possession, one even more valuable, delightful and suited to his way of life than the fish painting, but this criticism of Jellifer's Goodnight certainly annoyed him. He stroked the fleshy cheeks which in five years' time would become jowls, and said, "There was no doubt at all about it being his car. It's got a rent in the hood which I particularly noticed. I shall telephone the police."

"You're quite sure about seeing him on Saturday night with that woman, aren't you?" Rhoda Paget said to her daughter.

"Of course she's sure," Edgar broke in.

"Edgar," she said sharply. He was silent. Square and formidable, Rhoda confronted her daughter and repeated the question. Jennifer was unshaken.

"I couldn't mistake him."

"And you're sure it was her, too? You saw them go into the house."

"Yes, I'm sure."

Rhoda's manner changed to sudden, ferocious joviality.

"She only got what she deserved."

When Rex Lecky got back from rehearsals that evening Peter Clements, with an apron round his slightly thickening waist, was cooking in the kitchen. Half an hour later he dished up a meal to which Jack Jellifer would have given qualified approval. Rex, however, had come back in a bad temper. He said that the scampi had not been properly unfrozen and were like bits of gristle, that the *entrecote* steak which followed had been overcooked, and he refused chips altogether as bad for the figure.

"But of course you don't worry about that, do you, Peter?"

"Oh, really, you're intolerable."

"Not at all. just stating a fact. It's important to me, not to you. Lucky you." Peter defiantly shovelled more chips on to his plate. "In another couple of years you'll be as fat as a pig, but what does it matter to a producer?"

"I refuse to be provoked."

Rex showed his white teeth in a smile that made him look like some animal, a fox perhaps.

"Some people find fat men attractive. I can't say I do myself." There were nuts and fruit on the table and Rex cracked nuts with deliberate care, extracted them from their shells with delicate fingers, popped them into his mouth. "Sol Grundy, now, is a big man but he couldn't be called fat. He's just big all over. Tough."

"That girl he had a row with at the Weldons' has been killed."

"So I see. The penalty of leading a wicked life."

"Grundy was near there about the time she was murdered. I saw him. In his car."

"How interesting."

"He's the sort of man who might do anything."

"Now, Peter. You mustn't let your feelings show." Rex got up from the table, sat down on the sofa and picked up a book. Peter stared at him with impotent anger.

Chapter Four *Unprogress*

Forty-eight hours later, on Thursday evening, Manners sat in his office collating the reports from Ryan, Fastness, Jones, and two other detectives engaged on the case. He summarised them under several headings: Cridge Mews, Grundy, Kabanga, The Dell.

Everybody who lived in Cridge Mews had been questioned, in an attempt to find out whether the dead girl had really been a prostitute. The results had been unsatisfactory. Half a dozen people knew Estelle Simpson, and two couples had been asked up to drinks in her flat. They confirmed Seegal's view that she was a friendly girl, one very ready to stop and talk. She had said that she was a model, and also that she worked for stage and television, without going into many details. Men had been seen going into her flat, and the one seen most often recently was readily identifiable as Kabanga, but as Ryan had already discovered, people who lived in Cridge Mews were not inclined to be curious about their neighbours. Seegal, Harrison and Mrs Roberts had been questioned again, but nothing much had been learned from them. Mrs Roberts was indignantly insistent that no man had ever been in the flat when she arrived in the morning. Seegal and Harrison repeated their ambiguous stories about the men who came to call on her. Both of them identified Kabanga as her most frequent caller when his picture was shown to them, but neither of them could be sure about Grundy.

Seegal was inclined to think he had called occasionally, Harrison couldn't be sure.

Manners sighed and moved on to the postcard, the prints on which had proved too blurred for any positive identification. Certainly they did not appear to correspond with Grundy's, which he had obligingly provided on the sheets of paper he had handed to them. The handwriting, however, was another matter. Tissart, the handwriting expert, was prepared to stand up and say positively that Grundy had written the card.

Tissart was a short stout man who often gave evidence in cases that involved the identification of handwriting. His fees were considerable, and his evidence was always given with that absolute certainty of his own correctness that should in theory offer fine opportunities to opposing counsel, but in practice – as the great Spilsbury and others have shown – often overawes them. It was years since Tissart's opinions had been seriously challenged in Court.

He frowned and puffed out his cheeks when Manners said that they had nothing more than a postcard to offer him.

"It's very little, Mr Manners, but it may be enough. What about this little drawing, that's this Guffy McTuffie, right?"

"Yes. And the chap who interests us is one of the creators of this strip. But I don't think he does the drawing of it, only produces the ideas."

"Hah. Pity." Mr Tissart gave the impression that he would have welcomed the challenge of an identification by drawing as well as by calligraphy. He took the sheets of paper provided by Grundy. "And this is our guide, eh. Let's see now." He spent a quarter of an hour with the documents, measuring them and examining them under a magnifying glass, while Manners did other things. Then he straightened up, and wagged a finger. "You understand, Mr Manners, that the opinion I'm going to give you now is based on a quick examination, it's subject to the tests I shall carry out in full detail. At the same time, *at the same time,* this opinion is the fruit of thirty years' experience. And although I'm not the Pope, my opinion isn't often questioned. Eh?" Here Mr Tissart laughed, as though he had made a good joke. Manners expressed his appreciation of the importance of Mr Tissart's opinion.

"Now, Mr Manners, my opinion is – " Mr Tissart paused for a moment to puff and blow, "– quite shortly, that these documents were penned by the same individual. That is my opinion, sir."

Manners ventured to say that there were very few words on the postcard. Was it really possible to –

He was interrupted. "The trained eye, my dear sir, the trained eye is a remarkable organ. What you see and what I see when we look at a sheet of handwriting is not the same thing. Take, for example, the word 'same', which is repeated three times in the card. Compare it with the two 'sames' on these sheets of paper, and you will see –" And Mr Tissart was launched on a tide of comparisons which Manners did not trouble to follow in detail, but which would he knew be immensely impressive to a jury when backed up by the twenty large albums of handwriting specimens which Mr Tissart brought into Court.

If Tissart's view was accepted – and detailed examination had confirmed him in it – then Grundy had intended to meet Estelle Simpson (to call her by the name she had used in Cridge Mews) on Monday evening. "Same time, same place, same object." No doubt the object was sexual intercourse, but what about the time and the place? The place might have been Cridge Mews, but if by any chance they had met somewhere else and had been seen, that would be an invaluable piece of evidence. Manners turned to the account of Grundy's movements on Monday.

These had been closely plotted by Sergeant Fastness. He had talked to Mrs Langham and Miss Pringle, and also to the newspaper editor, Clacton. It was clear that Grundy had been in a very emotional state on Monday afternoon. Manners himself had talked to Grundy's partner Werner, in Werner's large ramshackle flat in Earl's Court Square. A long-haired languid young woman, who was introduced only as Lily, poured them drinks and then sat with her feet up on a sofa looking at Private Eye.

Werner was a lively little man, agreeable to talk to. He said that Grundy had been upset by the interview with Clacton.

"Mrs Langham says that when you got back there was an argument."

"For the first time, Superintendent, for the first time we have a quarrel. Generally we are very sympathetic, we are in rapport. That surprises you? We are different types, but we have a good understanding. Sunday afternoon I went to see him, I saw that he was worried, I said, 'When anything bothers you I know it,' and that's the way it was."

"But what could have been bothering him on Sunday afternoon? You didn't see Mr Clacton until Monday morning."

"No, but Sol is a temperamental man. When it comes to presenting a new idea, talking about a new series, he is jumpy."

The answer seemed inadequate, but Manners didn't press the point. "And on Monday?"

"On Monday – well, I have never seen him like it before. He shouted at me, said my drawing was poor, said we must start revising the series straight away. Now, this was foolish and I said so, you understand. To do something like this when you are angry, that is no good, but when I said this he didn't like it. I turned round and he caught hold of me and pulled my tie. I am a good-natured man, Superintendent – isn't that so, Lily?" Lily looked up, gave him a dreamy smile, returned to Private Eye. "But at that moment I was annoyed, really angry. I told him to get out, and he did. Then I left the office myself. The next day, well, we said no more about it. But you understand, although I am sorry he is mixed up in this silly business, I do not feel quite the same."

"This silly business" – for Werner was sure that Grundy had had no connection with the murder. He had never heard of Estelle Simpson, he knew nothing of any extra-marital affairs that Grundy might have conducted.

"I do not believe he had such an affair. You know this place where he lives, The Dell?" Werner shuddered, a little exaggeratedly. "For me this kind of living is – well, it is not for me. But Sol likes it." He looked thoughtful, amended this. "Sol accepts it. Marion likes it."

"He hates it," Lily said unexpectedly from the sofa.

"He only stays there because of that bloody woman."

Werner laughed. "Marion and Lily don't get on."

"I don't like English frigid bitches," Lily said, and added, "If Sol's in trouble I don't blame him, I blame her."

That was interesting but didn't, Manners reflected, take him much further. At an interview in his office, Grundy had said that on Monday afternoon he had gone drinking in two or three Soho clubs. He had then returned to the office and had stayed there throughout the evening, except for a visit at about half past seven to a pub round the corner called *The Wild Peacock,* where he had eaten sandwiches. This was confirmed, and there was nothing to disprove his story that he had then returned to the office and stayed there until eleven o'clock – and nothing to prove it either.

Manners abandoned Grundy, and turned to consider Ryan's report on Tony Kabanga. Kabanga had no alibi, in the sense that he would have had no difficulty in leaving his Clarges Street club for half an hour, time enough for him to have gone round to Cridge Mews and strangled the girl. But that presupposed a premeditated murder, and everything suggested that the crime had been carried out on sudden impulse. Kabanga's clubs were well conducted, and appeared to have no association with prostitution. Neither his handwriting nor Werner's bore any resemblance to that on the postcard. And Kabanga seemed so genuinely grief-stricken by the girl's death – at one session with

Ryan he had broken down in tears – that even the hard-bitten inspector was inclined to think him innocent.

There remained The Dell. From The Dell had come the statement of Jennifer Paget's which, if it was true, proved that Grundy was associating with the dead woman. From The Dell also had come statements from a Mr Jellifer and a Mr Clements which placed Grundy's car near Cridge Mews at about the right time. In the close community of The Dell, Manners felt, lay the answers to many of his questions, but this was no more than a feeling, and in any case what could he do about it?

To sum up, then: the case against Grundy rested on the handwriting identification, the car identification, and the word of Jennifer Paget. It was not enough. Manners had little doubt that Grundy had killed the girl, but unless some other witnesses came forward, or Grundy made some false move, or it proved possible to link him directly with the dead girl, there was little hope of charging him. After coming to this conclusion Manners put away the file and then, with no particular purpose in mind other than the thought that personal interrogation of Grundy might induce him to make some slip, he telephoned Marion Grundy and announced his intention of calling on her husband that evening.

Chapter Six *In The Dell*

It was the belief of those who lived in The Dell, although this was a belief that they would never have been so vulgar as to express openly, that they were upon the whole more intelligent, liberal and humane than the majority of their fellow citizens. Subconsciously they regarded themselves as a fragment of a new élite establishing itself in the big cities of England, an élite not marked by its adherence to an ideal of wealth, class or profession, but simply one attuned, as most people were not, to the realities of life in the middle of the twentieth century. The plate glass windows, the landscaped gardens, the underfloor central heating, the garbage disposers, the rooms that made provision for just so many books and gramophone records, these appeared to them not as desirable adjuncts to comfort, but as the badge of modernity itself. The idea that they might ostracise one of their number would have seemed to Dell-dwellers deeply shocking, yet the groundswell of gossip that linked Grundy to the death of the girl in Cridge Mews changed subtly to a feeling that anybody about whom such gossip could be circulated was not really the right sort of person to be living in The Dell.

Edgar and Jennifer Paget had told their stories to several people, but these stories had radiated out also through Adrienne Facey and Jill Mayfield and their parents. Adrienne had happened to see the police car draw up outside the Grundys' on Tuesday evening. In less than an hour it was known that the superintendent in charge of the case had called on Grundy, and within twenty-four hours Jack Jellifer's identification of Grundy's car in Mayfair and the police visits to the AdArts office were being talked about. Gossip placed the car not just in Mayfair but in Cridge Mews itself, and the police visit to the AdArts office was transformed into "a thorough grilling of everybody there which went on for hours," as Felicity Facey delightedly put it. In such matters The Dell was not, after all, very different from any other community.

On Thursday evening Grundy turned left into Brambly Way and stopped at the garage on the corner to fill up, and make arrangements for the Alvis to be serviced. Sir Edmund Stone stood beside his Mini Minor at another petrol pump. He made no response to Grundy's greeting, but turned away and spoke to the garage attendant.

"Just a minute," Grundy said to the foreman with whom he was talking. He marched across the forecourt and took Sir Edmund by the arm. "I said good evening."

Sir Edmund slowly turned. "Good evening."

Grundy's face was brick red. "When I said it before you turned away from me. Deliberately."

Sir Edmund's complexion was completely white, and never showed the faintest touch of colour, but his long nose quivered with emotion. "I did not."

"You did. I saw you. He saw you." Grundy gestured at the foreman, who was watching with interest.

"You are mistaken. Really, this – this altercation – is most unseemly."

"Is it? When I say good evening to someone I know I expect them to answer."

"I have already done so. Kindly let go of my arm."

Grundy's hand was in fact still touching Sir Edmund's arm. He let go and marched back across the forecourt to his car. The foreman looked at him sideways, but made no comment. He arranged for the servicing of the car and drove out of the garage, revving up unnecessarily as he did so.

When he got home Marion was upstairs. She came slowly into the living-room. Her manner was composed, but she did not look well. "Superintendent Manners telephoned. He is coming at eight o'clock to see you."

"Sod him. He's been talking to Theo, asking all sorts of questions." He took the evening paper out of his briefcase, tossed it over to her. "Shall I tell you something? That clot Stone tried to cut me this evening. At the garage. He didn't do it, though. I made him say hallo."

"You quarrelled with him?"

"How can you quarrel with a dummy?"

"You don't understand. You simply don't realise what people are saying, how awful things are for me."

"They're not too cheerful for me, either, but I'm very sorry." He tried to embrace her. She stood with statuesque immobility and said:

"Please."

"Christ, now you've turned into a dummy too. All right, if that's the way you want it. What are we eating?"

"I've telephoned Daddy."

"Your father?" He looked at her in astonishment. "What for?"

"I don't feel I can go on. I must go away. Or at least I must ask Daddy's advice. He's very – wise, you know."

"No, I don't know. He's a bloody old bore, that's what your father is. Now I'll tell you something. If you go away now, at a time like this, you needn't come back, do you understand?" He advanced across the room and she shrank back. When he touched her she gave an experimental scream.

"Don't come near me. Don't dare to come near me."

He dropped his hands in a gesture of despair. Marion ran upstairs again.

The scream was distinctly heard next door by the Faceys. Felicity was making a raffia lampshade and her husband was looking at, rather than reading, a book about art by Sir Herbert

Read. Adrienne, who had been denied a television programme on the ground that it would affect her parents' concentration, was sulking upstairs.

Felicity paused and let a long string of raffia dangle like spaghetti towards the floor.

"Bill, did you hear that?"

Bill Facey was small, thin and weedy. He had heard, but he did not wish to acknowledge. "What?"

"That scream. It was Marion. You must go in."

"Oh, no." Bill looked desperately at Herbert Read for help. "I couldn't. I mean, you can't interfere."

"We don't know what he may have done. He may be murdering her." There was a silence, heavy with the implications of the words.

"You've no right to say such things." But Bill Facey said it feebly. There was no doubt in anybody's mind that Felicity was the dominant partner in their marriage.

"Listen." They listened, but heard nothing. "You ought to go in."

"No, really Felicity, you can't do things like that."

"Very well. I shall go myself." She rose, vigorous and mannish, and moved towards the door. Her husband sheepishly watched her go, and then returned to his book.

Grundy looking, as she afterwards said, really wild, opened the door. With a casualness obviously assumed she said that she had run out of milk and wondered whether Marion could lend her a little. Grundy went away and came back with a pint bottle, which he thrust at her.

"Are you sure you can spare this? Is Marion sure?"

"Yes."

"Perhaps I should just ask her."

He glared at her, teeth showing in a sort of grin that, as she said afterwards, frightened her. "She's gone to bed."

"Oh, really. I thought –"

"Got a bad headache." Now there could be no doubt of it, he was grinning at her. He made a small mock bow before closing the door. He was, she thought – to use a favourite word of hers – a most obnoxious man. She saw the police car drive up a few minutes later.

Manners could adopt when he wished a severity of tone that was often disturbing to suspects under questioning. He used this tone now in talking to Grundy, and his manner without being in the least impolite conveyed clearly enough his certainty that Grundy knew more than he was telling. Sergeant Fastness chipped in occasionally with a question pointed to the edge of rudeness. Beneath this barrage of questions about his movements on Monday evening and his knowledge of the dead woman the suspect remained commendably, if that was the word, unperturbed. He still denied ever meeting her except at the party.

"Come now, I have a witness who saw you with her on Saturday evening. You went into Kabanga's house with her."

"Nonsense."

"We have a positive identification. Do you still deny it?"

"Absolutely." Grundy's big hands rested placidly on his knees.

"And your handwriting on the postcard has been identified too." That was Fastness. "You slipped up badly there, you should have taken it away. Silly to sign it with that little figure too. Guffy McTuffie."

"Rubbish."

Fastness laughed unpleasantly. "Did you think we wouldn't be able to identify the writing just because you didn't sign it?"

"I didn't write the postcard."

Fastness was confidential. "From you we just want the details, that's all. You save us trouble, you'll save yourself a hard time."

"Sergeant." Manners's voice was sharp, his tone to Grundy apologetic. "There's no need to talk like that. It's just that we feel sure you haven't told us everything you know. It will be in your own interest to amend your statement now rather than later on."

"Nothing more to say."

The most difficult suspect to deal with is the one who answers questions so briefly. Manners felt his temper slipping slightly. "Where's Mrs Grundy?"

"Lying down upstairs. She's got a headache."

Manners debated whether or not he should ask to speak to her, and decided against it. What could she say that she had not said before? He said a curt good night. Outside, in the car, Sergeant Fastness said, "He keeps his mouth zipped tight, doesn't he sir?"

"Yes. We just have to find something that will unzip it."

They drove away. Felicity Facey watched them. "They haven't taken him," she said to her husband.

"Oh, really, Felicity."

"It's poor Marion I feel sorry for. I hope he hasn't done her an injury. I shall go and see her in the morning."

"I don't think you should interfere," he said without conviction. He knew that he was fighting a lost battle.

The alarm clock which should have wakened Grundy had remained unset. When he woke and looked at his watch the time was nine o'clock. In the other bed Marion lay sleeping still, curled like a child, her face unlined and young. He woke her, washed, cut himself shaving, dressed hurriedly. When he came downstairs he found her standing in the dining annexe beside the toast and coffee.

"I heard what they said last night, the detectives."

"I thought you'd gone to sleep. You had your eyes shut when I got upstairs."

"I wanted to think."

He opened the paper, looked for news of the murder, read that police inquiries had taken them to a high-class residential estate called The Dell.

"You did it, didn't you?"

He looked up from the paper. "What?"

"I think I've known it ever since Tuesday evening, when you showed me her picture in the paper. But don't worry, a wife can't give evidence against her husband, can she? And anyway, I wouldn't if I could. I blame myself as much as you. If we'd had a properly integrated relationship you would never have needed to –"

Grundy was not listening. He was staring in astonishment at the Rover that had just drawn up outside the house. Out of it stepped the burly figure of Mr Hayward. He looked at Marion.

"I told you I'd spoken to Daddy." In her voice there was a note of appeal or regret. She went to the door. Grundy furiously thrust a piece of toast into his mouth, washed it down with coffee, crumpled the napkin in his big hand, stood up.

"A very good run up," Mr Hayward was saying as he came in. "An hour and a half, door to door. I took that short cut just after Crawley."

"The one by Sumpter's factory?" Marion broke off, looked nervously at her husband.

"Solomon. This is a bad business." Mr Hayward was grave as a publican at a funeral.

"What are you here for?"

"Because my little girl asked me to come, because she's worried. And she's frightened, Solomon, frightened."

"Dad. Don't talk about it."

"Frightened of me, you mean? She thinks I killed this girl, she's just told me so. She said we hadn't got a *properly integrated relationship,* and do you know why we haven't? Because she's been able to run to Mum and Dad all the time and discuss the fifteen different routes to Hayward's Heath." His voice had

105

risen to a shout. "Why don't you keep your nose out of our affairs?"

"I don't think I need to answer that."

"Dad, I won't be a minute. I'm packed." Marion ran up the stairs.

"Packed?" Grundy glared after her, then swung round on her father.

"You must understand the position, Solomon."

"I'll tell you what I understand. If Marion goes she doesn't come back."

Mr Hayward's gravity was wonderful. "Perhaps that will be for the best."

Marion came down the stairs carrying two suitcases. Her face was very pale.

"You'd packed last night," Grundy said accusingly.

She looked surprised. "I said I must get away. I thought you understood."

Mr Hayward intoned a valediction over the grave.

"It's possible that when this sad affair is cleared up some arrangement may be –"

"Shut up."

Marion said, with a look of anguish, "Sol. Please try to understand."

"Goodbye. Have a good relationship."

"Oh, you're intolerable."

"Take a good short cut on the way down."

The door closed after them. He stood in the picture window and watched them go, Mr Hayward carrying the suitcases. Marion got into the Rover without a backward glance.

He turned and stood looking at the fragments of his breakfast. Then he took them into the kitchen, said, "That's that," put on his overcoat, and went to the office.

Chapter Six *Flight?*

The office, as Mrs Langham said to Miss Pringle, was not what it had been. There was an atmosphere about it these days, and in view of everything that was of course, as Mrs Langham said also, not surprising. Mr Werner was still very polite, he was a man who would never fail in politeness, but he was obviously worried. And he had reason to be, Mrs Langham meaningfully said. As for Mr Grundy, well, of course, Mr Grundy was the cause of the worry.

He came in this Friday morning, Mr Grundy, obviously in such a hurry or in such a temper that he flung them a bare grunt over his shoulder as he charged into his office. A few minutes later, Mr Werner, who had been in for an hour, came out of his own office and entered Mr Grundy's.

"Well," said Mrs Langham, "I'd sooner him than me."

Miss Pringle giggled.

Werner found his partner moodily looking at the morning's post, and obviously in a bad mood. It was not perhaps the best time to say something which might be misunderstood, but he had made up his mind to say it anyway. He told Grundy of his interview with Manners, and added that the situation was a difficult one. "What do you think we ought to do about it?"

"Do?"

"Quite frankly, my dear, we're in a turmoil. Our little firm, I mean. And you and I, we're in a state too, aren't we? I don't like it that we should be bad friends, we've been good friends for so long."

He was looking a very neat little cock sparrow this morning, and his smile was appealing.

"Say what you mean."

"Don't misunderstand me. I'll tell you what's the matter with you, Sol, you're too bloody suspicious. You take everything too hard."

"I expect you're right." Grundy smiled, or half smiled, back at him. "I'll try not to misunderstand."

"What has happened is bad for business, you must see that. To be mixed up with a murder case, that is not very nice."

"So?"

"You ought to take a rest, stay away from the office, oh, for a month. Don't worry at all. Have a holiday, take Marion away. By then they will have found out who did this thing, everything will be forgotten."

"And Guffy?"

"Quite honestly, old dear, do you suppose that Clacton or anybody else is going to buy a Guffy series just now?"

"Take Marion away." Grundy barked sharply, then got up and paced about the room. Theo watched him nervously. Suddenly he shouted, "I won't do it, I won't bloody well do it."

Outside, Mrs Langham and Miss Pringle looked at each other. Mrs Langham whispered, "Oh dear."

"Sol. You said you would not misunderstand."

"Why should I run away?" He glared at Theo. "Do you know what happened last night? Some bloody old snob at home tried to cut me. I made him speak, though. He didn't like it, I can tell you."

"You made him speak?" Theo looked baffled. "I shall never understand you English."

"I'm not English, I'm Irish. You're trying to get rid of me."

"No, no."

"I won't have it. I'm not going to be mucked about by anybody, you or the police or anybody." Theo backed away as Grundy, half a head taller, advanced. His foot caught in a threadbare patch of carpet and he fell over backwards, knocking a tray of papers to the floor.

In the outer office Mrs Langham looked significantly at Miss Pringle, got up and opened Grundy's door after the most perfunctory of knocks. She took in the scene at a glance. Mr Werner was on the floor, and Mr Grundy was standing over him. Mr Werner looked at her ruefully. Mr Grundy said, "Mr Werner caught his foot in the carpet."

"So I see," Mrs Langharn said coldly. She stayed long enough to see Mr Werner get to his feet, and then closed the door again. It was her belief, as she said afterwards to Miss Pringle, that if she had not opened the door when she did, violence would have been done. This belief was not affected by the sound of Mr Grundy laughing, for the laughter had, she thought, a sinister sound.

Inside the office Grundy was saying, "I must be losing my sense of proportion. It's coming to something when you're nervous of me, Theo. I'm sorry."

Theo laughed too, uncertainly. "Do not misunderstand me, Sol."

"No. I'm just the original Irish clot, that's all. The hell of a situation like this is that you begin to suspect the motives of everybody, even your best friends. You'll know soon enough, so I may as well tell you now. Marion's left me, gone home to Mum and Dad."

Theo digested this news, then smiled. "You're a bachelor. Isn't that all the more reason for taking a holiday, old dear?"

Grundy smiled back at him.

The man who sat in Manners's office was about forty, pale, fattish, a little above medium height. Inspector Ryan watched him with the anxious pride of a father whose son is about to read his essay on a school prize day.

"Mr Leighton lives at 11 Cridge Mews, sir, just opposite Miss Gresham. Remember I told you he was up in Manchester, we couldn't get hold of him? Well, he came back today and I think you'll be interested in what he's got to say. Just tell the superintendent what you told me, Mr Leighton. Take your time."

Mr Leighton cleared his throat and began to speak in a flat Cockney whine. He was, like many people who came to tell their stories in Manners's office, distinctly nervous.

"I'm a scrap metal dealer, you understand, sir, old cars and that sort of thing really, and on Tuesday I had this appointment in Manchester with a Mr Hinchcliffe, so I thought I'll go up on the night train, otherwise it means getting up at the crack of dawn –"

"Take it steady, man," admonished Ryan, now rather in the role of a second advising an over-eager boxer.

"So, oh, just about ten o'clock that night I was getting ready, you know, changing and packing up and so on, and I saw this chap arrive, a big geezer he was."

"What room were you in?"

"Front room, that's my bedroom. just happened to be looking out of the window."

"Did you know Miss Simpson?"

Mr Leighton's bloodshot eyes looked away from the superintendent, his glance flickered around the room. What's the matter, Manners wondered, has he had it off with her himself and doesn't want me to know about it? "Just to talk to, you know, just to pass the time of day with, that's all. Very pleasant she always was too, always cheerful and nice."

"And you happened to be looking out of the window?"

Mr Leighton rolled his eyes and looked appealingly at Ryan, who laughed.

"I think he was interested in her male visitors, sir, put it that way. He says there were quite a few."

"Quite a few," Mr Leighton agreed eagerly. "There was the darkie, he used to come often, and then, oh, several others. Once or twice they stayed the night. I mean, I saw them leave in the morning."

"I see. You just happened to be looking," Manners said neutrally.

"I was dressing. But this chap, now, I'd seen him once before, or maybe twice. I noticed him specially, because he had ginger hair."

Manners felt the tingling in his stomach that he associated with the break-through in a case. "Can you describe him?"

"He was big, not all that tall maybe, but very broad, bulky sort of chap altogether. He was wearing some sort of light tweed coat, no hat of course. I saw his face under the lamp. Then he rang the bell and she came down, they spoke for a minute or so and she let him in. I saw them together upstairs. Then she drew the curtain."

"About ten o'clock, you say. You can't get the time more exactly?"

"No. But I left at ten-thirty, and it was a few minutes before that. Say ten to ten-fifteen."

"You didn't see him come out?"

"No. Still there when I left."

"Didn't see him drive up, get out of a car, anything like that?"

"No. He walked into the Mews."

"How sure are you that you'd recognise this man again?"

Leighton's cheek was twitching slightly. "Pretty sure. I think I'm sure."

"Would you be willing to attend an identification parade?"

"I – yes, I suppose so." He paused, gathering confidence. "Yes, definitely."

111

Manners avoided Ryan's look of triumph. Something about the situation bothered him, and suddenly he knew what it was. He said quietly, "Have you got form, Mr Leighton?"

"I –" the man said, and swallowed. Ryan looked first astonished, then disgusted.

"Come on, then. Let's have it."

"It was years ago, seven years. I got twelve months for receiving. It was a mistake. I had nothing to do with it."

"I sent you up, didn't I?" Leighton nodded. "And since then you've kept your nose clean?"

"I told you, it was a mistake."

When Leighton had gone, Ryan said, "Sorry, Super. I should have realised."

"How could you? I remembered him because I sent him up, that's all. You don't know anything about him? Then you'd better ask around, see what you can find."

"If there is anything to find."

"Of course. Scrap metal dealer doesn't sound too good. Pity."

"He didn't have to come forward. If there was anything against him, you'd think he'd keep quiet."

"I know. We can't show him a photograph, but if he does make an identification it puts Grundy in the right place at the right time. That's why it would be nice if Leighton were a solid citizen. As it is –" He sighed, and left the sentence uncompleted. The telephone rang. He lifted the receiver and listened with growing excitement to what was said at the other end. Then he turned to Ryan. "That was Clavering, the local super. It looks as though Grundy's trying to slip the country, may have killed his wife. We'll have to get the word to ports and airfields. Then let's get down there."

"How's Clavering got news of it?"

"Some woman phoned the station."

Felicity Facey always took Adrienne and their son Edward to school in the car, and on this Friday morning she did some shopping, and so did not return to The Dell until after eleven o'clock. She called on Marion, partly because she was curious to know exactly what had happened on the previous night, partly because they often had a cup of coffee and a chat in the morning. There was no reply to the bell. Marion must be out, then, although it was unusual for her to be out shopping in the morning, she was an afternoon shopper. Unusual, too, for her to be out on a Friday which, as Felicity knew, was not one of the days on which her cleaner came. Looking through the picture window she saw what was more unusual still, the living-room left untidy. She kept a lookout while she was making lunch, and told her husband about it when he came home.

Bill Facey said in his worried way, "You shouldn't interfere."

"Interfere! For all you know, she may be lying dead in the bedroom." He made a slight, incredulous noise, which she resented. "Where is she then, tell me that?"

"I expect she's home now, and you didn't notice her come in."

"We'll see." Felicity dialled the Grundys' number and held out the receiver so that he could hear the ring. There was no reply.

"She may have gone up to town to shop. Or out to see someone."

Felicity snorted her disapproval of these suggestions. When her husband had gone again she decided to have another look next door. Perhaps a glance through the kitchen window at the back might reveal something vital. Before going round, however, she pressed the front-door bell again, as a matter of form. There were footsteps, the door opened, and Grundy stood there.

"Oh," Felicity retreated a step. "Is Marion – can I speak to Marion."

"Not possible. She's gone away."

"Gone away? That's very sudden, isn't it?" She was taking in what she saw behind Grundy, the large suitcase, the overcoat on a table, and on top of the overcoat the passport.

"Quite sudden. She wanted a rest."

"When did she go, then?"

"This morning. Don't bother about the milk."

"Milk?"

"I thought perhaps you'd come to return it. But I see you haven't got it with you."

There could be no doubt about it, he was jeering at her in the most unpleasant way. Greatly daring, she said, "I see you're going away too. To join her, I suppose?"

"You suppose wrong. And now will you just go home and mind your own business." The half-grin on his face changed to a snarl, and the door was banged against her. She went home, and there quite openly sat in her window to watch. Less than five minutes had passed when Grundy came out, fetched his old Alvis from the parking space, brought out the case, put it in the boot and drove away. Felicity pondered the implications of what she had seen and heard. It did not take her long to decide that it was her duty to telephone the police.

"We can't enter by invitation, there's nobody to invite us. But I think that window round the back, you know, the one slightly open, looks as if it had been forced, don't you, sir?" Ryan winked one eye. "And if that's so, we ought to go in and have a look."

Manners's nose was wrinkled. "I don't like it."

"But we want to get in."

There had been no legitimate grounds for obtaining a search warrant, but Manners agreed that they wanted to get in. It was one of those problems which often confront the police.

"Well, then, if you just stay here a couple of minutes –" Ryan said cheerfully. Five minutes later they were inside, and ten minutes after that Ryan was saying, "If you ask me, this is a bit of a sell. Her clothes have gone, and he can't have got rid of her body round here. Where would you put a body in one of these super-modern places? And you can't bury it outside, you'd be disturbing the landscape gardens."

But the caution with which Manners had approached the case earlier had gone. He felt certain now that Grundy was the man they wanted. "Where is his wife, then? And why has he slipped the country?"

"I don't know. But I don't see much to help us here."

Ryan went downstairs, and Manners into the small study that Grundy used for working. He searched through the papers on the desk without finding, or expecting to find, anything relevant to the case. He did, however, discover several notes from Werner, and two of these were signed with the little Guffy McTuffie figure on the postcard. Werner was in the clear, but was it possible that Grundy and his partner had used this figure as a signature in writing to each other? He was thinking about this when the telephone rang. He went downstairs and Ryan, at the telephone, covered the mouthpiece and raised a thumb.

"They've got him. London Airport. He had an air ticket for Belgrade. One way. What do you want them to do?"

"Send him along to the station. We'll keep him for questioning."

"There's just one thing. He's been talking to the officers out at the airport. He said something about Mrs Facey causing this trouble, that she believed he'd killed his wife and he was stringing her along. He says he quarrelled with his wife, and she's staying with her father." Ryan hesitated. "We've got the number."

"All right, then. Ring it."

Ten minutes later, Manners himself had talked to Marion Grundy. "She's like an icicle, that one," he said to Ryan. Doesn't intend to come back to London to see him, or not at the moment. She confirms the quarrel, but had no idea he was going away. Wasn't surprised, though. 'I've given up being surprised at anything he does' she said. It's damning, though, we couldn't want anything better. His nerve broke."

"He said he was going for a holiday."

Manners's earlier doubts had vanished like snow in an oven. "What do you suppose he'd say? But running away at a time like this, what can it mean except that he did it? Shouldn't be surprised if we have a confession out of him in an hour."

"Pity Mrs Nosy wasn't right. If he had killed his wife that would really have been straightforward," Ryan said cheerfully. Manners was not amused.

They did not get a confession out of Grundy, not after one hour or five hours. He sat glowering at them all, an ape of a man with arms swinging, face brick red (Manners could not help reflecting that his appearance was likely to impress a jury unfavourably), and denied everything. Manners, Ryan, Fastness and Jones, questioned him in couples.

"Why did you suddenly decide to leave this country?"

"My partner, Theo Werner, suggested it. I made up my mind he was right."

"Did you tell him you were going?"

"It wasn't necessary."

"When he suggested it, what did you say?"

"Said I'd think about it."

"Why go so suddenly? Why the one-way ticket?"

"Why not. Nothing to keep me. I didn't know when I'd be coming back –"

"Nothing to keep you. We wanted you for questioning, you knew that."

"You didn't say so."

"Come on now, that won't wash. You aren't a fool. Are you?"

"I don't know. You tell me."

"You say you didn't leave in a hurry."

"No special hurry."

"At an hour's notice. Getting on the first plane you could. Without telling your wife?"

"I'd have sent her a postcard."

They left it and came back to it, talked about Estelle Simpson and came back to that.

"Your car's been identified – seen near her flat – you were seen going in – she opened the door to you, stood talking – because of Kabanga, was it? – you didn't want to share her – she was threatening to tell your wife – demanding money – is that why you did it? – come on now, if she was blackmailing you that's your story – you've got a story and we want to hear it – if you were innocent why run away – ?"

To these and hundreds of other questions Grundy's replies were that he had not known Estelle Simpson, had not visited her in Cridge Mews, had not run away. He had been going on holiday.

"I don't see much sign of that broken nerve," Ryan said after five hours had passed.

Manners was pale, and his face was covered with sweat. He disliked these sessions.

"No."

"If anything, he's in better shape than we are. Tough as old rope. What do we do, soldier on?"

"I think so, yes."

"He goes on helping us with our inquiries, you might say."

"If Leighton recognises him we're all right." "And if he doesn't?" Manners did not reply.

The identification parade was more than usually difficult to arrange. The procedure is that plain-clothes policemen go out into the street about half an hour before the time fixed for the parade and collect people from the street. They had tried to find ginger-haired men, but had only discovered a couple, and the other men had hair ranging in colour from flaxen to mouse. Only two or three of them much resembled Grundy in appearance.

Grundy had been told that he could have his solicitor or a friend present. He had first of all said that he wouldn't bother, but had then changed his mind and asked for a neighbour from The Dell named Weldon.

"Weldon?" Ryan said.

"Dick Weldon. And you'd better look out. Dick's a civic-minded type, if he finds you doing anything out of line you'll be for it."

Manners had nothing to do with the parade, which was conducted by the station officer. The two witnesses were Seegal, the garage man, and Leighton. Dick Weldon stood in a corner beside the station officer, large nose slightly raised. He had voiced a protest as soon as he saw the other people on the parade.

"They don't look like Sol."

"We've done the best we can, sir."

"Look at that little shrimp there, he's not more than half Sol's size. And that chap in the brown coat, he looks like a tramp."

"He had the option of refusing the parade, sir. He didn't choose to do so."

"If you ask me the thing's a bit of a farce. I suppose he realised that, and wanted to get it over."

The station officer made no reply. He had already marked Weldon down as an objectionable barrack-room lawyer type. He went into the room where the witnesses were waiting, with a police officer, and said to them: "You understand, walk slowly down the line. Take your time, don't hurry, you can go back and look at any of them twice. If you make an identification there's no need to say anything, just touch the person you identify on the shoulder so that there's no mistake. You will go out by another door, and as soon as you have gone out you must leave the building. You must not talk to each other. Do you understand?"

They said that they understood. Seegal, small and swarthy, was the first to go in. He took some time, looking carefully at Grundy, who stood next to last in the line, and at two of the others. Then he said to the station officer, "I think it's the one next to the door. The biggest one, with the tweed overcoat on."

"You're sure?"

"I'm ninety per cent certain that's the chap I've seen." "You mean it might have been someone else?"

"No, I'm sure that's the chap." Seegal touched Grundy on the shoulder.

Leighton followed him. He walked up and down the line two or three times, twitching nervously.

"Do you want any help?" the station officer asked.

"Want them to take their coats off, anything like that?"

"No. He was wearing an overcoat. I just want to make sure."

He walked up and down twice more, and then tapped Grundy on the shoulder.

"You're certain of the identification?"

"Definitely, oh yes, definitely."

The other members of the parade dispersed. Dick Weldon asked the station officer,

"What happens now?"

"They identified him, you saw that. I tell the super."

"And then?"

"That's up to him."

Manners listened to what the station officer had to say. Then Grundy was called.

"You have been identified today as a man who went with Sylvia Gresham into Mr Kabanga's house at The Dell on the evening of Saturday, 21st September, as a frequent caller at her Cridge Mews flat, and as a man seen to enter that flat on Monday evening, the 23rd, at about ten o'clock. Do you want to amend your statement in any way?"

"It's all bloody nonsense."

"That is all you have to say?"

"Yes. Except – can I talk to Dick Weldon?"

"In a moment."

He was formally charged with the murder by strangulation of Sylvia Gresham, also known as Estelle Simpson. Then he saw Dick, who said firmly, "That identity parade was a farce. You should never have agreed to it. No use worrying about that now, though. Who's your solicitor?"

Grundy's big hands clasped each other tightly. "Solicitor? I haven't got one."

"Shall I get in touch with old Trapsell, then, my own solicitor? He's on the ball, you'll find."

"Yes. All right."

"Just a matter of mistaken identification," Dick said heartily. "Trapsell will get it straightened out soon enough. What about Marion?"

"She's gone off to stay with her father."

"I know. Damned bad, running out like that. Still, she ought to be told. And I'll tell your office partner, shall I, what's his name – Werner."

He provided encouraging conversation for another five minutes, until Grundy was taken away.

PART THREE

Chapter One *Counsel's Opinion*

Marion and her father sat in Magnus Newton's chambers while he walked up and down on the rather dirty carpet and talked about the case in brief interjectory gusts. Newton was a red-faced puffy little man with a high reputation which, according to some of his critics, he had done little to earn. He was, however, a fashionable QC and Trapsell said they had been lucky to get him.

"Nothing but the best," Mr Hayward had boomed.

"Only the best is good enough for my girl."

Trapsell, a dapper and cynical little man who looked rather like a waiter, thought: *and your girl's husband.* Aloud he said, "It's a matter of availability, largely. It so happens Newton is free. If he hadn't been – " *His* shrug indicated the depths to which they might have been compelled to sink. "Mind, it will cost you money."

"Only the best," reiterated Mr Hayward. And now the best was in front of them, talking with his customary air of frayed irritability about the case.

"Spoke to your husband, Mrs Grundy, simply says he didn't know the girl at all, the whole thing's a mistake. You can't offer any opinion on that?"

"No. I was there at the party when she slapped his face. But he had never mentioned her to me. And when I spoke about the – the incident afterwards, he said he didn't know her." She paused. "Will you want me to give evidence?"

"I should think so, yes. Don't you want to?"

"If it's necessary."

"I don't want my little girl exposed to more unpleasantness than necessary," Mr Hayward said.

Newton glared. "Murder is an unpleasant business, Mr Hayward. Did you quarrel much? There's this story about a scream, that's a bit of nonsense I suppose, hysterical woman, Mrs what's her name, Facey."

"We had had an argument, and I think I probably did cry out. But for the most part we had a good relationship."

"Ha." Newton looked at her, seemed about to say more, didn't. "Now, I'll tell you the way I see this case. The evidence on the other side is divided into two Parts. First the evidence linking your husband with Simpson at The Dell, then the evidence putting him at her flat on the night she was killed. And there are three important points." He held up three stubby fingers. "One, this girl Paget who's supposed to have seen him with Simpson on Saturday night. Know anything about her, any grudge against your husband, that sort of thing?"

"Sol didn't – doesn't – get on too well with her father. But I don't think he even knew who she was. I've only spoken to her half a dozen times myself. I don't know any reason why she should have a grudge against us."

"Because that particular bit of evidence, seeing your husband going into the house with Simpson, that's something we've got to shake. You've tested the light?" he asked Trapsell.

"Yes. It's not all that good, but there was enough for her to see by."

"Ha. Then there's the postcard. They have Tissart. I suggest we try to get hold of Borritt." He turned again to Trapsell, who nodded sagely. Newton coughed, beamed, and then, conscious that he had not been entirely explicit, explained. "Tissart, the handwriting expert they will call, is quite positive your husband wrote the card. I hope that we shall be able to call an expert just as eminent, just as eminent I assure you, to say that he didn't.

And then the third point is this identification by the man Liston."

"Leighton," said Trapsell.

"Leighton. That places your husband at the right spot, more or less at the right time. I don't like that. No, I don't like that at all."

"Just a few seconds," Mr Hayward boomed, as though he were in Court himself. "A man can easily be mistaken."

Newton looked at him, swelled up a little, appeared likely to burst out in wrath, but in fact only said mildly, "We have to convince the jury of that, Mr Hayward." He went back to his desk, looked through the depositions. "Jellifer and Clements, they're supposed to have seen your husband in his car, or seen the car rather. What about them? Any grudge against you?"

"Why, no. They're – we've always thought of them as friends."

"All right. They're not important, it's the three principal points we've got to hammer away at. One more thing. You're still staying with your father?"

"Just outside Hayward's Heath," Mr Hayward said. "Same name but it doesn't belong to me, worse luck."

Newton went on as though he had not spoken. "The question of your husband leaving the country is bound to be raised. As you know, he was going for a holiday, but the prosecution are bound to say otherwise. It would help if you could make it plain that you went to stay with your parents by mutual agreement. That's one reason why I should like you to give evidence."

"I see," Marion said. "All right."

Newton said slowly, "It would help to scotch any rumours – and in my opinion a good part of this case is the product of rumour – if you went back to live again at home. In The Dell, I mean."

For a moment Marion's gaze met the stare of Newton's little eyes. Then she looked down. "I don't think I could do that. Not yet, at any rate."

"Ha." Newton continued to look at her for a few moments. Then his manner changed to jocular urbanity as he wished them good day, and told Marion not to worry. To Trapsell, who stayed behind for a few more words, he said, "She thinks he did it."

"Oh, I wouldn't say that."

"Trouble is I shall have to call her so that we can put something up against this story of his running off to Belgrade. But I don't like putting her into the box, I don't trust her. For that matter, I don't like him. Uncouth devil. Doesn't seem to take any interest in the case."

"I'd noticed that myself."

"You'd think he didn't care what happened. Oh, well, wouldn't do to take only the clients we liked, would it?" Mr Trapsell laughed dutifully. Newton tapped his nose. "Something I forgot. You might find out if he's got any form at all, our client."

"I checked. He hasn't."

"Good. Shouldn't have been surprised if he had, you know, punching a policeman on the nose, that sort of thing. I wish he didn't look such a violent type, I must say."

Chapter Two *Down in The Dell*

Caroline Weldon wheeled in a trolley from the other side of the room divider, and shouted "Supper." Cyprian did not stop looking at the television set, but stretched out a hand, picked up a bowl of soup and a spoon and began to convey the soup to his mouth. Gloria came in, said, "Oh, Mummy, look at him, honestly he's too much."

She walked over to the television and switched it off. Cyprian protested. Gloria appealed to her mother.

"Honestly, he just sits looking at that thing and shovelling food into himself, can you wonder he's fat?"

"Bum to you, sis," said Cyprian.

"And disgusting."

"Shut up," said their mother. Brawny arms akimbo she went to the door and shouted again, "Dick. Supper."

Dick came down the stairs, wearing the dirty old clothes he always put on as soon as he got home. He was met by protests from Gloria and Cyprian, which he ignored. He took his bowl of soup and began to drink it standing in front of the television set,rather as a few years earlier he might have stood in front of a fireplace. There were no fireplaces in The Dell.

Caroline sat on the arm of a chair with her own soup, and looked respectfully up at him. She knew the signs. Dick was about to make some serious pronouncement. It was the kind of thing that made her feel they were really a tremendously united family, and sure enough when he spoke it was to use the out-of-date slang which for Dick was always a sign of emotion.

"Rally round now, all of you, and listen to me. I want to talk about Sol."

"Is he a killer?" Cyprian asked. Gloria gave an exasperated sigh.

"Of course he's not. We all know Sol, he's a bit of a rough diamond but he wouldn't do anything like that. He never even knew the girl." In spite of himself, Dick could not help letting a slight note of scepticism enter his voice as he said these words.

"Then why did he tear her dress? And why did she slap his face?" Cyprian asked.

"Honestly, doesn't he butt in, Daddy, isn't he the most terrible bore?"

"You're both being pretty tiresome." Dick was a quick eater. He had finished his soup, and now took a hunk of bread and cheese. "If you'll listen to me for five minutes we might get on a bit. Sol's going to be tried for murder on some of the flimsiest evidence I ever saw. That identification parade was a scandal, he should never have let himself be put up for it. I'm sorry to say that some of our friends here seem just to be taking it for granted that he did it. Very bad show, that is. Now, what I suggest is that we should form a little group to try to discover the evidence that shows Sol didn't do it."

"Suppose he did?" It was Cyprian again.

Dick Weldon rarely lost his temper, and he did not do so even under this provocation. He said calmly, "He didn't, Cyprian. Let's not argue about that."

Caroline was looking puzzled. "What have you got in mind?"

"First of all, there's what Jennifer Paget said about seeing them outside on Saturday night. I believe she was – mistaken, let's put it that way. I thought we might just go over and make sure exactly what she could see."

Half an hour later, the four of them stood at the entrance into The Dell from Brambly Way. Gloria and Cyprian had reluctantly agreed to play the parts of Estelle Simpson and Sol, and were standing close together almost opposite Kabanga's house. Caroline, leading an imaginary dog, entered The Dell from Brambly Way and walked past them. Afterwards Gloria and Cyprian went together towards Kabanga's house. Dick stood watching.

"Did you see them?"

"Don't be silly, of course I did. I knew they were there. And they were standing almost under the lamp. They could have moved farther into the shadow."

"It's damp farther in," Gloria said. "She wouldn't have wanted to get her shoes dirty, would she?"

Dick had his pipe going. Now he said, "Why should they have been standing outside anyway, running the risk of someone seeing them, why not go into the house straight away?"

Felicity Facey bore down upon them, with Adrienne in trail. They exchanged sharp "Good nights". Felicity's suggestion that Marion had been murdered had become known in The Dell and had aroused indignation in some households, approval in others. Caroline had made clear her own feeling that Felicity had behaved badly, and the two women were barely on speaking terms. When she had gone by Dick repeated his question, to which nobody had an answer. "I think I'll just have a word with old Trapsell about that."

After they were indoors again Gloria said, "I tell you what I might do, I might talk to Adrienne. At school, I mean. She's quite thick with Jennifer, and she keeps on saying things about her that are – well, sort of mysterious."

"But I thought you didn't like Adrienne."

"I don't much. But still I could try and find out about this, couldn't I? Whatever it is."

"Do that," Dick said indulgently. His pipe had gone out, and he relit it. "I must say I don't feel we've wasted our time, do you?"

The question was rhetorical, and remained unanswered. Much later, in bed, Caroline said, "Do you think Sol can't have done it? Not possibly, I mean?"

Dick's large nose pointed to the ceiling. "Yes."

"I don't know what I think. He's a funny sort of man, Sol, and I always thought Marion didn't give him – I mean, I shouldn't say they were really compatible, would you?"

Dick turned and gripped her shoulders firmly. "I don't want to hear you talking like that. They're our friends. Nobody would have said anything like that before this happened. The way people behave –" He did not finish the sentence, but started another. "If you're not going to believe the best about your friends when they're in trouble, what hope is there for anybody? I mean, supposing it had happened to us, a frightful series of coincidences like this."

Caroline moved closer into his arms. "Yes, that's what it is. A series of coincidences."

On the following day Dick rang up Trapsell, and told him his deductions. The solicitor was unimpressed.

"Yes, Mr Weldon. I think you can take it that's the kind of thing that won't be overlooked."

"You mean you'd realised it already? It will be brought out in evidence?"

"The conduct of the case is in the hands of Mr Newton."

"But surely you must see –"

"Your friend Mr Grundy has every faith in Mr Newton, and I suggest we leave it to him."

When he had put down the telephone Trapsell told his clerk that he was out if Mr Weldon called again. It was by pure error that Dick's next telephone call, a couple of days later, was put straight through to Trapsell's office. This time the solicitor's impatience turned to interest within half a minute. He listened attentively, told Dick to ring him at any time without hesitation, and put through a telephone call at once to Magnus Newton.

After their guests had gone Jack Jellifer surveyed the debris of the dinner party with real distress. The main dish, steak cooked in the oven with wine and herbs, had not really been as tender as he would have wished, the burgundy had been a disappointment, there had been something disturbingly (he found himself searching for the right word even in his present anguish of mind) disturbingly *lush* about the sorbet which should have finished off the meal with tongue-cleaning freshness.

Perhaps these subtleties had gone unnoticed by the guests, two influential clods from New Zealand who might arrange a lecture tour for him, but Jack felt the pangs of the defeated artist. He had, also, a burning feeling, or something between a burning feeling and a knife-like pain, penetrating his chest. He said as much to Arlene.

"Indigestion."

"You know I never suffer from it."

"Conscience, then." Jack burped. "I knew it was indigestion. You haven't got a conscience."

"Arlene, my love, please don't go into all that again."

"I shall go into it as often as I like." She confronted him, a savage green and yellow and blue-hued parrot with scarlet claws. "Why didn't you let the bloody police do their own dirty work? If Sol did kill that bitch I expect she deserved it, and anyway what did you want to say anything for, why couldn't you wait till you were asked?"

"I've told you over and over again that I felt it to be a public duty –"

"Public duty be –ed," said Arlene, who was given to free use of language. "You went to them because you don't like Sol, that's all. And I don't believe you saw anything anyway."

"I feel one of my headaches coming on." Jack dropped into a chair and covered his eyes with one plump hand. Through his fingers he could see the abstract painting, but it lacked power to console him at the moment.

"I'll tell you something that will make it worse, then. The daily's not coming in tomorrow so there's the washing up to do, and I can tell you I'm not doing it on my bloody own."

"Pseudo," Edgar Paget said. "That's the trouble with this country today, too many pseudo people in it. You know what I mean, the sort of people who read *The Times* and the *Guardian* because the *Telegraph's* not good enough for 'em. Snobs. That place is packed full of 'em." His thumb jerked in the direction of The Dell.

"I never noticed it stopped you selling them houses," his wife said.

"Of course not, I'm a business man. But I'm a private citizen too, and a private citizen can have an opinion, can't he? This garage trouble, now, it comes from the pseudos like that man Grundy. You know I walked out, walked straight out of that meeting. 'I shall want an apology,' I said. Do you know what happened today? I had a telephone call from Sir Edmund, you know Sir Edmund, a real gentleman of the old school. He told me they were all very sorry for what had happened and the Committee had met again and they'd like to go ahead on the basis I suggested. It just needs a little common-sense and goodwill, that's all, to make the world go round. Get rid of the trouble makers and pseudos like this fellow Grundy." His wife glanced at him warningly, but Edgar took no notice. "Playing around with a woman who was going with a coloured man, and then strangling her. I knew he was a bad one, a real pseudo, the first time I set eyes on him. I wish I was going to give evidence instead of you, my girl, I can tell you that."

Jennifer had been sitting reading, or pretending to read, the evening paper. Now she threw it down. "Oh, Daddy, I wish you'd shut up talking about that horrible man."

She ran out of the room. Edgar looked after her, shook his head. "I don't know what's got into the girl, turning on the waterworks like that. She did it after the identification you know, but not when she was at the Magistrates' Court. Stood up there cool as a cucumber, I was proud of her."

Rhoda looked as if she was about to make some protest. In fact she said simply that she had some washing to do, and stumped out of the room.

"But giving evidence for the *prosecution,*" Lily said. "I mean, darling, I just don't see it."

Werner shrugged his elegant shoulders. "English law, it's crazy. You heard what I told what's his name, Manners, every word of it. Could I have said less? Did I say anything that was not true? But now they are telling me that I must go to the Old Bailey and say it, and I don't want to." They were sitting on the sofa, and he tugged her hair.

"Can't you just tell them that?"

"My sweetie pie, don't you think I'd like to? This whole thing is ruin, I can tell you. Guffy, he's finished, nobody will look at him. Business is not good, in fact it is lousy, and it is going to get lousier. Don't you think I wish I could get out of the whole thing, and get old Sol out too?"

"What did he say when you saw him last week? How did he seem?"

"I don't understand the way his mind works. He might almost be enjoying it."

He tugged her hair again, sharply. She turned her head towards him, and he kissed her.

Letter from Solomon Grundy to Marion Grundy:

Thanks for letters. Feeling the way you do, you're probably right in saying there is no point in coming to see me. We don't want to argue across a prison table. Theo has been in, very agitated because he's being called to give evidence for the prosecution. Dick's been twice, full of news, very cheerful. He's playing detective, I gather. I hope he enjoys it.

They treat me pretty well here. Food not bad, warders friendly, nothing to complain of. Peaceful, too. Prison is extremely interesting, a closed society, an image of what the world is going to be like in fifty years. Everything is ordered here for you by authority, it isn't like The Dell, where the residents were doing the ordering – that is the thing you like and I object to! Once you accept the fact that in all the trivial, inessential things you have to do what you are told, you have all the time that's left to think about your life and errors. You are free! Do you understand what I mean?

But it is not my life and errors I think about as much as yours. However did you come to marry me? What one has done is done and there's no use in regretting it, but I do feel that in the past I did you the maximum harm, and that I've now done you almost the maximum good by getting put in prison. If I am found guilty you will be able to get a divorce, and you are young enough to make a fresh start. You may get a good relationship yet! I'm sorry. I don't mean to be ironical or to hurt you. When I'm in prison, what's the point?

I want you to understand that I shall do nothing to influence the course of events, the result of the trial, that I shall accept whatever happens. Every event springs from a prime cause, isn't that so? And as a prisoner, as "the accused", I feel myself completely detached from any possible outcome. If I were outside it would be a very different matter. Try to believe that what happens is inevitable. And don't worry about the result of the trial. As you can see, I don't.

Sol

"Well," Mr Hayward asked. "What's the news, what does he say?"

Marion had aged in the weeks since her husband's arrest, not dramatically but in small ways. The lines of discontent in her face were more deeply drawn, the eager look characteristic of her had turned into an anxious stare, she found it hard to keep her hands still.

"He says, oh, I don't know. He says I shouldn't worry about the result of the trial."

Mr Hayward's pork butcher's face was solemn. "My poor little girl."

Her voice was high. "What do you mean?"

"What your dad means is he may be found guilty," said Mrs Hayward, never in favour of indirection.

"Oh, Mum."

Mr Hayward had crossed to the square bay window and now stood looking out, with his back to them. The main road ran outside the house, beyond the few feet of front garden. "Lot of traffic."

"I feel I'm being – inadequate."

"You'd think it would get less, this time of year, winter coming on." Without turning round he said, "Might be best to let us see what he says." It was a sore point that she had not shown them the letters that came from prison in her husband's firm angular hand.

"No."

"Suit yourself, my dear. You must be the judge." His voice made it clear that he thought the judge's decision wrong.

Marion looked at her mother, who seemed wrapped in a private dream. Then Mrs Hayward said slowly, "It gets worse and worse. Every year it gets worse."

"What does?"

"The traffic."

Inspector Ryan found himself dropping in rather often on Tony Kabanga as the days and weeks went by, and this was surprising because Ryan had no particular liking for spades or coloureds or whatever you liked to call them. At first Ryan had kept an eye on him, because it was after all in practical terms possible that Kabanga had left the Windswept Club, gone to Cridge Mews and killed his girl friend. A practical possibility, yes, although Ryan had never considered it seriously since that first interview. The clubs seemed to be respectably conducted, as such places went, and there was no question of Kabanga being a ponce, for the dead girl or for any other woman. Apart from that, though, as Ryan said to Manners, he could see when a man was genuinely upset, and he would have been prepared to stake his reputation that Kabanga had had nothing to do with the girl's death.

After the arrest of Grundy, of course, the reason for seeing Kabanga no longer existed, but Ryan continued to drop in on him at the Windswept, where he was almost always to be found in the early evening. The inspector justified this to himself by saying that you could often pick up useful bits of information in clubs like this, and also by saying (to Manners as well as to himself) that Kabanga was a good contact. The truth was, though, that Ryan, whose family had come over from Ireland during the Troubles and had done no good for themselves at all, was fascinated by the speedy success of this smooth African. He said as much to Kabanga one evening as he sat in the office of the Windswept drinking malt whisky, the sort of whisky he wasn't normally able to afford.

"Look at me now, Tony. Came out of the Army after the war, went into the police because I liked the routine, the discipline. Now I'm an inspector, you know how much I get?" He said how much it was. "Chicken feed, eh? But I'm the success of the family, you know that. Then I look at myself and I look at you and I think, how's he done it? You've been here how long, four years. And you're set up for life."

Kabanga now called the Inspector "Buck". He smiled his slow sad smile. "To some of us money just sticks, Buck. Put it that way."

"I'll say it does. I call it bloody marvellous."

"I would give all the money I've got if it would bring Sylvia back."

"Come on now. You'd known her seven weeks."

"You think that isn't long enough? He did it, this Grundy?"

"Sure he did it." Ryan drained his glass. "And we've got him – like *that*."

"He has been bad luck to me all the time." On this Ryan made no comment. "He will be hanged?"

"Not hanged, Tony boy. Life imprisonment. But they haven't found him guilty yet."

"I do not think much of English justice." It was a tribute to Ryan's friendly feeling for Kabanga that he forbore to say that a spade should be thankful he was let into this country at all. "It is too slow. It is silly. A man who would kill somebody as beautiful as Sylvia should be killed. I should like to kill him, Buck, I should like to kill him with my own hands."

"And he really means it too," Ryan said afterwards to Manners. "Shouldn't be surprised if he did something silly, if Grundy did get off. I tell you, he really loved that girl."

Once Manners had made up his mind about Grundy's guilt he never wavered in that belief, but set about preparing the case against him with his usual conscientiousness. All the reports, odds and ends, false alarms, that poured in were faithfully investigated, but only those possibly relating to Grundy seemed to Manners really important. Without conscious unfairness he tended to relegate that unsolved question about the dead girl's sexual activities to the background. In spite of what had been said, there was no proof that she had been a prostitute, and this aspect of the case was given up. She had been Grundy's mistress, he had become jealous of her association with and prospective marriage to Kabanga, he had killed her. Accept this pattern, and every coin fell into its slot.

Manners liked to do a tidy job of work, and he was quite pleased with the file he finally presented to the Director of Public Prosecutions.

The file was studied carefully, and it was decided that there was a case to answer. In due course the Prison Medical Officer's report arrived too. From the time of his arrest Grundy had, as is customary, been under constant surveillance in the prison hospital. The report read:

> I have had several interviews myself with the accused, and have had reports from the officers who have had nursing charge of him. I have studied the reports on his history, and have also read the depositions in the case.

There followed a detailed account of Grundy's upbringing and career, his intelligence test rating (which was 135, well above average), and his illnesses. There was nothing significant here, the barrister handling the case in the DPP's office thought, except possibly that Grundy's Army CO said that he had always been ready for a fight, and on one occasion had attacked another officer in the mess after some trivial argument. But his conduct was listed officially as "Very good," and the CO had evidently had a soft spot for a dashing young officer. The report went on:

> In my discussions with him, his married life naturally came up as a subject. He was quite ready to talk about it, but what he said seemed to conceal some inner amusement at my questions. When I asked him what importance he attached to the sexual relationship in marriage, for instance, he said that he attached the same importance as any other normal man. In reply to my questions as to whether his own relationship with his wife was satisfactory, he said it was an average one, and refused to enlarge on that. My impression is that it was probably

unsatisfactory for both of them, but this can only be called a personal impression.

It would be wrong to say that he was evasive. I would rather use the word "withdrawn". He seemed to enjoy our conversation. He referred often to the uselessness of trying to struggle against fate, in reference to his own situation, and said that if he was meant to be found guilty he would be found guilty. This remark did not spring from any religious belief, for he said rather aggressively that he had none, but apparently from a feeling that all human effort was useless, and that it is impossible for human beings to organise their own lives. When I asked if he regarded himself as responsible for his actions, he replied that he did not acknowledge human responsibility in that sense.

The barrister read this with a frown, without making much sense of it. He read it again and made less, and passed on to what was for the Department the most important part of the report.

He showed no sign of depression, but there were marked indications of a dissociation of the personality, of a schizoid kind. These were evident in the opinions he expressed, although it would be too much to call him a divided personality. There seemed to me no defect of reason, due to a disease of the mind, such as would suggest that at the material time he did not know that what he was doing was wrong. He has a perfectly good appreciation of the situation, even though his attitude to it is unusual, and in my opinion he is fit to plead to the indictment and to stand trial.

That seemed to be all right then, the barrister thought as he added the document to the file. There was little chance of a successful plea of diminished responsibility.

THE TRIAL

WITHIN THE

CENTRAL CRIMINAL COURT

OLD BAILEY,
LONDON

Judge

MR JUSTICE CRUMBLE

Counsel for the Crown

MR EUSTACE HARDY
MR L. P. STEVENAGE

Counsel for the Acused

MR MAGNUS NEWTON, QC
MR TOBY BANDER

Chapter Three *Trial, First Day*

Trial Transcript – 1

THE CLERK OF COURT "Solomon Grundy, you are charged on indictment that on the 23rd of September, within the jurisdiction of the Central Criminal Court, you murdered one Sylvia Gresham. Well, Solomon Grundy, are you guilty or not guilty?"
THE ACCUSED "Not guilty."

Opening Speech for the Crown

MR HARDY "My lord, ladies and gentlemen of the jury, the accused man who stands before you is charged with the most serious crime known to our law. He is charged with having, on the evening of September 23rd, strangled the woman whose name was Sylvia Gresham but who passed under the name of Estelle Simpson, in her flat at Cridge Mews, Mayfair. It is suggested that the motive for the crime was frustrated sexual passion, that the woman Gresham was or had been Grundy's mistress, and that when he met her quite unexpectedly in the company of a coloured African named Anthony Kabanga, and realised that she contemplated marriage with Kabanga, a marriage which must undoubtedly have meant the severance of her relationship with the accused, he went to see her in her flat, to which he was a frequent visitor, and there strangled her. I have to tell you that it is for the prosecution to establish the guilt of the accused beyond reasonable doubt, and not for the accused to establish his innocence, and that if you think the prosecution has not so established his guilt you will acquit him. It is my duty to make clear to you the facts of the case as we know them, and this I shall do without any flourish of rhetoric, so that on hearing these facts you may do justice according to the evidence.

Now, members of the jury, I will try to deal first of all with one of the features of the case of which I do not doubt you will hear more from the defence: they will say that all the evidence is circumstantial. They will be quite right, but, members of the jury, what is circumstantial evidence? I will not bother you with the whole column afforded the word in the Oxford Dictionary, but give you the kernel of it that concerns us. It is "indirect evidence inferred from circumstances which afford a certain presumption, or appear explainable only on one hypothesis". And I must say to you that much of the evidence in a murder case is always circumstantial, in the sense that there are rarely any witnesses who see the act itself at the moment of commission. You should feel no prejudice against circumstantial evidence providing always that, to quote the definition again, it is "explainable only on one hypothesis". I shall show you that the accused is by nature a coarse, brutal and quarrelsome man; that three days before the murder he met the deceased woman unexpectedly at a party, and quarrelled with her so violently that he tore her dress and she scratched his cheek; that he was seen talking to and embracing her the following evening, and then entering a house with her; that on the day of the murder he quarrelled with his partner in the firm which they owned together, and that during the whole of this day he appeared to be under great mental strain; that he had sent a postcard to Miss Gresham, arranging to call on her on Monday evening, that his car was seen near her flat at a time when the accused says he was in his office, and that he was seen actually entering the flat. These actions are, I suggest to you, "explainable only on one hypothesis", that the accused knew Sylvia Gresham, that she was his mistress, and that he strangled her in a fit of rage. And when, a few days later, the accused felt the net tightening round him, what did he do? He packed his bags hastily and without telling anybody of his intention – his wife, his partner, his neighbours – he tried to leave the country. He was stopped at the airport. His explanation of his action was that he had quarrelled with his wife who had gone to stay with her family, and he acted upon impulse. That is his explanation. Can you, as reasonable men and women, members of the jury, believe that it is true?

I think I shall start my story by describing to you the events of Friday evening, the 20th of September. On that evening the accused and his wife, Marion, went to a party at the house of some friends and neighbours of theirs named Weldon..."

(end of transcript)

Very few English courts of justice are impressive. They seem rather, to our eyes which have been sophisticated by seeing so many such courts on stage and screen, rather like a stage set. That oak panelling – surely it is a fake, something that will be removed at the end of the scene? And the counsel who sit so close to each other, nod so knowingly at the messages whispered by their juniors, and refer to each other upon occasion with such studied distaste or indignation, they are surely actors whose legal personalities will be taken off with their wigs, leaving behind a couple of young men who say to each other, "Gets pretty boring playing lawyers, doesn't it? I'll really be glad when this one's finished its run". Number 1 Court at the Old Bailey gives little hint of the dramas enacted there. It is oak panelled, of average courtroom size, anonymous in character. Its dignity is derived from the wigs and robes, the formality of the speech, the raised platform upon which the judge sits in his scarlet and ermine.

Upon this platform, Mr Justice Crumble sat now listening patiently to Eustace Hardy as he unwound the tale of what Solomon Grundy was alleged to have done. Mr Justice Crumble really did look as though he was crumbling away. His large red nose was manifestly rotting and the hands that occasionally peeped like mice out of his scarlet sleeves had backs visibly scaly with age, from which thick plum-coloured fingers depended like over-ripe fruits ready to drop from the bough. These fruity appendages were obviously not ideal instruments for taking notes, and the pencil which Mr Justice Crumble used wavered considerably. Yet he was a judge well regarded, not particularly for his knowledge of law, but for his patience with and courtesy to counsel.

Eustace Hardy's junior, Leslie Stevenage, thought as he listened to his eminent senior what a laboured opening it was, and how much better he could have done it himself. Hardy had a beautiful speaking voice, a fact of which he was only too well aware, he was lucid, he had a style markedly individual, but there was no feeling, no *warmth*. And to open on such an apologetic note, with all that stuff about circumstantial evidence, wasn't that a mistake, wouldn't it have been better to let the defence say some of that and then counter it? Leslie Stevenage knew the theory that it was a good thing to spike your opponent's guns before he had a chance to fire them, but personally he believed in firing your own guns first.

Magnus Newton sat with his little legs stuck out in front of him and his lower lip critically outthrust, which was a habit he had recently developed. He listened to Hardy's opening without ever giving it his full attention. His own line of defence was fairly clearly mapped out in his mind, and nothing he heard in Court was likely to alter it. He thought that the prosecution had a fairly flimsy case, and that there was good hope of an acquittal. If only, he thought, looking at the prisoner in the dock, if only he didn't look such a hulking great bruiser. His principal worry, indeed, was the effect that Grundy would produce when giving evidence. He would have liked to keep Grundy out of the witness box altogether, but knew that the omission to do so might be irreparably damaging. Newton had talked it over with his junior, Toby Bander, and they had agreed that they couldn't risk it.

Toby Bander, a bachelor, thought about the girl he was taking out that night. He looked at the jury, nine men and three women, and thought that they seemed a pretty averagely awful lot.

And the prisoner, what did he think about? He sat with his big hands gripping the sides of the dock and looked sometimes straight ahead of him at the judge, sometimes down at his counsel and the solicitor who sat in front of them. The corners of his mouth twitched occasionally. Was this a tic, or was he really amused by what he saw?

Eustace Hardy came to the end of his opening. He had spoken for an hour and a quarter with his usual clarity, so that every member of the jury must or should have a picture of the exact sequence of events, and the motives that had prompted the man Grundy to kill the woman Gresham. There was nothing wrong with his performance, yet he was conscious that he was not quite at his best. He found prosecution in a sex crime of this sort slightly distasteful, because he had a good deal of sympathy with the accused. His view of sex relations was tolerant in a rather eighteenth-century manner. He regarded it as perfectly reasonable that Grundy should keep a mistress, since apparently he didn't get on with his wife. And then when he found out that his mistress was playing around with a coloured chap and apparently actually proposing to marry the fellow – well, Hardy felt nobody should be surprised by what happened. But of course, these feelings lay below the level of consciousness. Eustace Hardy was too experienced not to order and present his case in the most effective way possible.

Trial Transcript-2

JENNIFER LOIS PAGET, *examined by Mr Eustace Hardy.*
"I am seventeen years of age, and I am a student at Malhearne Grammar School. I went to the party at Mr and Mrs Weldon's on the night of Friday, September 22nd. At about ten-thirty in the evening I had gone upstairs to the toilet, and while I was in there I heard a scream. I opened the door and I saw Mr Grundy, and a lady who was a stranger to me, but whom I now know to have been Miss Gresham."
MR HARDY "What were they doing?"
"They were standing in the bedroom doorway, the bedroom that was used for coats. He was holding her shoulder."
"Was he trying to detain her?"
"That's what it looked like."
"What else did you notice?"
"Well, I could see her dress was torn. I noticed that because she was holding it up with one hand."
"Did you see any mark on the accused's face?"
"No, I didn't see that."
"What happened next?"
"Well, then she sort of broke away from him and came down the stairs. And after a moment he followed her."
"What did you do then?"
"I was – rather frightened. I went back into the toilet. I'd never really come out of it, you see, and I locked the door and didn't come out till they'd gone."
"In order to go down the stairs both Miss Gresham and the accused would have had to pass you. Did they see you?"
"I don't think so. They were too intent on what had been happening. And I shut the door quickly."
"As to what happened afterwards, you can't help us?"
"No."
"Now, let me move on to the following evening. I believe you had taken your dog for a walk."

"That's right."

"What time would this have been?"

"About, I wouldn't like to say exactly, but about half past ten."

"Now, just tell the Court where you went and what you saw."

"Puggy and I walked up Brambly Way and just into The Dell. I often go that way for an evening walk. Just a few yards inside The Dell I saw Mr Grundy and Miss Simpson – Gresham. He was holding her and saying something, I didn't hear what. Then he kissed her. Then Puggy went back into Brambly Way again and I went with him, but I just looked back and they were going into the corner house, Mr Kabanga's house."

"Will you tell the jury how you can be certain of the identification?"

"Well, you see, I keep Puggy on a lead mostly because he wanders about, but it didn't seem necessary because this was at night, and he went rather near them, so I had to go rather near too."

"And how near is the nearest street light?"

"Just a few feet away, I should say six feet."

"And how near were you to them?"

"Puggy went almost up to them, you see. So I went – oh, about three or four feet away. They didn't take any notice of me."

"If they were holding each other, how can you be so certain of your identification?"

"First of all they were just holding and talking to each other, and I could see her quite clearly. Mr Grundy had his back to me, though I could see his hair. It's sort of ginger even under the light. Then when they were going into the house – you know, when I turned round I saw his face."

"Are you quite sure of your identification?"

"Quite sure." *(end of transcript)*

Edgar and Rhoda both attended this first day of the trial, and they took Jennifer to a small restaurant opposite the Old Bailey for lunch. Jennifer's hair had been done for the occasion, she had spots of colour in her cheeks, and she looked almost pretty. Edgar was in high spirits. As the days had passed he had more and more identified the case with his struggle against the pseudos, a battle in which victory was important to the spiritual health of the nation. He ordered a bottle of wine, and insisted that Jennifer should be allowed to have a glass.

"Can't possibly do the little girl any harm. You spoke up very well, very good clear answers, didn't she?"

"Very well." Rhoda, square-bodied, wearing square-toed shoes, cut firmly into her chop.

"Wonderful thing. English justice." Edgar leaned back in his chair, picked at his teeth. "First one side has its chance, then the other. Couldn't be fairer. That chap Newton will be having a go at you this afternoon."

"I know, Daddy." Jennifer drank the wine in little sips.

"Don't suppose he'll try to bully you, but if he does, stand up to him. Nothing to be afraid of. And don't be provoked, just keep calm."

"Oh, really, Daddy, please."

Rhoda cut a potato into four almost identical pieces.

"Listen to what your father says. This is serious, you're not here to enjoy it." She speared one piece of potato and conveyed it to her mouth, which shut on it.

"I'm not enjoying it." But the colour in Jennifer's cheeks belied her words.

Back in Court, all the actors were in their places. Mr Justice Crumble's fingers shook more than usual as he picked up his pencil – how had they managed to cut the charcoal-grilled steak he had eaten, avoided spilling the Guinness he had drunk? Eustace Hardy, an arm swept out in casual abandonment, rested, a greyhound out of the slips. Jennifer, a composed respectable schoolgirl, stood in the witness box. Magnus Newton got up, gave a preliminary cough, twitched at his gown.

Trial Transcript – 3

JENNIFER LOIS PAGET, *cross-examined by Mr Newton.*
MR NEWTON "Are you proud of your powers of observation, Miss Paget?"

"Not particularly."

"I ask because you seem to have shown them in this case. You were very much on the spot at the time things happened, weren't you?"

"I just happened to be there, that's all."

"So you say. Take the evening of the party. You say you were in the lavatory. Did anyone see you when you came out?"

"I don't think so."

"You must have come down the stairs when all the commotion was over, but nobody noticed."

"No. I stayed there afterwards for – oh, perhaps a minute. Or more."

"I see. But you'd really seen everything that mattered, hadn't you? Did you tell anybody?"

"My mother and father."

"Nobody else?"

"No."

"You were discreet. Then we will pass on to the following evening, Saturday. You were on the spot again in the right place at the right time. Did it strike you that these two people you saw were behaving in an extraordinarily foolish way?"

"Not particularly."

"Anybody could have seen them?"

"I suppose so."

"But it just happened to be you. Did it occur to you that they could have gone into the house straight away, and not stood about in the open?"

"I didn't think about it."

"But that's true, isn't it? If Grundy had wanted to go and see Miss Gresham in that house, it would have been sensible to go straight to it, isn't that so? And extremely foolish to stand about in the roadway embracing – and so near a street lamp too?"

THE JUDGE "The witness has told you what she saw, Mr Newton. I do not think she should be required to provide any explanation of it."

MR NEWTON "As your lordship pleases. I will be plain with you, Miss Paget. I suggest that the whole of your evidence is the product of your highly romantic imagination."

"That is quite untrue."

"We shall see. You have done this kind of thing before, have you not?"

"I don't know what you mean."

"You have a short memory. Do you remember that last year you produced at school anonymous letters that you said had been sent to you? Do you remember that, Miss Paget?"

"Yes."

"And that you suggested that a particular girl had sent them? And that an investigation was made, with no result except the strong suspicion that you had written the letters yourself?"

"That's not true. They never found – the one who sent them."

"Let us cast back a little further. Do you remember an incident three years ago, when you were at another school, before you went to Malhearne? Do you remember that some money was missing, and you accused another girl of stealing it? Answer me, please."

"I – yes."

"And was the money found simply to have been mislaid?"

"Yes."

"And was it suggested to your parents that it would be as well for you to leave, because of the feeling of other pupils against you?"

"No. No, that isn't true."

"Why did you leave, then?"

"I didn't like it there. I wanted to go. I asked to leave."

THE JUDGE "You will be calling evidence in support, Mr Newton?"

MR NEWTON "The headmistresses of the schools, my lord. Do you long for the limelight, Miss Paget?"

"No."

"I am bound to suggest to you that the whole of your evidence is an invention."

"No."

"You have made it all up, have you not, to gain a little notoriety, to become for a short time an important person."

"No. No, you shouldn't say such things."

"You never saw the scenes you describe, any more than you saw the girl steal the money at school, one is just as much an invention as the other."

"No, I did see them."

Re-examined by Mr Hardy.

MR.HARDY "Please don't distress yourself, Miss Paget. I just want to ask you this. Forgetting these incidents at school which occurred some time ago and have nothing to do with this case, you are quite sure of what you saw on the night of the party, and the following night."

"Yes."

"Everything happened just as you said, and you are sure of the identification?"

"Yes." *(end of transcript)*

To understand the feeling of a trial, the impact of evidence upon a jury, it is necessary to have been present, as lawyers often tell us. The words are there on the printed page, but the emotion, the drama, the momentary sense of triumph or defeat, is missing. When Jennifer Paget, tear-stained and trembling, stepped down at last from the witness box, Eustace Hardy knew

151

that he had lost the first round in the struggle to convict Grundy, and he knew too that the first round is often the most vital one, that the impression made on a jury's mind at the beginning of a case may be very difficult to eradicate. He did not waste time in worrying about whether she had been telling the truth, or what inadequacies of staff work had failed to unearth the school incidents, but as he proceeded with the examination of Tony Kabanga, establishing his relationship with the dead girl, their love for each other, her agreement to the suggestion that they should get married, he was conscious that the case had got away to the worst possible start.

Magnus Newton was correspondingly pleased with himself. To Trapsell's congratulations afterwards he replied modestly that it had been given to him on a plate, but still he hummed a little tune. "It was that friend of yours who did it," he said to Trapsell.

"Weldon, yes. He's a bit of a bore, but a good chap." That evening Trapsell rang up Dick to thank him. The solicitor added that if Dick made any further discoveries or had any suggestions to make, he would be delighted to hear from him at any time.

Edgar and Rhoda drove their daughter home. Edgar maintained a flow of vituperation against Newton in particular and the unscrupulousness of defence counsel in general, almost all the way. When they got indoors his wife said, "That's enough."

"What?" He stared at her. "They rake up all this dirt out of the past, and make my girl cry, and I'm to say nothing about it?"

"It's not that far past." To Jennifer she said grimly, "You can go upstairs and change."

The girl looked from one to the other of them and said in a high voice, "I did see them, I tell you, I did."

"Of course you did, love," her father said soothingly. He went across to the cocktail cabinet, poured two drinks.

"I want one," Jennifer said. "I had one at lunch, didn't I? I want one now."

Edgar looked helplessly at his wife who said, "Upstairs."

"Why? Why must I go upstairs? I'm seventeen, I'm not a child."

"Upstairs." When she had gone, shrieking and crying incoherently, Rhoda said, "I was afraid of this."

"I don't know what you mean. All that business about the money, I'd never heard about that."

"We didn't tell you. It was a secret between us, Jennifer and I. You knew about the letters."

"It's coming to something when a man's wife and daughter keep secrets from him." Edgar's face was shifting, wobbling, as if he also were going to cry.

"Don't be a fool."

Feebly he said, "I, really, I just won't be spoken to like that."

She sat with thick legs placed apart like small tree trunks. "What you'd better be thinking about is the effect on business. People aren't going to like it. It's going to raise a lot of sympathy for Grundy."

The movement to find further evidence to clear Solomon Grundy of the murder charge was already splitting The Dell into pro- and anti-Grundy camps. The leader of the Grundyites was of course Dick Weldon, who was inclined to take full credit for the information provided by Gloria which had been responsible for Jennifer's discomfiture. Dick and Caroline called personally on almost every family in The Dell to ask them whether they knew anything that might help. "Any bit of information," Dick said in his earnest way. "About Sol or about this chap Kabanga or about the girl – if anybody saw her talking to anyone else at some time, that kind of thing – anything at all that the police may have missed might help, if you see what I mean."

And Dick talked at length about the iniquities of the identification parade, and the way in which Sol was being victimised. Most of the people they talked to were sympathetic, but nobody seemed to remember anything significant. Afterwards Dick and Caroline talked it over in their living-room. This was the sort of social experience they very much enjoyed, although they would not have put it in that way. Gloria was upstairs doing her prep. Cyprian sat, for once not watching television but reading. They drank Irish coffee.

"I'll tell you something," Dick said, pulling at his pipe. "Marion's not been to see Sol. Not once."

"She ought to come back. It looks bad for her to stay away."

"Why don't you try to arrange it?"

"Me?" Caroline was one of those women whose physical vivacity is so abundant that they find it impossible to sit down to read a book, and fidget if they are compelled to watch a film or a play right through. Now her eyes positively sparkled at the prospect of action.

"Do you really think –"

"Why not? After all, you're a friend of hers. She must realise what people think about her staying away like this. She's got to come back and face the music." It is difficult for the utterer of a cliché to distinguish it from a profundity, and Dick rolled out this last phrase with satisfaction.

"Do you really think I should go down? Where is it her father lives, Hayward's Heath?"

" 'Doesn't belong to me, this Heath, you know'," Dick mimicked. Caroline laughed encouragingly. "In the meantime I'll make a few inquiries about friend Kabanga."

They were interrupted by Cyprian saying "– off," to the cat, Timmy, which was digging its claws into his knee.

"Cyprian. You are *not* to use that word."

"Why not?"

"Because I say so."

"Now, darling." Dick's voice took on a patiently reasonable tone, through which could be faintly heard a sort of whinnying annoyance. "I've explained before Cyprian, that the objection to bad language is that it is crudely anti-social. It may relieve your feelings –"

"It does."

"But it's disagreeable for others. This is a social custom, polite manners."

"Not any more. I've heard girls say –"

"Not nice girls." Caroline, more conventional than Dick, ignored his frown.

Cyprian shrugged. "I think it's stupid. But all right."

"Please don't use bad language any more," Caroline said.

"I won't. Not when you're around, anyway. I'll tell you something."

"What?" Caroline was nervous of some fresh enormity.

"That girl who was strangled. I'd seen her before. On television. You might get a lead out of that."

Dick and Caroline looked at each other. Dick said, "It's an idea."

"She wasn't raped, so it might have been a queer who did it," Cyprian said. "I believe television's full of queers."

"I give up." Caroline took the cups out to the kitchen.

Cyprian smiled happily at his father. "Did I say something wrong?"

The Weldons did not call on Jack Jellifer, because they had heard that he was a witness, but Caroline had called upon Peter Clements, who had told her with an air of offended dignity that he did not wish to be involved on either side. When she had gone, he said sheepishly to Rex, "A bit difficult. I didn't like to tell her I was giving evidence."

"Giving evidence?"

"You remember I told you I saw his car near Cridge Mews, the place where –"

"I know, of course, I know."

Peter said falteringly, excusingly, "I was with Jack Jellifer. He saw it too."

"You didn't give evidence at the Magistrate's Court."

"I hadn't made up my mind then."

"Oh, really." Rex walked out of the room. Peter watched him go, helplessly. Five minutes later Rex came down carrying his two suitcases. He came into the living room wearing his sheepskin, velvet-collared coat, went across to the telephone. Peter asked what he was doing.

"Calling a taxi. I'm moving out." When he had put down the telephone Rex said, "We're finished. We have been for a long time."

"Because of Grundy?"

"Oh, he's just part of it. Helping the rozzers, that's something you don't do in my book, you wouldn't understand." He stood with his hands in the pockets of the sheepskin coat, looking at his friend with contempt and curiosity.

"I mean, what will you do, where will you go?"

"I'll manage. I've got friends."

"Please don't go. You don't know what it – means to me."

"For Christ's sake don't let's make a performance out of it." Rex gave his foxy smile. "As a matter of fact I should be careful if I were you."

"I don't know what you're talking about."

"Just be careful, Peter boy, when you get up in that witness box."

Shrilly Peter said, "Are you threatening me?"

"I'm not. I wouldn't touch the police with a barge pole." The taxi could be heard outside. Rex paused at the door. "But somebody else might. Think about it. So long. No hard feelings."

Then he had gone. Self-respect forbade Peter to watch the cases being put in the taxi, but he did lift the curtains in time to see the rear lights going away down the gravel path. He stood looking out into the night for several seconds, and when he turned to face the empty room his eyes were wet.

Chapter Four *Trial, Second Day*

Kabanga made upon the whole a good impression in his evidence in chief. Slight, neat, perhaps a little too well-dressed, he spoke of the dead girl with such evident sincerity, such an obvious sense of loss, that it seemed the jury must be impressed. He looked only once at the man in the dock, when he was speaking of the incident at the party, but then the look in his brown eyes was one of such dislike, almost hatred, that Newton raised his brows when he saw it. The most dramatic moment in his evidence came when Hardy asked him to say what had happened when they left the party.

"We went home, I mean to this house I have bought in The Dell. Sylvia was upset. I asked what had made this man attack her. She told me that he was somebody she had known a long time ago, and he had wanted her to – take up with him again. She refused and said she did not want any more to do with him. Then he attacked her, and she defended herself."

"She told you that he had attacked her."

"Yes."

"And you believed her."

"I did. She was very upset."

On Saturday night, Kabanga said, he had attended the committee meeting, and then had driven back to London, where he had spent the night at one of his clubs, The Windswept. He had not seen Sylvia that evening.

The question of how a cross-examiner should treat a dead woman of dubious character is an uncertain one. By using kid gloves he may lose an opportunity of making valuable points, by attacking the dead who cannot answer back he runs a risk of outraging a jury's sense of fair play. Newton had no doubt, however, that this was a risk he should be prepared to take. His manner throughout cross-examination was one of sustained hostility, verging on deliberate insult.

Trial transcript – 4

ANTHONY KABANGA, *cross-examined by Mr Newton.*
MR NEWTON "You said you had known Sylvia Gresham for seven weeks, Mr Kabanga. How long had you known her when she became your mistress?"

"I think two weeks."

"You think – you are not sure?"

"It was about that time."

"I suggest to you that this was a casual affair, and that you both understood it as such."

"That is not the case. We were in love."

"Have you had other mistresses during your stay in this country."

"Yes."

"How many, would you say?"

"I am not sure."

"Come now, you must have some idea. You have been here, what is it, almost five years? Have you had two mistresses, thirty, two hundred?"

"Perhaps six."

"That is a round number. Suppose I said it was eight, would you contradict me?"

"Perhaps that might be so, but these were not like –"

"Just answer my question. Could it have been eight?"

"Yes, but these were not the same thing. They were just – nothing."

"And this was true love. Is that what you are trying to tell the jury?"

"We were going to get married. That was why I bought a house."

"Are you going to tell me that you regarded Sylvia Gresham as a pure young virgin?"

"No, but –"

"Just answer my questions, Mr Kabanga. You know of the pair of knickers that she was wearing when she was found, and what was written on them. Here they are. May they be passed round for the jury to look at, my lord."

(Exhibit 19 was shown to the jury.)

MR NEWTON "Perhaps you gave them to her?"

"No, I did not. She bought them herself."

"What did you think of them? Did they excite you?"

"I thought there was no harm in them."

"You know that certain photographs were found in her flat? May these be passed to the jury also, my lord?"

(Exhibit 20 was shown to the jury.)

MR NEWTON "Perhaps you gave these to her – as a token of your love?"

(Witness did not reply)

THE JUDGE "Will you be good enough to rephrase the question, Mr Newton, in a form that is not offensive to the witness."

MR NEWTON "Very well, my lord. Did you know that Sylvia Gresham had these photographs?"

"I have never seen them before. I do not believe that Sylvia would have –"

"We are not concerned with what you believe, only with the facts. I suggest to you that you know perfectly well that she was the kind of woman who took a new lover as casually as – as she bought a new pair of knickers, shall I say?"

"No. It is not true."

"And that you knew she was a woman likely to distribute her favours among three or four men at the same time."

"It is not so. Sylvia was not like that. She was not like that." *(The witness appeared distressed.)*

"By your own account you saw her only three or four nights a week. Have you any idea what she did on the other nights?"

"She was working."

"That is what she told you. Now let us come to the evening of the party. When Sylvia Gresham told you that the prisoner had attacked her, by your account she said that she already knew him."

"Yes, that is right."

"And did you not then ask her how and when she knew him, under what circumstances they had met?"

"No. I thought this was not my business."

"Not your business! And she was to be your wife – !"

(end of transcript)

The end of this savage cross-examination left Kabanga almost in tears. What had it achieved? It was difficult to know. Newton was satisfied with it, and so was Hardy, the one feeling that Sylvia Gresham had been shown conclusively to be little other than an amateur tart, the other believing that this aspect was not really important, and that the cross-examination had enlisted sympathy for her and for Kabanga.

Hardy was calling his evidence so as to trace Grundy's movements throughout the day of the murder, with the object of building up a cumulative picture of a man driven to desperate action by his internal frustration and by the pressure of external events. The evidence of Theo Werner, supported by that of Mrs Langham and Miss Pringle, was therefore important to him. Theo, when he took the stand, was obviously nervous. Hardy established that he was giving evidence only with reluctance, and then launched into a long series of questions about the interview with Clacton, and Grundy's extreme disappointment about the rejection of the strip cartoon. Mr Justice Crumble began to show signs of impatience. His thick red shaking fingers moved up to touch the great red ruin of a nose, explored the recesses of pendulous wrinkled ears, picked up and relinquished a pencil. At last he spoke, gently enough.

"What is the object of this part of your examination, Mr Hardy?"

"To show the prisoner's state of mind on the day of the murder, my lord."

"And do his feelings about this strip cartoon character, Guffy McTuffie, really carry your case forward?"

"I think so. If your lordship will permit me to develop the matter a little further, I think the jury will appreciate its relevance."

"Very well, Mr Hardy." Mr Justice Crumble gave up the struggle with a still-amiable sigh, and with such a fierce rubbing of his nose that it seemed likely to fall off.

Hardy moved on to the quarrel in the office. Werner said that there had been an argument between them about the reasons for the rejection of the strip cartoon. He had maintained that there was too much social comment, Grundy had said that the social comment was what gave the cartoon its flavour.

"What happened then?"

"Sol was angry." Theo smiled nervously at his red-haired partner, who stared stonily back at him from the dock. "He took hold of me, I pulled away from him, and he caught my bow tie and tore it a little. Then I went out."

"You were annoyed?"

"At the time, yes, very."

"Did you say to Miss Pringle in the outer office that your tie was ruined?"

"Something like that, yes."

"And now another point, Mr Werner." Hardy leaned forward to emphasise it. "Do you sometimes exchange memoranda with the accused?"

"That is so, yes. If I am working at home, or he is, and we want to put forward some idea which, you know, has to go on paper."

"How does he sign such memoranda? With his name or initials?"

"No. He just puts a little drawing of Guffy at the bottom."

"That is, a drawing of your strip cartoon character, Guffy McTuffie?"

"Yes."

Finally, Hardy took Theo through the conversation he had had with Grundy on the day of his attempted departure. It was perfectly true, Theo said, that he had suggested Grundy should take a holiday to let everything blow over. At the time Grundy had rejected the idea. He, Theo, had tripped and fallen over as he was leaving the office, it was nothing more than that, there had been no attack. Yes, it was true that he had been surprised that his partner should have tried to leave without telling him, but no doubt he would have sent word as soon as he had arrived. Newton left the cross-examination to Toby Bander. It was brief.

"I suggest to you, Mr Werner, that this little squabble was a storm in a teacup."

"Oh, precisely, yes." But Theo spoilt the effect of this answer by adding, "It was something that had never happened before."

"On the following day you had both forgotten it?"

"Forgotten and forgiven, yes." Theo smiled sweetly.

Tony Bander read a note handed down by Grundy from the dock, and said, "I suggest that you are mistaken in saying that your partner always signed memos to you with this little figure. I suggest that he sometimes signed them Sol."

Theo smiled at Grundy. "It is possible, yes."

"Can you confirm that?"

"If Sol says so, I am sure it is right."

"I suggest also that some of your own memos to him are signed with this little figure, that you both used it occasionally?"

"Yes, that is so."

Theo agreed readily, or rather repeated, that he had mentioned the question of a holiday, and that there had been nothing in the way of business to prevent his partner from going. Toby Bander left it at that, but he could not prevent Hardy from establishing in re-examination that Theo could not remember receiving any memo signed "Sol". There followed Mrs Langham and Miss Pringle, eager for their moments of glory, ready to testify to Grundy's bad temper on Monday morning and drunkenness on Monday afternoon. Followed the landlord of The Wild Peacock, who said that Grundy had come in about seven-thirty on Monday evening and left twenty minutes later. The pub was just round the corner from the office, but Grundy had been wearing an overcoat, and the implication that Hardy tried to draw from this was that he had finished work for the night. Cross-examined, the landlord agreed that it had been a cold night, and that he could not remember whether Grundy was carrying a briefcase. Followed Jack Jellifer, handsome, plummy, grave.

Trial Transcript – 5

JOHN JASPER JELLIFER, *examined by Mr Hardy.*

"I am a journalist and an expert on matters connected with food and drink. I live in The Dell, and am well acquainted with the prisoner and also with his car, which is distinctive, as it is an old gunmetal grey Alvis. At approximately nine o'clock on the evening of Monday the 23rd of September I was walking along Curzon Street, and saw the prisoner's car pass me. I pointed it out to my companion, Mr Clements. I am quite sure of the identification of the car."

MR HARDY "Could you see who was driving the car?"

"No, sir, I could not."

"Then how can you be sure that it was the accused's car?"

"His car has a rent in the hood, on the driver's side, just above his head. I have commented on it more than once, as a joke, asking when it would be mended. I noticed the rent in this car."

"When did you come forward?"

"As soon as I knew that the – ah – that Grundy's name was connected with the case."

"One final question. Do you bear a grudge of any kind against the prisoner?"

"Absolutely none. One has a duty in these matters, that was my feeling."

Cross-examined by Mr Newton.

MR NEWTON "You are an expert on wine and food, Mr Jellifer. That involves you, I expect, in eating a good deal of delicious food and drinking some remarkable wine."

"That is my duty."

"You are much to be envied. I hope that I may consult you about my own cellar."

"I shall be delighted to advise you, Mr Newton."

"Not today, however. Now on this particular evening, Mr Jellifer, I wonder where you dined?"

"I dined with my friend Peter Clements at a little restaurant recently opened, called The Emperor's New Clothes."

MR JUSTICE CRUMBLE "I trust that the food is not imaginary, in accordance with Hans Andersen's fable?"

"No, my lord, I can thoroughly recommend the restaurant."

MR NEWTON "I am happy to hear it. No doubt you were a welcome guest. Perhaps you would tell us what you ate."

"I always like to eat the speciality of any restaurant. Here we began with a *bisque d'homard*, and I can assure you that it was one that did not come out of a packet, and then we shared a duck which had been prepared in quite a special way with cherries, nuts and olives. We finished with *fraises de bois,* specially flown over from Southern Italy."

"That sounds a memorable meal. I hope the wines did not disgrace it?"

"Not at all. With the soup we drank a Gewurztraminer, fine but a little too aromatic, with the duck an excellent Aloxe Corton, with the *fraises de bois* a Barsac, Chateau Coutet, that complemented them perfectly, and with our coffee a Napoleon brandy."

"Does it not occur to you, Mr Jellifer, that this consumption of wine and spirits impaired your faculties of observation?"

"No. I am accustomed to it."

"A bottle and a half of wine at a meal, and brandy on top of it? Come now, Mr Jellifer."

"I don't regard that as excessive. Drink has no effect on me."

"Really? No doubt the jury will take note of that fact. Now, you had just one guest."

"Yes, Mr Peter Clements, the television producer, who is a neighbour of mine."

"He also lives in The Dell, I believe. Did you discuss your acquaintance Grundy at all?"

"His name was mentioned. I don't think we discussed him particularly."

"But his name was mentioned. He was in your mind. And now will you tell us exactly the circumstances in which you think you saw your friend's Alvis. You were walking along Curzon Street. Was the car coming towards you?"

"Yes, it was."

"Travelling at what speed?"

"Oh, well, really – an ordinary speed."

"An ordinary speed. Would that be fifteen miles an hour, thirty, forty?"

"About twenty, I suppose."

"And how far away was it when you recognised it?"

"Oh, a few yards, I suppose. Say fifteen yards."

"Do you know how long it took the car to travel fifteen yards and pass you at the rate of twenty miles an hour, Mr Jellifer? Approximately two seconds."

"But I commented on it to Peter Clements at the time. 'Good lord,' I said. 'There he goes.' "

"So Clements had not noticed it at that time."

"Well, no, I suppose not. He turned round to look."

"Your identification, then, is based on what you saw during two seconds of time."

"It was longer than that."

"How can it have been?"

"Perhaps the car was going more slowly. Much more slowly."

"So you are not sure of the speed. Are you really sure of anything, Mr Jellifer?"

"I tell you I recognised the car. I'd know it anywhere."

"Mr Jellifer, you had drunk approximately a bottle and a half of wine, and a glass of brandy. You were talking about your friend Grundy. You saw this car for two, or at most three seconds. You did not notice the number. You could not see the driver. Are you seriously telling the jury that you recognised the car by the rent in its hood?"

"It wasn't only that. The colour is very distinctive."

Re-examined by Mr Hardy.

MR HARDY "Whatever counsel for the defence may say, you remain quite certain that it was the prisoner's car you saw?"

"Absolutely sure, yes."

THE JUDGE "Even though it has been demonstrated that you can have seen the car for only two or three seconds, that makes no difference to you?"

"No difference at all, my lord."

"Very well."   *(end of transcript)*

"You made a fine bloody fool of yourself," Arlene Jellifer said when her husband got home that night. She had not gone to the

Old Bailey because she refused, she said, to have anything to do with the persecution of old Sol.

"Not at all." Jack sat down rather heavily in a chair and stared at the fish painting.

"You've been drinking." She snatched up the evening paper and read, " 'A bottle and a half of wine and brandy on top of it, that wasn't excessive?' "Who do you think you're fooling? You let him walk all over you."

"Not at all."

"If I'd known how much you'd drunk I'd never have let you give evidence."

He murmured something as he bent down to untie his shoes.

"What?"

"Couldn't have stopped me."

"You're an absolute fool, Jack. I love you, but you're an absolute fool."

"Peter's giving evidence tomorrow. Then you'll see."

Arlene looked for a moment as though she would like to tear him to pieces with her parrot claws, then turned and went up the stairs. Jack sat where he was for a minute or two – holding one shoe in his hand.

"You said the other day you wanted to get out of giving evidence, and get old Sol out of trouble too. You seem to have shoved him farther in," Lily said. They were lying naked on the bed in the Earl's Court Square flat. Theo stroked her buttocks, shifted his hand. "No, shut up, I want to talk."

"What is there to talk about? I had to give evidence."

"*Had* to?"

"I am a foreigner. When you're a foreigner in any country, doesn't matter where, you try not to get into trouble with the police."

"Why should you help the police? I hate those bastards."

"My sweetiepie, you have to be a little realistic. Foreigners do what they're told. And you ought to be realistic about something else too. He did it."

"What?" She sat up on one elbow, and stared at him.

Theo said with apparent seriousness, "He didn't get enough from Marion, so he had this other bit, and then – I don't know what, she tried to blackmail him perhaps – and he did for her."

"You don't know, how can you?"

"I know Sol. I know his temper."

She stared at him wide-eyed. "But if you think that, you ought to –"

"What?"

"I don't know. I just can't believe you really think it."

"I do, you know, my sweetiepie. And talking about not getting enough of it –" He moved over quickly and held her arms, "– I haven't had enough either."

Squared-off before a television set, and with food put in front of him, Cyprian would eat away steadily until everything was finished, almost irrespective of the quantity and the quality of the food. When he had done so on this evening he belched. "When's Mummy coming back?"

"I don't know," Dick said, busy with the *New Statesman*. "She's gone to see Mrs Grundy."

"I'll tell you something. Just been watching a play done by that old queer Clements."

"Don't talk like that," Dick said automatically.

"I'll tell you something about him."

Cyprian told his father, and what he said was sufficient to make Dick put down his paper. After a little thought he telephoned Trapsell. When he came back he was smiling.

"Cyprian, old chap, I'll never say again that there's no point in watching television."

"It's a modern art form." Cyprian turned on the set again. "Anything else to eat?"

Caroline Weldon sang in a loud, rather tuneful voice as she drove towards Hayward's Heath, after paying a duty visit on an old aunt in Brighton. She cut in on other drivers and then smiled at them so happily that they were unable to resist smiling back. She was a happy woman – happy in her husband, whose work as an architect she regarded as socially valuable, happy in the cleverness of her children, happy to live in The Dell, which was for her the symbol of a new community spirit in England. Behind her happiness, it might fairly be said, was a complacent self-satisfaction at having managed life so well, but behind the self-satisfaction was a genuine desire to be of service to the community which was expressed in her work for half a dozen local welfare and artistic organisations, work which took her into the homes of the distressed, the maladjusted, the poor. Into these homes she brought her wide smile, her overwhelming physical vitality, her insatiable curiosity about people. Others might have been embarrassed by the idea of paying such a visit as hers, with such a purpose. Caroline felt simply the tingling of anticipation that for her preceded any sort of contact with other human beings. What would the house be like, what would Marion say, would she have any luck in getting her back?

The house was as bad as she had expected, a little semi-detached villa in a row of similar villas, set back a few yards from the main road. Caroline slammed the car door, opened the little wooden gate, walked briskly up the crazy paving drive. She had telephoned to announce her presence in the neighbourhood, and had been invited to have a cup of tea. Before she could ring the bell the door opened and Mr Hayward, solid, square, pork-butcherly, filled the space.

"You found us all right, then. Come along in."

A hideous little hall, cream paint, a dado, an umbrella stand. How could people, people who had money to be elsewhere, live in such places? The living-room, which was two rooms knocked into one, had a square bay window in front and at the back french windows through which a small, carefully-tended garden could be seen. Tea things stood on a trolley. There was nobody else in the room.

"Did you have a good journey down? Which way did you come?"

Caroline, who had been exposed before to what she and Dick called the travel game, answered with caution, but did not stop Mr Hayward from describing an infinitely better route from Brighton. Her attention wandered. Where was Marion, where was Mrs Hayward? Even as these thoughts passed through her mind, Mrs Hayward came in carrying a silver teapot and a plate of bread and butter cut very thin. In response to Mr Hayward's question, "Where's that girl?" his wife said that she would be down in a minute. They drank tea, and Mr Hayward talked about the dryness of the summer, and about the harvest. Even Caroline, who was not susceptible to what people thought and felt, sensed something uneasy in the conversation.

When Marion did come in, while they were drinking their second cup of tea, Caroline was shocked. She had always admired the sharp prettiness and brittle elegance of Marion's looks, and often said that she certainly had a sense of style. The woman who came into the room, walking as carefully as though she were treading some invisible line across the carpet, had untidy hair in which the streaks of grey were now obvious, a face thin as though with illness, twitching hands. Caroline got up, said, "Hallo, my dear," warmly, kissed her. As she did so, she could not fail to be aware that Marion had been drinking gin.

Marion accepted a cup of tea but only sipped at it, crossed her hands over each other, and looked at the opposite wall. Her father and mother bent their gazes upon Caroline, rather as though she were a specialist who had been called in to give that vital second opinion. When Caroline, whose extrovert self-confidence was a little shaken, suggested that she and Marion should have a talk, they left the room almost eagerly.

"How are you?"

"I'm all right."

Inane question, uncommunicative answer. Caroline was warm-hearted, and she was especially distressed by mental misery because she was really incapable of understanding it. She said, "Oh, my dear, what's the matter?"

"I don't know. I feel –" Marion left the sentence unfinished. "I've been drinking, you know that, don't you? I've been drinking for three days. But I can't get drunk."

"But why?"

"He writes me such terrible letters, no, I don't mean that, it's that he – he *accepts* everything so. I don't know what to do. I don't understand him."

She took a letter out of a pocket, passed it over. Even in the midst of her deep, genuine sympathy for Marion, Caroline could not help feeling satisfaction as she read the lines on prison paper, with their acceptance of blame for whatever was wrong in their relationship, their assurance that nothing whatever should be done about it. This kind of satisfaction was something she and Dick always felt at glimpses into the recesses of other lives. She handed back the letter.

"I haven't shown it to *them*." Marion gestured in the direction of her mother and father, almost as if they were enemies. "I write back, but it's no good. I keep thinking about the past, the way I've failed him."

"Nonsense."

"No. We were never – it was never – much good. In bed, you know. I think I'm frigid." Caroline, the warmth of whose responses were such that frigidity was for her something almost unimaginable, was silent. "And yet it wasn't like that, really. I mean, it wasn't all my fault. He never thought about me. He wasn't like these letters," she cried out, protesting against the unfairness of the gap between what is written and what is done.

"Come back. My dear, do come back. You'll be better at home."

Marion turned upon her a dark anguished gaze. "It will be just the same anywhere."

Caroline seized her advantage. "If it's the same anywhere, then come back. People talk about you having left Sol. It will be better for him if you come back."

"Better for him. But could I ever go on with it? Does he even want me to? I don't understand, I've never understood him. Oh, help me to understand."

Oh, dear, Caroline thought, she really is rather drunk. Firmly, practically, commonsensically, she said, "I'm going to take you back with me, that's settled. You'll stay with us for the time being, then you can decide whether you want to move back home. I'm quite sure you'll feel better."

So it was settled. They went upstairs and packed Marion's things together. Caroline announced magisterially that Marion had decided that her proper place was in her own home, and the Haywards, far from objecting, seemed relieved. On the way back in the car Marion fell asleep. She did not wake up until they had reached The Dell. Caroline took her in, helped her to undress, put her to bed in Cyprian's room. Then she went down and said triumphantly, "Mission accomplished."

"Was she drunk?" Cyprian asked. "She looked drunk to me."

Gloria rebuked him. "You don't say that sort of thing. It's disgusting."

"Yes, it is," Caroline said. "And don't you dare to repeat what you've just said. If you do I shall be very angry indeed."

She spoke with such uncharacteristic sharpness that even Cyprian was quelled. "Where am I going to sleep?"

"We'll make up a bed for you down here."

"Good, I needn't go to bed yet then. Can I watch TV?"

"No."

"Don't be hard on him. I'll tell you what he remembered," Dick said. He told her.

Chapter Five *Trial, Third Day*

Trial Transcript – 6

PETER JAMES CLEMENTS, *examined by Mr Eustace Hardy*.

"I am a television producer and I live in The Dell, where the accused lives also. The accused is well-known to me, and so also is his Alvis car. On the evening of the 23rd of September I had dinner with Mr Jellifer. After dinner we were walking down Curzon Street when he pointed out the accused's Alvis car to me. I saw it myself, and I have no doubt that it was his car. I recognised the number."

MR HARDY "What subjects were discussed during dinner?"

"Principally a possible television series featuring Mr Jellifer. I shouldn't have been handling this myself, but another producer was interested. We talked about the idea."

"Did you discuss the accused?"

"Not particularly. His name was mentioned."

"In connection with the incident at the party?"

"And his odious behaviour at the garage committee on the following evening, yes."

"But you discussed these matters only in passing."

"Quite."

"If it were suggested that the accused was very much in your mind, would that be correct?"

"No, not at all. We only mentioned him because he had been more boorish than usual."

"There is one further point. If it were suggested that you had dined so well that you were likely to be mistaken about the car number, what would you say?"

"I should say it was nonsense. It was a pleasant dinner, no more than that. We weren't in the least drunk, if that is what you mean."

"And you are quite sure you recognised the car?"

"Quite sure."

Cross-examined by Mr Newton.

MR NEWTON "Three bottles of wine between two people, and then brandy. Do you call that 'just a pleasant dinner', Mr Clements?"

"I've often drunk more, if that is what you mean."

"Very possibly, but you haven't always had to identify a car number afterwards."

"I did recognise it."

"Mr Clements, do you know anything about the way in which alcohol slows down human reactions?"

"I know I recognised the car number."

THE JUDGE "Mr Clements, we have had it already that the car could have been seen for a few seconds, no more. Do you agree with that?"

"Yes, I suppose so."

"What do you mean, you suppose so? Do you want to dispute it? Look at your watch, if you have one. Estimate the time. Does two seconds seem right to you?"

"I saw the car number, my lord."

"That is not what I asked."

"I – no, I couldn't dispute the time."

"Now, turning round, as I understand you did, and looking at the back of this passing car for two or three seconds, did you look specially for the number?"

"No, I suppose not."

"You must surely know whether you looked for it."

"Well, no, I didn't."

"Then how did you happen to see it?"

"I just noticed it, that's all."

"You just noticed it. Very well."

MR NEWTON "I must thank your lordship for eliciting answers to several questions I should have asked."

THE JUDGE "We have had it all before, Mr Newton, with another witness. I thought it would save time."

MR NEWTON "But I still have one or two more questions. Do you like the accused, Mr Clements?"

"Not particularly."

"What does that mean?"

"He is very boorish, rude. I thought he behaved atrociously, both at the party and on another occasion, at the garage committee."

"In your opinion, does he often behave badly?"

"He is often rude and always uncouth."

"You don't like him, then?"

"I certainly shouldn't choose him as a friend."

"Were you jealous of him?"

"What? That's absurd?"

"Is it? Do you know a Mr Rex Lecky?"

"Yes."

"Is he a friend of yours?"

"I –"

"Come along. Is he a friend or not."

"We've quarrelled."

"Mr Lecky was sharing a house with you, was he not?"

"Yes."

"And now he has left it?"

"Yes."

"Why did he leave? Did you quarrel about the accused?"

"No, it was nothing like that."

"Did Mr Lecky say that the accused was an attractive man, and did that upset you?"

(The witness showed signs of distress.)

THE JUDGE "You may sit, if you wish."

(Questioning was resumed after a short delay.)

MR NEWTON "Do you remember the incident?"

"No. I am not sure."

"You are not sure. Your memory is hardly equal to your powers of observation. Do you remember that Mr Lecky disapproved of your going to the police?"

"I don't know. Perhaps."

"My lord, I shall be calling Mr Lecky, so that the jury will have an opportunity of hearing him. Is that why Mr Lecky left your house?"

"No. Certainly not."

"Why did he leave, then?"

"There were personal reasons."

"Personal reasons! Well, I will inquire no further."

"Would you agree that you had an argument about the accused?"

"I think that's right. Yes."

"Good. I am glad to have got so far. Now, we have been dealing with your memory. Let us consider your powers of observation. Had you ever seen the dead woman before that Friday night of the party?"

"No."

"You are quite sure of that?"

"Absolutely."

"Will you please look at this paper, and see if you recognise it."

"It seems to be a casting list."

"It is a casting list for a television play called *The Springs of Justice,* is it not? Did you produce this play?"

"Yes."

"My lord, I have further copies of this casting flist, which I should like to enter as Exhibit Number 61. Perhaps the jury would like to look at it." *(Copies of the list were passed to Mr Justice Crumble and the jury.)* "Now, Mr Clements, will you look at the second page, the second entry down. Will you tell us what actress was chosen to play the part of Celia Reston?"

"It says here Estelle Simpson."

"Do you dispute the accuracy of this list?"

"No."

"Below her name there is her address, and then it says here: 'Availability. For a total of twenty rehearsals plus ampexing'. Will you tell the jury what that means."

"It means that we had twenty days of rehearsal and then the play was ampexed, put on tape, ready to go out."

"You were the producer, and Estelle Simpson, that is Sylvia Gresham, was in the cast. That means you saw her every day for three weeks?"

"Not every day, but most days. She had a very small part. I remember now."

"You remember now, Mr Clements? You had no recollection of it?"

"It was two years ago. I've produced several plays since then."

"Just think what you are saying. Two years ago you saw this girl almost every day, for three weeks. Yet it is only a few minutes since, speaking on oath in that witness box, you told me that you had never seen her before the night of the party. I asked whether you were sure of that, and you replied that you were absolutely sure. You were quite wrong, weren't you?"

"Yes."

"Yet although you were utterly wrong about a girl you had seen for three weeks, you are still asking the jury to believe that you recognised the number plate and identity of a car which you saw for two or three seconds?"

"I – yes."   *(end of transcript)*

Hardy did not re-examine. When Peter Clements, white and shaking, left the witness box, he knew that the damage done to his case by the stupidity of this wretched television producer might be considerable. He felt, as he said to Stevenage during the luncheon recess, that there was no cause for them to blame themselves. Clements was not an important witness, he provided no more than confirmation of Jellifer's story. The fact that his recollection had proved faulty was not important either. But the effect on the jury of his equivocation and discomfiture, and of Newton's adroit suggestion that Clements was a homosexual and that for some reason other inhabitants of The Dell were ganging up on Grundy, all this might be very important. The case was not going smoothly, yet Hardy was far from depressed. He was not a man who was ever greatly elated by a triumph or depressed by a defeat, being accustomed to treat those two impostors just the same. He did not, however, expect defeat.

Magnus Newton, on his side, had in his broad nostrils the smell of victory, which he was inclined to scent perhaps too easily. As he and Toby Bander carved away at their chump chops in a nearby pub he made grandiloquent gestures with his knife, which was one of his bad habits when carried away by enthusiasm. They wasted little time in consideration of the wretched Clements, except that Newton said Trapsell had done a good job in getting hold of the casting list.

"It was really that architect chap in The Dell," Toby Bander said. "He found out about it somehow, yesterday."

Newton took a large draught from his tankard of beer.

"The chap's a regular detective."

"None of this removes the real obstacle, does it?"

"No. He's certainly no oil painting."

They both contemplated without pleasure the appearance their client would present when he gave evidence, face brutish or sullenly louring, hairy hands gripping the edge of the box, body bearishly clumsy.

"I don't like to think what Hardy will do to him," Toby Bander said.

They drank the rest of their beer and talked about other, more important things. Magnus's daughter had just won a scholarship to go to Cambridge. Toby had got his handicap down from eight to four.

Peter Clements walked out of the Old Bailey as unsteadily as a punch-drunk boxer. He took a taxi to a pub which was frequented a great deal by actors and boxers, and drank several whiskies. In the afternoon he visited other pubs and clubs, asking for Rex Lecky. He found him eventually in a club called the Fallout Shelter. Rex was with another young actor named Jackie Levine. He smiled his foxy smile.

"You made the headlines."

Peter stood swaying, looking down at him. "You went to –" the word escaped him, "– to *them*."

"I told you to be careful."

"Betrayed me. Let me down. I've been humiliated."

"Isn't that what you like, humiliation?"

"Let him alone, Rex, he's half sloshed," Jackie Levine said.

"Judas." Peter stretched his arms wide. "Judas, come back to me. I didn't want you to go away."

"Oh, for crying out loud, she's maudlin."

Jackie giggled. "Morbid."

"Maudlin *and* morbid, both. And she's wet. You can see it dripping off her." The two young men got up. Peter put out a hand, Rex pushed it away, they went out laughing. The barman suggested that Peter had better go home. He was a good-looking boy and Peter smiled at him, but the barman did not smile back.

He had the same experience during what was left of the afternoon. He no longer felt sad, rather as though his head had been removed from his body. He wanted to explain this to people, and to tell them something of how he had been betrayed, both in his personal life and through that cruel ordeal in the witness box, but nobody would listen. Driven by the need to empty his bladder he went down into a lavatory, and there one man at whom he smiled seemed to smile back at him, but rudely shrugged him off when spoken to. Just by the exit another man, a boy really, seemed to be smiling at him.

It was unavoidable that he should go out that way, and really it seemed inevitable that he should speak.

"Thank goodness," he said. "I thought I should never find anyone to talk to. Come back with me."

"Where?"

"Home, of course, The Dell."

"You were smiling at me."

"Was I? You looked so nice."

Now another young man, not so young really, was standing beside him, and the boy didn't look nice at all. "We are police officers and we have been keeping you under observation," he said. "We have seen you speak to several men, importuning them. Come along."

He tried to tell them that it was all a mistake, that he was not really like that, but they took hold of his arms and he could not get away. In the street he became angry – after all, hadn't he volunteered to give evidence, wasn't he on the side of the police? – and at the station he protested quite vigorously. In the corridor leading to the cells they had to restrain him, which they were not unwilling to do, for neither of them liked queers.

That afternoon, also Inspector Ryan dropped in to have a chat with Kabanga, to tell him how things were going. The African felt, as he said, too personally involved to stay in court. Kabanga began to pace up and down the room as Ryan told him in detail of Clements's debacle.

"The fool," he said. "Why did he give evidence at all. Oh, it is all rubbish, this British justice of yours, it can let a guilty man get away."

"Can happen." Ryan used a toothpick.

"But what kind of justice do you call that? Grundy did it, he should hang."

They had had all this before, more than once, and Ryan tried again to put Kabanga right about it.

"First thing to bear in mind is he won't hang." He pointed the toothpick. "And the next is, it's not up to you to go on about Britain. We let you in here, Tony, let you make a fat living out of this country."

"I know that."

"You loved this girl, I know you did. All right. I respect you for it. But don't you say anything about British justice, it's the best in the world."

"Listen, Buck. This man Grundy, we know he did it."

"We *think* he did it. It's the jury that *knows*."

"We know, you and I. Don't we? And you are saying he could be let off?"

"It could happen. I don't think it will, but it could."

"And you call that justice? The defence man twists and argues and lies and you call that justice?" Kabanga was trembling with passion. Ryan tried to argue with him but it was no use. In the end he got browned off with it, and left. He felt that he had had enough of Kabanga. You tried to make a friend out of one of them, he told himself, but really it was impossible, they just didn't think the same way. East was east and all that. He might have imparted some of these philosophical reflections to Manners, but the superintendent greeted him with a quiet anger that forbade such observations.

"I'm told you've been seeing Kabanga frequently."

"Not frequently. I've dropped in once or twice to –"

"Don't you know enough not to talk to a witness in a case, especially one like this?"

"But he's given his evidence. What harm can it do?"

"What *harm*!" And then the super really tore him off a strip about the duty, incorruptibility, etcetera, of a police officer (would he have done so, Ryan wondered, had the case been going well?), and came to the real point, which was that Kabanga was suspected of pushing drugs in quite a big way.

Certainly they were being distributed through his clubs, and it didn't seem likely that he would be ignorant of it. He had obviously been laughing his head off over Ryan, and had very likely talked to his friends about this nark who was so stupid you didn't have to pull the wool over his eyes, he wore blinkers anyway. More and worse, when they did catch Kabanga with the stuff, the other side would certainly suggest either that Ryan had helped to plant it or that he had been taking dropsy from Kabanga...

It was as nasty a twenty minutes as Ryan had had for years, and the worst thing about it was that he didn't feel he could put up any defence. He *had* been stupid, he *had* stuck his neck out, and it was no sort of use saying that Kabanga hadn't seemed to be anything but genuine. Put not your trust in spades was the lesson to be learned from the whole thing, not even when the spades seemed to be trumps.

The afternoon was given to the evidence of Stanley Leighton, who survived the ordeal better than Hardy had dared to expect. Witnesses may alienate a jury by uncertainty or over-confidence, so that under pressure they either become totally unsure of what they have seen or take refuge in the dogmatic assertion of "facts" which are obviously no more than suppositions. That Leighton steered his way between this Scylla and Charybdis was due largely to the skill of Eustace Hardy. Thinking over the judge's intervention during Clements's cross-examination, an intervention in which he had almost taken on the role of cross-examiner himself, it seemed to him that Crumble was showing, most unusually, a bit of feeling. And then also Hardy had gathered from something in Stevenage's manner – nothing that he could put his finger on, yet it was quite perceptibly there – that his junior was critical of his handling of the case. He had also become aware, when he sneezed three times and then blew his long thin aquiline nose, that he was developing a cold. The fact and the thoughts together stung him into self-examination. He was a man who would have been disgusted to feel that he was carrying through a case to anything but the best of his ability, and he handled the potentially shaky Leighton quite brilliantly.

"Why were you looking out of the window, Mr Leighton?" A smile touched his face and vanished, like sunlight glancing over ice. "Come now, you needn't mind saying."

"Well, I was kind of interested in Miss Simpson, see, in her visitors. I'm a bit naturally curious, put it like that."

"Especially in Miss Simpson, Miss Gresham, perhaps?"

"She was a good-looking girl, you know," Leighton admitted.

"And you are interested in good-looking girls?"

"Definitely. I mean, who isn't?"

"Now, I want to be quite clear about what you saw on the evening of the 23rd."

"What I saw was this big ginger-haired chap walking down the Mews. He went by my house, and after that I stopped looking a minute, because I was getting dressed so that I could get off to catch my train, see."

"But then you looked again?"

"That's right. And he was ringing the bell. Then she came down and they spoke for a minute or so. She let him in and they went upstairs."

"Had you see this man before?"

"Definitely. I'd seen him go into her flat before, two or three times."

"You are sure it was the same man that you saw on this night?"

"Yes, definitely."

"Did you later pick out this man at an identification parade?"

"I did."

"And do you see him in Court now?"

"There." Leighton flung out a hand quite dramatically at Grundy in the dock. Grundy glared back at him and suddenly shouted, "Don't be such a bloody show off!"

"Silence."

"He's enjoying himself. Look at him." Grundy pounded the dock in front of him. There was uproar in the Court. Mr Justice Crumble's great nose and thick raddled cheeks began quite perceptibly to shake, and his ten fingers played by what seemed their own volition a kind of dance in front of him, so that his pen dropped to the floor and had to be retrieved. Magnus Newton, face very red, hurried across and spoke to his client, who could be heard saying something like, "Get this bloody farce over." There was a stir and murmur in the public gallery. Two or three members of the jury could be seen looking at Grundy with the sidewise, fascinated glance that means no good for an accused man. Then the judge said, "Mr Newton, I cannot have this. Your client must control himself."

"He will do so, my lord. He wishes to apologise to the Court."

"Very well. But he must control himself." Slowly Mr Justice Crumble's shaking subsided. Eustace Hardy, well satisfied, sat down.

It is the law that the prosecution must tell the defence of any criminal record that their witnesses may have if it is relevant to the case being tried, although the defence is under no such obligation in relation to their own witnesses. Hardy had, then, begun by frankly admitting Leighton's previous conviction, but had said that this was seven years ago. Newton went into details of the conviction, and carried on from there.

"I see that you are now a scrap metal dealer. Where is your yard?"

"Yard?"

"Yes. Where do you keep the scrap you buy?"

"I don't have a yard. I'm more of a middleman, see."

"You don't have a yard!" Newton allowed astonishment and incredulity to pass over his puffy features. "Do you mean that you don't handle any scrap metal yourself, that you never see it or store it or stock it?"

"That's right. I'm definitely a middleman."

"Very much so, I should say. And your friend Mr Hinchcliffe, the gentleman in Birmingham, is he a middleman too?"

"Oh no, he's just a friend of mine."

"Can you give me the name of any firm who has bought scrap metal from you, or through you, in the past six months?"

But here Newton over-reached himself, for Leighton gave him the names of three firms, and the judge showed signs of impatience, so that he had to give up this line of questioning. Nor was he more successful in shaking Leighton's conviction that he had seen Grundy, and nobody else, enter the Cridge Mews flat that night. The only point he was able to make was that Leighton had seen other men going into the house, but this was too vague to be particularly revealing. At one moment Leighton appealed to the judge, in answer to a question from Newton.

"My lord, why should I make up this story to let Mr Newton make aspersions on my character?"

"I suppose you are going to tell us that you have come here simply as a good citizen concerned to see justice done?" Newton asked with a sneer.

"Definitely, yes. Estelle was a nice girl."

The gibe had been unfortunate, and Leighton's reply was not lacking in dignity. Newton sat down.

He got no more change out of Seegal and Harrison, who told their stories as they had before. The faint degree of uncertainty about their identification was almost more convincing than positiveness would have been. Altogether, if the morning had gone to the defence the afternoon decidedly belonged to the prosecution.

Newton went back to his house in Hampton Court. He had been in a good temper for a fortnight, ever since the news about his daughter's scholarship came through. His wife recognised that he wanted to talk about the case and she let him do so throughout dinner and most of the evening, although legal talk bored her.

Eustace Hardy stayed at his club when he had an important case on. He found the atmosphere congenial, and was able to work there after dinner with greater concentration than he would have achieved at home. On this evening, however, he could feel the cold creeping up on, and over, him. He had decided on hot whisky and bed when one of the assistant directors of the DPP's office telephoned, in a state of perturbation unusual in him, to ask if he might come round with Manners to talk about some fresh evidence.

Hardy saw them in a little room where he knew they would not be disturbed. A coal fire burned brightly, brandy and whisky were in front of them, but still Hardy shivered and sneezed. "I've got a cold," he explained.

The assistant director expressed sympathy, even alarm. Hardy waved away his concern. He knew from experience that his cold, now that he was fully aware of it, would not prevent him from handling the case to the end, and might even spur him to a sharper point of acuity. He would have been prepared to concede that the cold was perhaps psychosomatic, a consequence of the fact that the case had not been going too well. Now he lay back in his chair and waited for Manners to speak.

Manners did not feel at home in these surroundings. At the station he was regarded as a cut above his fellows and a little remote from them, a man whose opinions on any subject were to be heard with respect. Here, among all these leather chairs and dark brown pictures, in the presence of a man whose response to his presence as bearer of important news was the remark that he had a cold, Manners felt awkward, resentful, almost inferior. It was in his mind that Hardy did not take the case with proper seriousness, and the thought persisted even though he knew it to be unjust.

"It's a woman called Mrs Stenson," he said. "She came to the Yard late this afternoon. Her story is that she parked her car in Cridge Mews just after ten o'clock on the evening of the 22nd, occasionally parks it there because it's conveniently near a friend of hers in Cridge Street. A man friend, I gather she's divorced."

"Ten o'clock. Fits in with Leighton," the assistant director said. He had a jerky, attractive eagerness that in Manners's eyes contrasted favourably with Hardy's languor.

"That's right, sir. Must have been when Leighton turned back and started dressing, that's why he didn't notice it. Well, she parked her car, started to walk out of the Mews to her friend's house, and saw a ginger-haired man come down the Mews, stop at the door of No. 12, ring the bell. A woman came down, they stood talking, and the man went in. She's identified the man as Grundy from a photograph."

Hardy had his eyes closed. He murmured, "Why hasn't she come forward before? It's two months ago."

"She went away the following afternoon, Tuesday, to Paris, staying with some friends over there, didn't come back until a few days ago. Wasn't until she read about the case in the papers that it came back to her. Natural enough."

"It really pins Grundy there," the assistant director made a pinning gesture. "Right place, right time. In a sense it's only confirmation of Leighton, but two is much better than one when the one is Leighton, I'm sure you'll agree. He stood up wonderfully, though. I thought your handling of him was masterly, masterly."

Eyes still closed (he looks like a bloody death mask, Manners thought), Hardy asked: "What's she like, this Mrs Stenson?"

At another time, in another place, Manners might have said that she was the rich bitch upper-class type, but he felt that this would not do. He summarised. "Says she's thirty-two, rather haggard but good-looking, bit of a rackety life I should say. I told you she was divorced. Lives on her own in half a house in Porchester Terrace – told me that herself. Obviously has plenty of money. Slightly nervous type, but seems determined. I should think she'd hold up all right in the box."

Hardy opened his eyes. "There's no question of her having been in your hands, like Mr Leighton?"

"No, sir." Manners permitted himself a brief laugh.

"I had a check, just to make sure, but she's got no record. You realise I saw her only a few hours ago, and I've had no time to get a life history, but she seems all right. Husband was a stockbroker, no children, she says they just didn't get on so they decided to part, only civilised thing to do and so on. That's the sort she is." More at ease, he permitted himself the remark he had held back a few minutes ago. "Society type."

Not by the flicker of an eyelid did Hardy indicate the distastefulness of the phrase. "Very well."

"This is what she says."

Hardy read the statement through. The assistant director wriggled enthusiastically in his chair. "It's exactly what we want, don't you agree, ties up the whole thing, just couldn't be better."

"It seems useful." He's a cold fish, thought Manners, who was sometimes accused of being a cold fish himself, if you cut him open it would be water inside instead of blood.

"We've got to give the defence twenty-four hours' notice. We'll serve a Notice of Additional Evidence and call her at the end, so that the defence can't make too much of a song and dance. All right?" The assistant director was referring to the rule by which the prosecution case may not be reopened once it has been concluded, so that it might be necessary for Hardy to spin out his examination of witnesses to allow for this.

Hardy sneezed. "Don't worry. We've got the boys who caught him at London Airport. There's your own evidence, Superintendent. And then there's Tissart. He'll talk all day if I let him."

"You ought to go to bed." The assistant director would have liked to add "Eustace," but something about Hardy forbade such familiarity.

"I'm going." He drained his glass. His guests dutifully rose.

They showed Marion into the little room, and she sat down. Sol came in and sat on the other side of the table that separated them. A police officer, sympathetic but watchful, stood by the door. It was all as she had seen it in half a dozen films.

Sol looked as he had before, looked well even. Nothing could ever refine his features, and he was certainly pale, but he looked well. When he smiled at her, which was something she didn't remember him doing for a long time, he really looked quite youthful, and she felt again the emotion, a blend of admiration and delicious nervousness – the sort of nervousness you might feel about the reactions of some self-contained but potentially fierce animal that you were proposing to adopt as a pet – that had moved her when she married him.

"I'm back, Sol," she said. "For good. Caroline came down to see me and made me see I ought to come back. They've been wonderful, Caroline and Dick. I think she came down specially to see me, though she didn't say so."

"They like to stick their noses into other people's business."

"But Sol, you know they found out about –"

"I know, I know." He ran a hand through his ginger hair. "Dell life doesn't suit me, but you're right, they're good neighbours."

She looked at the impassive policeman, lowered her voice. "I read about what happened, you ought to try and control yourself – you know, the jury will get a wrong impression, that's what Dick said."

"And of course Dick's right."

She felt the old barriers rising. "Please, Sol."

"You don't understand anything I've written to you, do you?"

"When you're in the box, when, you know, you're being cross-examined, you must keep calm then."

"I told you it didn't matter."

"Oh, how can you *say* that? Of course it matters."

"The purpose of living is what happens now," he began, and then said as though he were humouring a child, "All right. Perhaps it does matter."

They talked for another five minutes, but she could not be sure that he had taken in anything she said. Had it been worthwhile, she wondered afterwards, had there been any point in going, did he want to see her? Driving back in the car with Dick, who talked away with his usual enthusiasm, she could not be sure.

Chapter Six *Trial, Fourth Day*

Trial Transcript – 7

Detective-Constable LEONARD SIMS*, examined by Mr Stevenage*. "I was instructed, with Detective-Constable Larkin, to go to London Airport, watch for the accused, and detain him for questioning. I discovered at the Airport that he had booked a single air ticket for Belgrade, and when the Belgrade flight was called, Detective-Constable Larkin and I detained him as instructed. He expressed surprise, and said that he was going for a holiday in Yugoslavia. He made no objection to returning with us, although he was annoyed."

Cross-examined by MR NEWTON. "You say he was annoyed. That would be the natural reaction of an innocent man, would it not?"

"It might be, sir."

"Had he made any attempt to conceal his flight?"

"How do you mean?"

"Had he booked under a false name, did he try to board the plane at the last minute, anything like that?"

"No, sir."

"In fact his whole behaviour was perfectly consistent with innocence, was it not?"

"I had simply been asked to detain him."

"Let me put it this way. He behaved exactly like any other passenger?"

"That is so, yes."

"Now, when you detained him, I believe he said something. Will you tell us what it was?"

"It was something like this. 'I suppose it's because of that stupid bitch Facey. She thinks I've killed my wife. I shouldn't be surprised if she's got the police searching for her body.' He said further that he and his wife had quarrelled, and his wife had gone to stay with her father."

"And this was the truth?"

"I understand so, sir."

"Mrs Grundy was understandably upset, and had gone to stay with her family?"

"I couldn't say if that was the reason, sir."

"So really this order to detain the accused was the result of a ludicrous mistake?"

"I couldn't say, sir. I was simply carrying out instructions."

"The instructions of your superior officer, yes..."

Extract from the cross-examination of Superintendent JEFFREY MANNERS *by Mr Newton.* "... So you had been told by this neighbour, Mrs Facey, of her suspicions. You had no warrant for making a search, had you?"

"The kitchen window appeared to have been forced, and in all the circumstances it appeared right to investigate."

"I know, Superintendent, I know. And did you find anything suspicious when you searched the house without a warrant, anything at all?"

"No, sir."

"The whole tale of the accused murdering his wife was absolute nonsense, was it not?"

"It proved to be untrue, certainly."

"It came about because the prisoner quite naturally resented the insinuations of a silly neighbour?"

"There had been a quarrel, and Mrs Facey had heard it. Then Mrs Grundy disappeared. I think her conclusions were reasonable, a little alarmist perhaps."

"But they were utterly wrong?"

"They were wrong, yes."

"Now I want you to consider my next question very carefully, Superintendent. Supposing you had not been told this ridiculous story –"

THE JUDGE "The witness has already said he thought the conclusions of this Mrs Facey were reasonable, Mr Newton."

MR NEWTON "If your lordship pleases. This story. Supposing you had not been told this story, would you have arrested the accused?"

"Yes. The proof is that when he was detained at London Airport, Detective-Constable Sims telephoned me and told me that he said his wife was staying with her family. I confirmed this within a few minutes. At the time he was charged, therefore, I knew that Mrs Grundy was unharmed."

"But then why did you not arrest him earlier?"

"He hadn't tried to leave the country then."

"Had you told him not to do so?"

"No, sir."

"Why not?"

"He knew very well that he was a suspect in a murder case. Such a warning was unnecessary."

"This was a perfectly innocent and unconcealed flight, would you agree?"

"The most significant thing was that he booked a one way ticket."

"Please answer my question."

"He flew off at an hour's notice. He hadn't even told his partner."

"Superintendent, I must put it to you directly that you made an appalling mistake here in taking notice of local gossip, and that when you realised your error you felt you had to go on and make an arrest."

"No, sir. That is not correct."

"I ask you again, then, why you had not arrested him before."

"I have already explained that he had not then tried to leave the country."

"You still maintain that this was a panic decision on his part?"

"I do."

"In spite of the open way in which he did it, in spite of his spontaneous reaction at the airport that this had arisen because of Mrs Facey?"

"Yes, sir. I believe that he knew the net was closing on him, and that if he had got away he would not have returned voluntarily to England…"   *(end of transcript)*

Newton, Toby Bander and Trapsell considered the "Notice of Additional Evidence" at a gloomy conclave in the room set aside for the defence barristers. Their depression was caused chiefly by the fact that much the most damaging evidence against Grundy was that which professed to place him at Cridge Mews. Leighton was thus a far more important witness than Jellifer or Clements, and it was a pity that he had remained unshaken in cross-examination, but at least Newton had been able to convey the shadiness of Leighton and the doubtful character of his scrap metal dealings. Leighton unsupported was one thing, Leighton confirmed by a respectable witness who could have no possible motive other than a wish to see justice done quite another. It might, of course, turn out that Mrs Stenson was extremely short-sighted or that she was a lifelong enemy of Grundy's, but these were far-fetched suppositions. Altogether, there was reason for gloom.

"Better put your amateur detective on to it," Toby Bander said. Trapsell laughed dolefully. Newton sat with his little legs stuck out in front of him, his head sunk in his double chin. Toby continued, "Anyway, you might see what you can find out about her."

"Of course. But there isn't much time."

They both looked at Newton for hope, for inspiration. At last he lifted his head and spoke. "That's her story, and we're stuck with it. We shall just have to do the best we can."

It was hardly inspirational. Later Trapsell got busy, in the little time he had. He saw Grundy, who said that he had never heard of anybody named Olivia Stenson. He spoke to Dick Weldon, who had no knowledge of her. He had an inquiry, necessarily perfunctory, made in the area of Porchester Terrace. He found out that she was the daughter of a wealthy Irish peer, that stockbroker Stenson was wealthy too, and that she owned the house in which she lived. None of these discoveries was at all helpful.

During most of the day Hardy nursed his cold, spraying his throat with a product specially prepared for him on the recommendation of his man in Harley Street, preparing himself for the vital witness. It was Stevenage, therefore, who took Tissart through his examination, although to use such a phrase gives a wrong impression for Tissart was like a machine that, once started, could be guaranteed to run as long as was required, or even longer. His act, for it could be called nothing less, was impressive, consisting as it did of an encouragement to the jury to take part with him in a sort of guessing game about handwriting identifications with the aid of his enormous albums. Newton sat watching unhappily as the jury evidently warmed to the idea that they were the favourite and extremely intelligent pupils of a benevolent schoolmaster. Slowly Tissart led them through the maze of style characteristics and personal characteristics in handwriting, spoke of the mysteries of arcades and garlands, elaborated on terminal spurs and connecting strokes, pen-lifts and hesitations, shading and alignments. And when these technical points had been disposed of he told them of his own, not to be too modest about it, infallible system of handwriting comparison, a refinement of the old process by which every handwriting specimen was broken down and given a code number in terms of its precise characteristics in slope, shading, size ratio and shape. The infallibility, Tissart readily agreed, lay in the care and delicacy of perception with which his code system was carried out. An inferior sensibility would produce an inaccurate result.

"Do you claim that your system of giving a code number to each specimen is infallible?" Stevenage asked.

"By no means." Tissart smiled broadly. "There is always a possibility of human error, since we are all human beings."

"You have given evidence in many dozens, perhaps many hundreds of cases. Has your own evidence of identification ever been successfully queried?"

"It has been queried, sir. Never successfully."

"And with your immense knowledge, and using your personal and exclusive system, will you tell us what conclusion you have reached?"

"The conclusion I have reached, sir, is that the specimens of handwriting given me were of the same authorship."

"That is to say, that the accused wrote the postcard found in Miss Gresham's flat."

"That is the conclusion I have reached," Tissart said solemnly, and then smiled at the jury.

Newton had seen juries blossoming before under the sun of Tissart's smile. He would be able to cross-examine, but he knew from past experience that what he said was unlikely to smirch the image of infallible Tissart in the eyes of the jury. He left the cross-examination, therefore, in the hands of Toby Bander, as an indication of how little importance should be attached to the evidence of experts. It was twenty past three when Toby Bander rose, his light springy voice coming as an agreeable contrast to the ponderous weight of Newton's attack. He followed the well-established rule that one expert may cancel out another.

"You are familiar, of course, with Dr Wilson Harrison's classic work on *Suspect Documents?*"

Tissart bristled. "Of course."

"Do you agree with Dr Harrison when he says, 'The document examiner should insist on being provided with ample specimens, written over a fair period of time, before he ventures on the expression of opinion as to the authorship of a disputed writing'?"

Tissart smiled. "I think that Dr Harrison was referring particularly there to adolescent handwriting."

"Please answer my question. Do you agree with the quotation?"

"In a general way, yes."

"But here you have only one document for comparison, a postcard. Are there not immense possibilities of error?"

"When the examination is made truly scientifically, no."

"Dr Harrison gives a special warning, does he not, about the dangers of being too positive 'where the handwritings being compared are limited in amount'? And he says that even one dissimilarity, no more than that, just one, should make the examiner doubt the identification. What have you to say about that?"

"I have borne that warning in mind most carefully. I always do. But I have found no dissimilarity."

It was no good, Toby Bander could see, the jury were against him, they positively radiated their confidence in this odious little man. He made some menacing remarks about what would be said by their own expert but as he made them he was aware that Borritt was of much lower jury-impressing calibre than Tissart. Then he sat down.

"Olivia Stenson. I've never heard the name," Marion said. "Who is she?"

Dick stroked his nose. "Trapsell was mysterious, but I gather she's an unexpected witness, prosecution witness that is. He wondered if we knew anything about her."

"There's a villain named Stenson," Cyprian said, in that new crime series, *The Racketeers.* Last week he had a man killed by an electronic device which he operated from a thousand miles away. Frizzled the man up in the middle of a desert."

"Shut up, Cyprian," Gloria said. "Do you think Marion wants to hear about that sort of thing."

"I don't mind." It was forty-eight hours ago now that Marion had come back with Caroline, and the change in her was remarkable. She had had her hair done, much of the tenseness had gone out of her manner, she was prepared to talk cheerfully about life after Sol's acquittal.

"I just hope Sol keeps control of himself in the witness box," she said after the children had gone to bed. She smiled at Dick and Caroline. "Something like this shows you who your friends are. I'm not very good at saying it, but I can't tell you how grateful I am."

"You saw about Peter Clements?" The producer had been charged with persistently importuning, and released on bail. "I must say I was surprised."

"He's split up with Rex," Dick said. "You know what a thing like that can do to someone like Peter."

Marion had been staying at the Weldons', but now she returned home to sleep for the first time. It was strange to be in the bedroom without Sol, to be aware of his presence through clothes, shirts in the airing cupboard, shaving cream in the bathroom. The effect of all this unused maleness was confusing, rather as though Sol were dead and a compulsion rested on her to get rid of the things that belonged to him because they brought up recollections agonisingly painful. But that isn't true, she said to herself as she fingered the rough cloth of a tweed jacket, it's silly, it's wrong to think like that. To prove how wrong it was, she got out the trousers belonging to the tweed jacket – they were baggy, like all Sol's trousers – and pressed them. When he comes out, she told herself after she had bathed, taken a sleeping tablet and gone to bed, we shall have a really good relationship, and because she knew the importance of such a relationship she dwelt on images of Sol returning home in mid-afternoon and finding her stretched naked on the bed, of occasions when he forced her to submit to him as he had done sometimes in the past and which in imagination were not revolting as they had been in fact, but delightful. Thinking such thoughts, she fell asleep.

Chapter Seven *Trial, Fifth Day*

Mrs Stenson presented, there could be no doubt about it, an appearance of some elegance. She was a small thin dark woman, dressed in black coat and skirt and white blouse, and plain but expensive black shoes. She took the stand after Eustace Hardy had explained that this was an additional witness whose evidence had only just come to the notice of the prosecution, and was thought to be of importance. Mr Justice Crumble had graciously agreed to admit this evidence, and Hardy had devoted himself to eliciting Olivia Stenson's story so that the unexpected bonus was appreciated by the jury at its full worth. He had been disturbed that morning to find his nose stuffy and his throat sore. When he first spoke after waking the words came out in a dismal frog-like croak. Application of the throat spray and of a nasal spray containing some mixture which, as he understood it, temporarily froze the mucous membranes, had an effect little short of miraculous, so that when he got to Court and Stevenage solicitously asked how he felt, Hardy was able to reply in positively ringing tones that he was much, much better. Stevenage, who would have liked the chance of handling this witness himself, said that he was delighted and reflected, not for the first time, that Hardy had remarkably speedy powers of recovery.

There was no difficulty in handling Mrs Stenson. She was an excellent witness, positive but not dogmatic, sincere and straightforward. She was thirty-two, of independent means, divorced. On that particular September evening she had been to dinner with an old friend who lived in Cridge Street and had parked her car, as she had done before, in the Mews. There she had clearly seen a ginger-haired man ring the bell of Number 12 Cridge Mews. A woman had opened the door, the two had spoken together, the man had gone inside.

On the following day she had gone abroad to join a party of friends in Paris, and later on a long motoring holiday in France and Italy. At the end of this holiday she stayed in Venice with some other friends. She had returned to England only ten days ago. While she was away she had hardly looked at the papers, but when she read about the trial she remembered the incident in Cridge Mews, and got in touch with Scotland Yard.

There was not very much evidence, but every word of it was deeply damaging to Grundy, who sat in the dock glowering at the woman in the box and, as it seemed, restraining himself from shouting again only by an effort. At the end of a half-hour question and answer session Hardy sat down, content. If Grundy was acquitted, it would not be Mrs Stenson's fault.

It seemed useless to attack her credit. Newton made the only approach possible.

"I understand you went to the police the day before yesterday, Mrs Stenson."

"Yes, that's right."

"And you told them about something that you had seen on September 23rd, nearly three months ago, is that correct?"

"Yes."

"Now, these two people you saw standing in the doorway, was there anything special about their behaviour that made you notice them?"

"I'm not sure what you mean."

"I mean were their voices raised, did they kiss each other, did anything at all happen which made you look at them particularly?"

"Nothing in particular."

"It was simply that the woman opened the door, they spoke, the man went in. Something that happens in thousands, in tens of thousands of streets in this city every night, something there was no reason at all to notice specially." Oh dear, Toby Bander thought, the old thing is blustering about. Still he's on a sticky wicket no doubt about that. "Then why, why, Mrs Stenson, did you notice it?"

Mrs Stenson was not discomposed. She patted the pair of white gloves that she had brought with her. "I really can't say. Why does one remember a particular thing and forget a dozen others? I happened to notice this, that's the only answer I can give."

"Without any particular reason, none at all?"

Newton drew himself up to the top of his little height, put his thumbs into the top of his gown. "Something absolutely commonplace, but you just *happened* to notice it."

"That's right."

"Very well." He shook his head sadly, conveying his scepticism to the jury. He paused, as if quite at a loss for his next question, and then shot it at her suddenly. "I suggest, Mrs Stenson, that you were mistaken in the date you saw this."

She shook her head. "No."

"You had no particular reason for remembering this date –"

"Oh, but I had."

"And what was that?"

She patted the gloves again. Her eyes were brilliant, they shone like bits of glass.

"The man I had dinner with, Charles Craigie, is the man I hope to marry. He had been away, and I hadn't seen him for several weeks. It was an occasion for me, one I remembered."

Of course there would be something like that, Newton thought, there had to be something which fixed the date for her so patly. He hitched his gown up and went on asking questions with the desperate energy of a man pushing through a ploughed field, but when he sat down ten minutes later he had made no progress at all. Mrs Stenson, eyes shining, stepped down from the box, composed and neatly elegant, as she had stepped into it. Hardy rose and said that this completed the prosecution case.

Magnus Newton's opening was diffuse and over-emphatic. He had been badly shaken by the sudden transformation of a case which had seemed to be moving along favourably in the direction of acquittal. During the luncheon recess he went down to talk to Grundy, and confirmed that the big man knew nothing of Mrs Stenson.

"She couldn't possibly have a grudge of any kind against you?"

"How do I know? I told you I've never seen her before in my life. She made a mistake, that's all."

"She was very positive it was you."

"You know the definition of positive, being mistaken at the top of your voice."

"So we're left with another ginger-haired man, someone who looks like you."

"That seems to be right."

Newton controlled his irritation with difficulty.

"You'll be going in the box tomorrow. I want you to be careful. Just tell the story of what happened in your own way. Don't go in for long explanations, keep to the point. And when Hardy cross-examines, keep your temper."

Could it be possible that there was amusement in Grundy's eyes? "You've taken a lot of trouble."

Really, he's insufferable, Newton thought. "I'm being paid for it."

"Don't worry on my account." Newton stared. "I mean, I don't much mind what happens either way."

What could one do with such a man? Newton stumped off in something resembling a fury.

Borritt was cadaverous and gloomy, where Tissart had been short and choleric. He did not use albums but huge sheets of paper on a roller, which he draped over a blackboard, rather like a school map. With a long ruler he then tapped the sheets, and proceeded to explain precisely why it was that Grundy could not have written the vital postcard. Borritt did not radiate the impression of utter certainty that came from Tissart. His strength lay rather in a belief that the identification of any handwriting, and indeed by extension of anything that happened at all in the world, was so difficult, and the possibilities of error so immense, that no group of reasonable people could possibly convict one of their fellows on anything but the direct evidence of their own eyes – if, indeed, such evidence itself was not susceptible of error. A conviction of human error was engraved into his long marble cheeks, finely grained with the red lines of the drinker, and perhaps it was this conviction that made him a less convincing expert than Tissart, for where all else was questionable, might not his own opinion be questioned too?

Yet Borritt faced Stevenage's cross-examination with a sort of hangdog determination. He had his own system, one in which he awarded points for similarities in handwriting, and deducted points for dissimilarities, making a positive identification at the end only if he reached a total of one hundred. It was about this that Stevenage questioned him.

"I understood you to say, Mr Borritt, that you discovered sixteen points of dissimilarity between the postcard and the handwriting specimens of the accused."

"Yes."

"And you deducted points accordingly."

"That is so, yes."

"Sixteen sounds a great many for one small postcard."

"It is."

"Am I right in saying that six of these points were found in the letter 'a'?"

"Yes."

"But should this not be simply one point of dissimilarity, as it is a single letter repeated?"

"Certainly not."

"And your other points were concerned with punctuation marks, were they not?"

"And with diacritics. It is possible to learn a great deal from individual use of diacritics."

"Diacritics, in plain language they are the dots over the letter 'i,' the crossing bar of the 't,' that kind of thing."

"That is so, yes."

"And what you are saying is that these diacritics and punctuation marks show sufficient differences to establish a genuine dissimilarity."

"I am."

After fifty minutes of this, Stevenage decided that he had cast enough doubt on Borritt, and the tall man rolled up his sheets of paper, tucked the rollers under his arm, bowed to Mr Justice Crumble, and shuffled out of Court on very obviously flat feet. There was nothing wrong with Borritt, perhaps he knew as much as Tissart, but those flat feet were somehow a final dubious mark against him.

At this stage of the trial an air of boredom pervaded the Court. The day was stuffy, although it was December, and Mr Justice Crumble, head sunk low in his gown, plum fingers playing with each other, gave the impression that he was on the verge of sleep. Eustace Hardy had listened to Borritt's evidence with his eyes closed and a look of ineffable weariness on his face. Two of the jurors seemed to find it impossible to stop yawning, a third was occupied in creating a most intricately patterned doodle.

Elsewhere in Court there was the subdued rustling of papers, the popping up and down and in and out of altogether junior and unimportant figures, that can only take place during one of those periods in a trial when people feel that what is going on is not really worth their attention.

Borritt had been permitted to give his evidence first through that consideration often afforded to expert witnesses on the ground of their presumably extreme busyness, but everybody had been hoping that Grundy would go into the box that day. When Stevenage sat down, however, it was five minutes to four, and Mr Justice Crumble, emerging perhaps from a profound meditation on the nature of man, decided that it was time to adjourn. The Grundy fireworks, if there were to be Grundy fireworks, were left for the morrow.

There were no rejoicings in The Dell that evening. Cyprian put the matter with his usual brutality by asking about Mrs Stenson.

"What about her?"

"I mean, if what she says is right he's had it, hasn't he?"

"Cyprian," Caroline said. Marion tried to look as if she had not heard.

Cyprian stuffed veal and ham pie into his mouth.

"Has anyone investigated her?"

Dick answered. "Yes. George Trapsell's been looking into her background. Can't have turned up anything or they'd have used it." Cyprian mumbled something unintelligible. "What?"

"I said it was pretty funny her not knowing about the case."

"I don't know. She went abroad the next afternoon –"

"Did she? Has anyone checked on that?"

"Greedy," Gloria said. Cyprian's hand was stretched out for another piece of pie.

The Weldons had been right in thinking that Marion's return would sway opinion – that is Dell opinion, which within this narrow enclave was more important than anything said in the outer world – in her husband's favour. It was a mark of this changed opinion that Peter Clements, returning from a hard day's administrative argument about a new thriller series, in which everybody had been most painstakingly nice and there had been not a hint of a snide remark, had found himself decisively cut by Sir Edmund Stone. As Sir Edmund said afterwards to his wife, that fellow Grundy might be a perfectly awful character, but for somebody like that fellow Clements – a fellow who was, Sir Edmund said with a very inaccurate glance at the charge on which Peter Clements had been arrested, very likely no better than Grundy himself – to get up and give evidence against him was something that a gentleman really didn't do. Peter Clements was shaken almost equally by this and by the curt nod which was all he received from a neighbour named Adrian Leister, who was a saxophonist in a successful jazz band, and with whom he had always considered himself to be on the most friendly terms.

Back in the house where the blankness of Rex's room stared at him as though it were a symbol of some great gap suddenly created in his physical being, the nerves of the ears suddenly cut or the tongue torn out, he decided that life in The Dell was no longer bearable. He went that very evening to stay with an adoring aunt who lived at Penge, and a couple of days later wrote to Edgar Paget to say that he wanted to put up his house for sale. Edgar sold it for him within a month, to an advertising man who was rather pleased to be able to tell his friends that Peter Clements, the well-known queer mixed up in the Grundy murder case, had lived there. Peter was eventually fined ten pounds on the charge of importuning, but he did not lose his job. Nor was his heart actually broken, for shortly afterwards he rented a flat in a new, rather smart block in what used to be called Maida Vale. He shared this flat with a film executive of about his own age, and they got on awfully well together.

Edgar Paget also found himself no longer a hero of the Grundy saga but suddenly recast, to his disgust and astonishment, as a minor villain. When he went into his local for a pint that evening and the same thing happened, with slight variations, on many evenings to follow, unpleasant remarks were made in his hearing about pathologically untruthful schoolgirls who were encouraged by their fathers in the un-English pastime of kicking a man when he was down. To have his character as a bulldog Englishman attacked was for Edgar almost like an accusation of illegitimacy and he snapped vigorously at these cowards who, as he said to Rhoda, would never name names or say anything you could really get hold of. He refused to admit to Rhoda or even to himself, the possibility that Jennifer might not have been telling the truth.

Jack Jellifer found his relationship with Arlene quite distinctly changed by his performance in the witness box. One evening, for instance, he began to tell her about his activities and achievements during the day, as he always did when he came home, but she cut him short in a ruthless manner, with a remark to the effect that she had heard it all before. They passed most of the evening in watching television. Jack wore a martyr's cloak of sullenness, for after all he had done no more and no less than what he regarded as his duty.

All organisations are more or less bureaucratic, all engender in their chief executives a desire not so much for personal glory as for the assurance that their skill, intelligence and dexterity shall not be spoiled by the clumsiness of all those other fellows. Chief-Inspector Whiteface of the Narcotics Squad felt that he had gone as far as could possibly be expected when he warned Manners about the idiot Ryan, who for some bad reason or for no reason at all, had cultivated Kabanga's acquaintance. He did not, however, think it necessary or advisable to tell Manners about the raid on Kabanga's clubs. Suspicion that these clubs were being used as drug pushing outlets and that Kabanga himself was receiving and distributing the drugs in a big way had hardened into certainty, and it was certain too, or so Whiteface's man inside the Windswept said, that Kabanga had just received a consignment. He might have been made suspicious by Ryan's visits, and he would get the wind up properly when he realised that the visits had stopped. It was necessary to raid Kabanga, and to do it quickly. If Whiteface told Manners about it he would be certain to ask that the raid should be delayed until the trial was over, a request which Whiteface did not want to grant and would have found it awkward to deny, even though the result of the trial couldn't, as he saw it, possibly be affected. It was as a result of this reasoning that Whiteface left Manners in ignorance.

The raids were carried out on Kabanga's six clubs simultaneously, just after midnight. In four of the clubs drugs were found in considerable quantities. Kabanga himself was in the tiny flat that he kept at the Windswept. He was very high on heroin. With him was a woman who was also high on heroin. They made quite a fuss, Kabanga shouting obscenities about the inspector who had come to him as a friend and then shopped him, the woman shrieking and fighting, saying things and making threats that were incomprehensible to the officers arresting her. It was not until they got to the station that they discovered the woman's identity. She was Olivia Stenson.

Chapter Eight *Trial, Last Day*

Trial Transcript – 8

MR NEWTON "My lord, I wish to ask for the recall of one of the prosecution witnesses for further cross-examination, as a result of information that has become known both to my learned friend and to myself since yesterday."

THE JUDGE "This is an unusual request, Mr Newton. What is the name of the witness?"

MR NEWTON "Mrs Stenson."

THE JUDGE "I take it you have had an opportunity of consulting with Mr Hardy. What do you say, Mr Hardy?"

MR.HARDY "My lord, in the circumstances, I do not resist the application."

(Mrs Stenson was recalled to the witness box.)

MR NEWTON "Mrs Stenson, you gave evidence in this Court yesterday upon oath to the effect that you saw the accused on the night of September 23rd, in Cridge Mews. Was that evidence true?"

"No"

"Was it in fact wholly fictitious?"

"Yes."

"Let me put the truth to you, so that the jury may have it clearly. You said that on the night of September 23rd you were in Cridge Mews. That was a lie?"

"Yes."

"The truth is that you never saw the accused in your life before yesterday."

"Yes."

"You said that you went to Paris on the following day. That was a lie?"

"Yes."

"The truth is that you went three weeks later, so that you had every opportunity of knowing about the case in the papers?"

"Yes."

"Will you tell the Court your reason for perjuring yourself." *(The witness did not reply.)* "Perhaps it will be easier if I put certain matters to you. Are you a drug addict?"

"Yes."

THE JUDGE "Please speak up."

MR NEWTON "Who is your supplier?"

"Mr Kabanga."

"Now, will you tell the Court if an approach was made to you the day before yesterday."

"Yes. He told me –"

" 'He,' that is, Mr Kabanga."

"Yes. He told me that the trial didn't seem to be going well, that the man, Grundy, might get off, and that he was going to fix him."

"That was his expression, 'To fix him'?"

"Yes. He said I was to come forward as – as a last minute witness, and to corroborate another witness."

"That was Mr Leighton."

"Yes. He told me what to say, and said it would be all right, I should be believed."

"That is because you are, what shall I say, a woman of good social position."

"I suppose so."

"Whereas Leighton is a convicted felon?"

"Yes. I believe that is true."

211

"It is true. Now, you knew the serious nature of what you were doing, Mrs Stenson. Why did you do it?"

THE JUDGE "You must answer the question." *(The witness appeared distressed.)* "You may sit, if you wish."

MR NEWTON "I will repeat the question. Why did you do it?"

"He – Kabanga – threatened me."

"How did he threaten you?"

"He said he would cut off –"

"Cut off your supplies?"

"Yes."

"And it was because of this threat that you came here yesterday and perjured yourself?"

"Yes."

"And this perjury might not have been discovered but for the fact that you were arrested with Kabanga last night, in a raid on his club – " *(end of transcript)*

It is rarely, in truth, that cases are won and lost in a few minutes of so-called "deadly cross-examination". The process is generally much more a relentless piling up of facts which lead inexorably to only one possible conclusion. But Newton's treatment of the pathetic figure in the witness box, hardly recognisable as the poised, elegant Mrs Stenson of yesterday, was felt by those who saw it to be devastatingly effective. The other side were on a hiding to nothing, as Toby Bander said afterwards, but the old thing really rubbed their noses hard in the dirt, and did so in such a manner that he did not seem to be attacking the wretched Mrs Stenson so much as making clear that the villain of the piece was the sinister Kabanga. It was a situation of which nobody could have failed to take advantage but Newton really used it, as Toby Bander handsomely conceded, to the full.

Hardy, on his side, made no attempt to do the impossible, and resuscitate Mrs Stenson as a witness of truth. His face retained its customary impassivity. There is no armour against fate, he may have thought, and there is no redress when you have been saddled with a thorough-paced liar as a witness. He did not re-examine, nor attempt in any way to minimise what had happened. His cold had come back in full stream, and whether or not it was of psychosomatic origin, it was plain that, to put the thing simply, he should have been in bed. He made little attempt, even, to resuscitate Kabanga, who was called back when Mrs Stenson had left the box. The African did not conceal that he had told her what to say, and did not seem to understand at all the seriousness of his offence. Newton made full play with this and, without making any positive accusation, succeeded in leaving the impression that Kabanga had probably introduced Sylvia Gresham to the drug habit. Hardy's re-examination was brief.

"Mr Kabanga, I believe that in your country it is not unusual for false evidence to be given, even in a case of such seriousness as this?"

Kabanga was not the wreck that Mrs Stenson had been. He answered readily. "Of course. It is a matter of how much you pay to the witnesses."

"And your sole motive was that you believed the accused to be guilty, and wished justice to be done?"

"Of course, yes."

"You realise now that what you did was extremely wrong?"

Kabanga pointed dramatically to the man in the dock and shouted: "He did it. Will your justice say so? If it does not, I spit on British justice."

Hardy was barely able to repress his irritation. Didn't the man *know* what he should say? He ended his re-examination with a couple of perfunctory questions, sat down and blew heavily into his handkerchief. Stevenage might have felt sorry for him, except that he was almost sure that when the time for cross-examination of Grundy arrived, his senior would miraculously have recovered.

The crucial interview in the case, seen in retrospect, took place before these cross-examinations, before even the day's proceedings in Court, when Newton and Toby Bander, already apprised of the raids and arrests, went to see their client in his cell and told him what had happened. Grundy said nothing.

" Now," Newton said pontifically – he could not prevent his manner from being pontifical, and really did not try very hard. "Now, I shall recall this Mrs Stenson and Kabanga too, and I don't think there is any doubt that the questions I put will be extremely damaging to the other side, very damaging indeed. Isn't that so, Toby?" Toby Bander agreed, as forcibly and directly as possible, that it was so. "The question is whether, in these circumstances, you should go into the box yourself to give evidence."

Grundy raised his thick eyebrows and said that he was in their hands. He might have been talking about somebody else.

"No, that's not the way it is at all. *We* are in *your* hands." Newton could not resist putting his thumbs in his buttonholes. "On a similar occasion to this, where a vital witness might or might not be called, Marshall Hall left with his client two slips of paper, one saying that he wanted the witness called, the other saying that he didn't. He asked his client to return one of the slips. The man chose to call the witness, but wouldn't go into the box himself."

"What happened to him?"

Newton coughed. Toby Bander said. "He was hanged." He added after a moment's hesitation, "But under the 1957 Homicide Act that wouldn't be possible in this case."

"It's only life imprisonment now for strangling someone." Grundy seemed almost to be enjoying himself.

"I want you to understand clearly what the choices are, and what the effect may be," Newton said. "A man who is accused almost always goes into the witness box to explain his actions. If he doesn't, prosecuting counsel conveys to the jury that the reason he didn't do so was obviously that he was afraid – " here Newton paused, for Grundy had grinned at him in a very disconcerting manner. "– to face cross-examination and the judge also is likely to comment adversely in his summing up. Speaking generally, then, there are only two kinds of occasion when a defending counsel is likely to advise his client not to enter the box. The first is when the prosecution case is so weak that it doesn't require an answer. That doesn't apply here, although I don't think the case is a very strong one."

"And it will be weaker by the time we've done with Mrs Stenson," Toby Bander said cheerfully.

"The second sort of occasion," Newton said deliberately, "is when counsel's client is likely to make such an unfavourable impression if he goes into the box that it is better to keep him out of it."

Grundy smiled broadly. "And I come into that class?"

Silence. Toby Bander said, "You have a hot temper. Eustace Hardy knows how to stick in needles so that they really get under the skin. If you lost your temper under cross-examination it would be a pity."

"So what do you advise?"

The note of detached irony was so strong that Newton could not trust himself to speak. Toby Bander replied.

"What we would have said before today was that the case against you demanded that you should go into the box and answer it. Now there is the possibility that Mrs Stenson's perjury and the way Kabanga arranged it may leave such an unpleasant flavour in the jury's minds, and cause so much doubt, that we can obtain an acquittal anyway."

"The possibility," Newton said. "It can't be put higher than that. If you could guarantee to control yourself in the box –"

Grundy intervened, grinning. "Which of us can *guarantee* to control himself anywhere?"

Now Newton fairly shouted at his client. "Damn it, man, it's your skin we're worrying about."

"Very good of you. You gentlemen are the experts. What do you advise?"

"It must be your own decision."

"I see." Grundy pondered, but only for a moment.

"Let's toss for it, shall we? Heads I go in the box, tails I don't."

And toss for it, to the open fury of Magnus Newton and the secret amusement of Toby Bander, was what they did. A half-crown, produced by Toby Bander from his pocket, was spun by him and dropped to the floor. It came down tails.

So it was that Magnus Newton rose, after Kabanga left the box, and said solemnly that he proposed to call no further witnesses and that the case for the defence was closed. Red-faced, puffing irregularly like a car starting up from cold on a winter morning, he made a vigorous final speech. The half-crown incident had made him so angry that he would have preferred, for once, to find himself upon the prosecution side. It was not in his nature to be half-hearted, however, and he warmed to his words as he went on talking, telling the jury that the prosecution case was such a tissue of quarter-truths, terminological inexactitudes and confessed perjury that, after the most careful consideration, he and his learned junior had decided that it was not necessary for their client to go into the witness box. This, Newton said gravely, was his right and privilege, and it should not be thought that he was afraid to enter the box. Making the best of Grundy's appearance, he asked, "Do you think he would be afraid of anything?" Grundy scowled at them with obliging ferocity.

Then Newton listed some of the prosecution witnesses, the girl Paget who had been asked to leave one school and who had sworn to things that were almost self-evidently ridiculous, Jellifer the wine and food expert who sampled only too well the subject matter of his talks and articles, Clements who identified a car in a glimpse lasting two or three seconds but could not remember a girl he had seen every day for a fortnight, Leighton the convicted felon, and last and worst of all Mrs Stenson, the model of respectability who had turned out to be a drug addict and peddler. Was there a conspiracy, Newton could not help wondering, was there a conspiracy of some sort on the part of a sinister figure or figures behind Mrs Stenson, to victimise his client? He left the jury with this slightly improbable thought.

Perhaps the most important effect of the decision not to call Grundy was that it disconcerted Eustace Hardy, so far as that model of intelligent legal decorum could be disconcerted. Hardy's closing speech, like his opening one, was not one of the most notable in his career. There were many things which he would have liked to ask the accused, he said. What were the circumstances in which Sylvia Gresham's dress had been torn, and his face raked by her nails? It was, however, the accused man's right, as his learned friend had said, not to enter the witness box, but it did mean that the jury must try to find their answers to these and other questions without the help of the accused man. He referred to Grundy's "ungovernable temper," and then proceeded to answer all the rhetorical questions he had asked about the party, about Grundy's general behaviour, and about his attempted departure for Belgrade without a word to his wife or his partner. He skirted as delicately as possible the unfortunate incident of Mrs Stenson, and suggested that the total volume of evidence was overwhelming...

If Hardy was well below his best, Mr Justice Crumble's summing up was a model of the judge's art. A judge may be likened – well, to many things no doubt, but among others he may be likened to an apothecary who, holding those scales above the Old Bailey in his hands, delicately tips them this way and that, dropping in an inch of perjury on this side and an incontrovertible fact on the other, finally balancing them triumphantly with the aid of the necessary precious blobs of judge's opinion placed unobtrusively on one side or the other. On which side should the balance finally tilt? It was for the jury to say.

But Mr Justice Crumble came back again and again, as it would have been impermissible for Hardy to do, to the fact of Grundy's absence from the witness box. What of the party incident and of "what the prosecution has called his panic flight" to Belgrade? Well, they must try to explain these as best they could, because the person able to tell them had chosen not to do so. What of this, what of that, what of the other? They must make up their minds without the assistance of the accused man. At the same time, he was careful to add, no obligation rested on the accused to enter the witness box...

When Mr Justice Crumble had finished this balancing act with his ten fat red fingers and his nimble judicial brain, the jury filed out. They were back in a little more than an hour, and those wise in the ways of courts noticed that they abstained from looking at Grundy. The foreman, a neat sort of man with a well-kept toothbrush moustache, rose composedly when asked whether they had reached a verdict, and said that they had.

"Do you find the prisoner at the bar guilty, or not guilty?"

Fingering the little moustache he replied, "Not guilty."

It would be too much, far too much, to say that there was a sensation in court. Magnus Newton smiled a fat jolly kind of smile as Toby Bander patted him on the back and Trapsell shook hands with him. Hardy congratulated him also, his thin features paler than ever, his voice almost extinguished by the cold in which he was now visibly enfolded. Mr Justice Crumble stroked his rotting nose, entwined his over-ripe fingers, and said that the prisoner was discharged. Grundy, whose expression had not changed when the verdict was given, stepped out of the dock and came face to face with Magnus Newton. He did not thank his counsel, nor did he offer to shake hands. "Congratulations," he said.

"Thank you."

"That coin came down on the right side."

As Newton said to Toby Bander afterwards, the man was the most insufferable boor he had ever met. No word of thanks for sweating your guts out, nothing about the care with which every possibility had been pursued, every crack in the prosecution armour prised open, nothing but that atrocious joke. But when Grundy had gone to pass through the usual form of discharge Newton was able to put him out of mind, and to savour again the taste of triumph, that taste which never varies yet is endlessly fresh upon the tongue.

Now people in Court were busy gathering up papers, putting into order a case which was finished and could be tied up with pink ribbon and placed into its appropriate pigeon hole. It was finished for all of them and passed quickly out of their minds, for Newton who was defending in a couple of days' time two men accused of a bank robbery, for Hardy who got down to work on the details of a complicated security case, for Mr Justice Crumble who brought his ageing body and alert mind again to the Old Bailey on the following day, when he attended to a case of alleged rape. For them what was done was done. They had no second thoughts and no regrets.

Marion had not come to Court on this last day because she felt, as she wrote to her husband, that she might break down or do something foolish. Dick Weldon had told her that he would be there and would telephone her as soon as a verdict was reached, but Dick was trapped unexpectedly by a client who had come down from Newcastle and insisted on talking to him. He did not reach the Old Bailey until half an hour after the verdict had been reached. He learned what had happened from an usher, and then went to look for Sol, but was told that he had passed out of the jurisdiction of the Court, and had presumably left its precincts. He telephoned Marion in the expectation that Sol would have rung her already, but she had heard nothing.

What should have been an evening of celebration became increasingly muted through the absence of its subject. The champagne cocktails Dick made tasted sour on Marion's palate, the irrepressible energy that spilled out of Caroline made her feel for some reason uneasy, every word said by Gloria and Cyprian rasped her nerves. She knew that this was wrong, that Dick and Caroline had both been wonderful, and that only last night (could it really be no longer ago?) Cyprian had made the suggestion about checking with the airline that had helped to dispose of Mrs Stenson's story. But it was no use, she felt that she must be in her own home, to await Sol's arrival or a telephone call from him. It was logical enough to say that if Sol rang his own home and got no answer he would obviously try the Weldons', but still she felt she had to go and wait for him.

"I'll come with you," Caroline said at once.

"No, really. I'd rather be alone."

"But I don't like to think of you, sitting there waiting on your own. Let's go round together."

"Now, darling," Dick said. "Do you think Sol will want to find an old matron like you sitting there when he's expecting to see his wife?"

"I ought to have been in Court today, then this wouldn't have happened."

"Marion, my dear, it's I who ought to have been there." Dick was earnest. "I'm very sorry I wasn't."

They watched her go, her elegant legs put one before another with the abstracted accuracy of a sleepwalker's. All of them, even Gloria and Cyprian, felt an obscure disappointment, as though they had been rather disgracefully let down. They ate the salmon that Caroline had bought and cooked, but it did not really taste as it should have done. Dick expressed the feelings of the whole family accurately when he said, "I must say, Sol is a very odd cuss."

In the empty house the telephone did not ring. Marion wandered from one room to another, touching Sol's jackets in the cupboard, taking down a frying pan in the kitchen, putting salt, pepper, butter and eggs ready to make an omelette, switching the television on and quickly off again, looking out through the drawn curtains in the living-room and then letting them drop. She arranged a trayful of drinks, whisky, gin, pernod, but the very idea of taking a drink sickened her. Aloud she said, "My heart is full of love," wondered if the phrase was true, and decided that it was. Her legs were already smooth, but she went to the bathroom and shaved them carefully. Then she returned to the bedroom, took off her coat and skirt and put on a cocktail dress. She put on three times her usual modest ration of lipstick and used mascara liberally round her eyes. The process brought some relief to her feelings, but inevitably the relief was only temporary. She spoke aloud again in the empty room, saying, "I want sex."

She was painfully aware of the urgent need of her body. The apparatus of her life in this room, bits of china picked up cheaply, a collection of books about wild flowers, in which she had been passionately interested as a child, the curtains chosen with so much care at Heal's, what did they mean, what did they add up to in a life? She unlocked a drawer in her desk and took out a small photograph album in which were recorded scenes of her childhood, dogs and holidays, dead aunts and uncles. Looking at them she wept and made the mascara run. She cleaned herself up, put on fresh mascara, and poured a large whisky. The time was almost nine o'clock.

Just after eleven she was sitting, half-asleep and half-drunk, beside the picture window. She had opened the curtains to look for Sol so that he saw her at several yards' distance, framed with the light behind her, as he walked along the gravel road and opened the gate. He saw and was seen by Felicity Facey, who had been watching her neighbour's house all the evening. When she told her husband, who had moved on from Sir Herbert Read to Sir Kenneth Clark, he grunted and advised her not to make a fool of herself again. The Faceys too had found themselves unpopular in The Dell in the general reversion of feeling that had taken place during the trial.

When Grundy opened the living-room door it seemed to Marion for a few moments that she had been transported back to the night of the Weldons' party, for down one of his cheeks could be seen again the scratches that had been visible when he descended the stairs. Then she saw that these were not scratches but livid weals, and that they were upon the wrong cheek. The greeting she had imagined, in which she melted unquestioningly into his arms, was forgotten. She rose. "Sol," she said, as though uncertain of his identity. "Sol?"

He stood there, filling the doorway, looking at her.

"Where have you been, Sol? I've been waiting. So long." She heard with dismay a note of querulous complaint enter her voice.

"Seeing those bastards." He had been drinking, although he was not drunk, no more drunk than she.

"Seeing – who? What happened to your face?"

"What do you think?" He came cautiously into the room, stepping as though there might be a trapdoor beneath the carpet. "First went to see MY partner, my loving partner who tried to shop me."

"Theo?"

"Who else? Beat him up. His girl was there."

"But Sol, Theo only did what he had to do, he only –"

"Broke two of his teeth." He looked at his knuckles, and she saw that they too were scarred and bloody. "Little dummy, he'll have to get some dummy teeth. But I did a better job on the other."

"What other?"

"Took her away from me, the scheming little bastard. Doped her up to the eyes, I shouldn't wonder. Then tried to frame me."

"Sol," she cried out. "Sol."

"He's out on bail, you know that. He'll wish he wasn't, now. Two of his boys caught me, but I think I broke his jaw first." He began to laugh, then stopped.

Desperately she tried to preserve something at least of the dream with which she had begun the evening. She came towards him, entered the circle of his arms – or would have entered, if those arms had not been hanging, like great atrophied fins, by his sides. "Sol, I don't want to hear any more, I don't want to know, we can make a new start. We must make a new start."

"A new start."

"I want – " She could not say the word sex, it seemed wrong. "I want love. Make love to me, Sol."

"Too late."

"I don't understand."

"Too late, I tell you. You do what you've got to do, you see what I mean."

"No, I don't see what you mean. Tell me."

"With her it was always, it was all, she was sex, you see what I mean."

"*Her,*" she cried out, horrified. "Her?"

He sat down now, heavily, and talked, not looking at her, not coherently, yet with a total meaning in his words that she was unable to avoid.

"From the beginning it was like a revelation, you see what I mean. It was reality. All my life, I felt as if all my life had been wasted, not wasted exactly, but meaningless. Instant sensation, you see what I mean, that was what it was, and through it you get the whole meaning of life."

She tried to extract from this jumble something of what, for her, made sense. "It was true then, what they said."

"Who said?"

"Jack – Jack Jellifer, Peter Clements, that man – Leighton."

He might not have heard her. "It was reality, you see what I mean, nothing else existed. That's not right, though, no, you live in two worlds, but only one of them is real. And you don't – you don't control either of the worlds, they do things to you, not the other way round, you see."

"You strangled her because she was going to marry Kabanga, that's right, isn't it?"

"To destroy a world. I only did what I had to do."

"Oh, talk sense," she said, more angry than frightened, determined to know the truth. "They were all telling the truth, even that wretched little Jennifer."

"The truth," he said, and seemed to meditate on the words. "Jennifer saw us."

Gropingly she said, "But I don't see – why didn't you give yourself up?"

Before she had finished he was shaking his head.

"You live in two worlds and in both of them you have to *behave* as if they were real, you see? You play the game, you don't give anything away. But shall I tell you something terrible? When one world has gone it's impossible to live in the other." For a moment the eyes that looked now straight into hers seemed to clear, and she thought she saw in them an intense suffering. Then they were again opaque, milky, like the eyes of a sufferer from glaucoma. He took something out of his pocket. "I got this from Kabanga, he tried to shoot me with it."

For a moment she could not speak, then she said,

"You're not responsible."

"Do you know that if I'd been found guilty they wouldn't have hanged me. That's the law." He laughed.

"If you strangle someone they don't hang you. If you shoot someone, they do."

I have done nothing, she wanted to say, but she could not utter the words. "Those letters you wrote, how could you have written them?"

"They're part of the game. You have to pretend, that's one of the rules."

"The rules," she cried out. "Did you live by the rules?"

"I only did what I had to do," he said, as though the words were an answer with which she should be satisfied.

"But you don't have to do it to me." She was aware of a desire to live, the most intense desire she had ever known. "I am innocent. I'm not responsible."

"Which of us is innocent?" he said gently, almost chidingly. "And you said just now that I was not responsible. Do you mean that there is no such thing as responsibility?"

Then the revolver went off.

Felicity Facey heard it. "That was a shot."

"Don't be absurd, my dear."

"I don't care what you say. I'm going to telephone the police."

Her husband sighed.

When the police arrived they found Grundy sitting beside the window, as though he were expecting them. His wife lay on the floor. He had shot her once, through the temple. His hands, large, strong and hairy, rested on his knees. One of them held the revolver.

Epilogue: *The End of Solomon Grundy*

Solomon Grundy was held to be fit to plead to the murder of his wife, and he refused to accept his counsel's advice (his counsel was not Magnus Newton this time) to base a defence upon diminished responsibility. He refused also to enter the witness box. When he had been found guilty, and was asked if he had anything to say before sentence, he replied: "I am happy to accept the verdict of the Court, but I wish to go on record as saying that I do not regard the members of the jury as responsible for their actions." The judge made no comment upon this remark before pronouncing the death sentence. Grundy was hanged on a cold morning in March.

Shortly afterwards local school children began to sing a rhyme which, although (or perhaps because) they did not really understand the meaning of it, became very popular. It ran:

> Solomon Grundy
> Strangled her Monday.
> Arrested on Tuesday.
> Tried on a Wednesday.
> Acquitted on Thursday.
> Shot her Friday.
> Arrested on Saturday.
> Ate his dinner Sunday.
> Hanged on a Monday.
> That was the end of Solomon Grundy.

Julian Symons

The Broken Penny

An Eastern-bloc country, shaped like a broken penny, was being torn apart by warring resistance movements. Only one man could unite the hostile factions – Professor Jacob Arbitzer. Arbitzer, smuggled into the country by Charles Garden during the Second World War, has risen to become president, only to have to be smuggled out again when the communists gained control. Under pressure from the British Government who want him reinstated, Arbitzer agreed to return on one condition – that Charles Garden again escort him. *The Broken Penny* is a thrilling spy adventure brilliantly recreating the chilling conditions of the Cold War.

'Thrills, horrors, tears and irony' – *Times Literary Supplement*

'The most exciting, astonishing and believable spy thriller to appear in years' – *The New York Times*

Julian Symons

The Colour of Murder

John Wilkins was a gentle, mild-mannered man who lived a simple, predictable life. So when he met a beautiful, irresistible girl his world was turned upside down. Looking at his wife, and thinking of the girl, everything turned red before his eyes – the colour of murder. Later, his mind a blank, his only defence was that he loved his wife far too much to hurt her...

'A book to delight every puzzle-suspense enthusiast'
– *The New York Times*

Julian Symons

A Man Called Jones

The office party was in full swing so no one heard the shot – fired at close range through the back of Lionel Hargreaves, elder son of the founder of Hargreaves Advertising Agency. The killer left only one clue – a pair of yellow gloves – but it looked almost as if he had wanted them to be found. As Inspector Bland sets out to solve the murder, he encounters a deadly trail of deception, suspense – and two more dead bodies.

The Players and the Game

'Count Dracula meets Bonnie Parker. What will they do together? The vampire you'd hate to love, sinister and debonair, sinks those eye teeth into Bonnie's succulent throat.'

   Is this the beginning of a sadistic relationship or simply an extract from a psychopath's diary? Either way it marks the beginning of a dangerous game that is destined to end in chilling terror and bloody murder.

'Unusual, ingenious and fascinating as a poisonous snake'
– *Sunday Telegraph*

JULIAN SYMONS

THE PLOT AGAINST ROGER RIDER

Roger Rider and Geoffrey Paradine had known each other since childhood. Roger was the intelligent, good-looking, successful one and Geoffrey was the one everyone else picked on. When years of suppressed anger, jealousy and frustration finally surfaced, Geoffrey took his revenge by sleeping with Roger's beautiful wife. Was this price enough for all those miserable years of putdowns? When Roger turned up dead the police certainly didn't think so.

'[Symons] is in diabolical top form' – *Washington Post*

A THREE PIPE PROBLEM

Small-time actor, Sheridan Haynes, had a rather unhealthy preoccupation with Sherlock Holmes. So when the chance came for him to play the famous detective in a TV series, it seemed his dreams had come true. And when London was plagued by a series of unsolved murders, well it seemed only natural for him to take his role into real life. Was this a case of a laughable and misguided actor, or was Sheridan actually on to something?

'Mr Symons has never done anything so wholly delightful'
– *Sunday Times*

TITLES BY JULIAN SYMONS AVAILABLE DIRECT
FROM HOUSE OF STRATUS

Quantity		£	$(US)	$(CAN)	€
CRIME/SUSPENSE					
	THE 31ST FEBRUARY	6.99	11.50	15.99	11.50
	THE BELTING INHERITANCE	6.99	11.50	15.99	11.50
	BLAND BEGINNINGS	6.99	11.50	15.99	11.50
	THE BROKEN PENNY	6.99	11.50	15.99	11.50
	THE COLOUR OF MURDER	6.99	11.50	15.99	11.50
	THE GIGANTIC SHADOW	6.99	11.50	15.99	11.50
	THE IMMATERIAL MURDER CASE	6.99	11.50	15.99	11.50
	THE KILLING OF FRANCIE LAKE	6.99	11.50	15.99	11.50
	A MAN CALLED JONES	6.99	11.50	15.99	11.50
	THE MAN WHO KILLED HIMSELF	6.99	11.50	15.99	11.50
	THE MAN WHO LOST HIS WIFE	6.99	11.50	15.99	11.50
	THE MAN WHOSE DREAMS CAME TRUE	6.99	11.50	15.99	11.50
	THE NARROWING CIRCLE	6.99	11.50	15.99	11.50
	THE PAPER CHASE	6.99	11.50	15.99	11.50

ALL HOUSE OF STRATUS BOOKS ARE AVAILABLE FROM GOOD BOOKSHOPS
OR DIRECT FROM THE PUBLISHER:

Internet: www.houseofstratus.com including author interviews, reviews, features.

Email: sales@houseofstratus.com please quote author, title and credit card details.

TITLES BY JULIAN SYMONS AVAILABLE DIRECT
FROM HOUSE OF STRATUS

Quantity		£	$(US)	$(CAN)	€
	THE PLAYERS AND THE GAME	6.99	11.50	15.99	11.50
	THE PLOT AGAINST ROGER RIDER	6.99	11.50	15.99	11.50
	THE PROGRESS OF A CRIME	6.99	11.50	15.99	11.50
	A THREE PIPE PROBLEM	6.99	11.50	15.99	11.50
	HISTORY/CRITICISM				
	BULLER'S CAMPAIGN	8.99	14.99	22.50	15.00
	THE TELL-TALE HEART: THE LIFE AND WORKS OF EDGAR ALLEN POE	8.99	14.99	22.50	15.00
	ENGLAND'S PRIDE	8.99	14.99	22.50	15.00
	THE GENERAL STRIKE	8.99	14.99	22.50	15.00
	HORATIO BOTTOMLEY	8.99	14.99	22.50	15.00
	THE THIRTIES	8.99	14.99	22.50	15.00
	THOMAS CARLYLE	8.99	14.99	22.50	15.00

ALL HOUSE OF STRATUS BOOKS ARE AVAILABLE FROM GOOD BOOKSHOPS
OR DIRECT FROM THE PUBLISHER:

Hotline: UK ONLY: 0800 169 1780, please quote author, title and credit card details.
INTERNATIONAL: +44 (0) 20 7494 6400, please quote author, title, and credit card details.

Send to: House of Stratus Sales Department
24c Old Burlington Street
London
W1X 1RL
UK

Please allow for postage costs charged per order plus an amount per book as set out in the tables below:

	£(Sterling)	$(US)	$(CAN)	€(Euros)
Cost per order				
UK	1.50	2.25	3.50	2.50
Europe	3.00	4.50	6.75	5.00
North America	3.00	4.50	6.75	5.00
Rest of World	3.00	4.50	6.75	5.00
Additional cost per book				
UK	0.50	0.75	1.15	0.85
Europe	1.00	1.50	2.30	1.70
North America	2.00	3.00	4.60	3.40
Rest of World	2.50	3.75	5.75	4.25

PLEASE SEND CHEQUE, POSTAL ORDER (STERLING ONLY), EUROCHEQUE, OR INTERNATIONAL MONEY ORDER (PLEASE CIRCLE METHOD OF PAYMENT YOU WISH TO USE)
MAKE PAYABLE TO: STRATUS HOLDINGS plc

Cost of book(s):———————— Example: 3 x books at £6.99 each: £20.97

Cost of order:———————— Example: £2.00 (Delivery to UK address)

Additional cost per book:———— Example: 3 x £0.50: £1.50

Order total including postage:——— Example: £24.47

Please tick currency you wish to use and add total amount of order:

☐ £ (Sterling)   ☐ $ (US)   ☐ $ (CAN)   ☐ € (EUROS)

VISA, MASTERCARD, SWITCH, AMEX, SOLO, JCB:

☐☐☐☐☐☐☐☐☐☐☐☐☐☐☐☐☐☐☐☐

Issue number (Switch only):

☐☐☐

Start Date: **Expiry Date:**

☐☐/☐☐   ☐☐/☐☐

Signature: ————————————

NAME: ———————————————————————

ADDRESS: ———————————————————————

————————————————————————

POSTCODE: ——————————

Please allow 28 days for delivery.

Prices subject to change without notice.
Please tick box if you do not wish to receive any additional information. ☐

House of Stratus publishes many other titles in this genre; please check our website (**www.houseofstratus.com**) for more details.